S0-BIM-156

BURLY TALES

BURLY TALES

FAIRY TALES FOR THE HIRSUTE AND HEFTY GAY MAN

EDITED BY
STEVE BERMAN

LETHE
PRESS

WITHDRAWN FROM
RAPIDES PARISH LIBRARY
Alexandria, Louisiana WR

Copyright © 2021

ISBN: 1-59021-084-0

Cover and Interior Design by Inkspiral Design

Published by Lethe Press.
All rights reserved.

All the stories are copyright 2021, as is the intro and afterword.

This is a work of fiction. Names, characters, businesses, places, events and incidents are either the products of the authors' imagination or used in a fictitious manner. Any resemblance to actual persons, living or dead, or actual events is purely coincidental.

No part of this publication may be reproduced, stored in a retrieval system, or transmitted in any form or by any means, without the prior permission in writing of the publisher, nor be otherwise circulated in any form of binding or cover than that in which it is published and without a similar condition including this condition being imposed on the subsequent purchaser.

C O N T E N T S

INTRODUCTION
MATTHEW BRIGHT

ONCE UPON A TIME, WE told stories, and these stories shaped us. Stories always have. There are volumes written about how folklore both *reflects* and *creates* how we see the world. What else is myth and folklore but the power of pure narrative that has survived the passing of generations? Once upon a time, and still to this day.

If I were to mention 'fairy tales' in this day and age, most likely the first images that would spring to mind would be Disney's—but most of these films are only the pretty, sugary blooms on the branches of trees with much deeper, darker roots. These sanitised narratives have undoubtedly left their mouse-shaped imprint on our ideas of romance and love for several generations. the rescue from the sleep of death by the kiss of a kind and noble man; the humble girl who becomes a princess; Prince Charming, and his happily ever-after. The cultural implicatons of this has no doubt been covered in volume upon volume, but the debate of whether these ideas are warped or aspirational I shall leave to others, in other introductions, in other books. Instead, I'm here to ask: if fairy stories both reflect the world back to us and also shape our world, how about we try those stories with a different, well... shape?

Particularly, a round shape. A rotund shape. A hirsute shape.

Let's be realistic. The cast of Prince Charmings across the last few decades of pop culture are as white and indistinguishable from each other they may as well have been cast by Ryan Murphy, and modern female leads in fairy tales are little more diverse. And let's be further realistic: the gay community is hardly unfamiliar with placing the ideal of the young, thin and pretty on a pedestal, despite the astonishing diversity of those who comprise our community somewhere over the rainbow.

In recent years there has been a notable rise in 'recasting' the familiar homogenous faces of our pop cultural fairy tales, particularly where such fables intersect with queer culture. Think cartoons of the Prince's Grindr profiles. Gender-swapped princesses. Cosplays that shake up race and gender. But for all this ironic subversion, it is still impossible to escape from the fact from the bulk (pun unintended) of the iconography at play: the glittery hopes and dreams of the thin and beautiful. In the world of fairy tales, it's a culturally ingrained idea that the fat body belongs only to the realm of the inconsequential, sometimes the farcical, often the villainous—and these characters do decidedly do *not* get their happily ever after.

Here at Lethe, under the Unzipped imprint, we have often championed erotica and romance collections that put the more traditionally overlooked body type front and centre. It's easy to get *heavy* (pun still unintended) when talking about representation. It can so easily become fraught, laborious, *worthy*. But if some of our earliest ideas of love and romance can start in the uncomplicated roots of fairy tales, then we think everyone deserves the chance to be a part of that ever-after, that magic, maybe that darkness, too. We want to create stories full of joy and froth, silliness and escapism, lightness and sexiness, whimsy and hirsuteness. Inconsequential stories *are* consequential.

This time, we are taking on fairy tales as our theme. Sure, some of us fledgling queers might have grown up identifying more with the princesses in these stories, but if, in your later years, you have found yourself built more like LeFou than Prince Eric, then that happily ever-after might not seem a foregone conclusion at all. Balls to that! Consider us your fairy godmother. If you've been wondering if someday your prince will come, well... here he comes, and he's put on a few pounds.

Run away with us to the woods, where the cubs and bears are not going to eat you (not without informed, enthusiastic, consent), where no one will judge you if you take up residence in a house with seven bearded men and only one bed, and where, if you fall in love with a large, hairy man with a forbidding castle and well-stocked library, he will still be that way *after* you kiss him.

Come get your happily ever after. We hope it was worth the weight. (Okay, that one was intended.)

—MATTHEW BRIGHT
Manchester, England

THREE, TO THE SWIZZ'!

JAMES K. MORAN

ITHOUT MASKS, THEY ALL STOOD on the Alexandra Bridge that spanned Ontario and Quebec. Beneath it flowed the Ottawa River. Sunlight winked off the white caps and filled Tom, who said, "Oh my gods, guys, I fucking needed this."

Each of the friends inhaled and exhaled to savouring the taste of freedom, as well as the smells of dirt, trout, and perch. The mournful cry of a seagull drifted from afar.

"We can tell," Dave replied. "First time walking?" For a quiet coder who dressed emo in a black-on-black ensemble, sporting multiple earrings, Dave could bare the sharpest horns.

Tom growled through his beard and lunged toward Dave, becoming a marauding predator of red-black-and-white plaid shirt, sleeves rolled up, and denim jeans.

Dave retreated to Reece's far side. They hadn't horse-played like this since their twenties. But today was special.

"Don't poke the bear," Reece said, chuckling. In khakis and a button-down, his hair and goatee freshly shorn, Reece did not run. His was a quieter rejoicing, savouring a moment over a mixed drink, whether watching a televised Olympic victory at a bar or attending Ottawa's annual Pride parade.

And Tom couldn't stand his cool demeanour. They were out. They were alive. "I thought we could celebrate it being over."

"Spoken like a true therapist," Reece said.

"Coming from an accountant, I'll take that as a compliment."

Behind them, across the Ottawa River, the Museum of History stood on the Quebec side. Even today, the globular buildings appeared mixed contemporary. In May daylight, under a peacock-blue sky, surrounded by a verdant lawn, it looked like an H. R. Giger creature had wandered lost into Gatineau, and settled down by mistake.

"Ahem," Reece said. "Gentlemen ... if I may?" He lit a tightly rolled cigarette.

Dave sniffed. "The green where we graze."

Tom arched his eyebrows comically once, twice.

"Well, don't just stand looking all manly," Reece said. "Take it!"

Tom accepted, took a drag. The joint hidden under his paw, he shared with Dave.

It went around.

The river flowed westward. The museum hugged the shoreline on the left, before yielding to red brick and panelled residences, and green space. The water of the rapids shushed, far off. The sun, behind them, glazed the sight as though in an impressionistic painting.

Tom cleared his throat.

Reece saw tears in the man's eyes. "You okay, big guy?"

Tom nodded, wiped his nose. "Just thinking of the last time we got out. The last time that anyone got out."

"We can frolic in the fields again," Dave mused, his tone hushed, amazed.

Reece wrapped an arm around Tom's shoulders, stretching to do it. "We even all scrubbed up for the occasion."

Dave rubbed his goatee. "I didn't shave this."

"It took you a pandemic to grow it, so I don't blame you," Reece said.

Dave, his turn with the cigarette, dragged hard, hacking up a puff of smoke. The cloud streamed upward, briefly appearing like horns atop his head.

Sounds of yelling and of pumping music rose from below. The trio hurried to the railing and looked over and down. A ferry was passing under the bridge. Strobe lights roamed across it, from bow to stern. Multicoloured streamers flapped from the railings in the breeze. Men gyrated on the starboard. Reece counted a dozen. They were all large, and they all wore leather accessories of some sort. Two in the centre of the pulsating mass, broad-shoulders covered in leather, wore matching pants, chaps, and boots, all a move. The man on the right, trying to match his dark-skinned dance partner's contortions, looked up to see Tom, Reece, and Dave staring down.

"Who are you?" Tom yelled down to them.

"Can't you read, handsome?" The man tipped his cap and a swipe of his moustache, à la Freddie Mercury. He gestured to the banner on the port side, facing Tom, its garish, multicoloured letters—*The Twelve Dancing Princesses*—arranged in a prism of colours. Beside that, in equally large, letters, it said, *Ottawa Knights Pandemic Recovery Fund.* "We're sneaking off to party with the princes!"

The man's dance partner swished long, pitch-black hair. His coffee-dark eyes were discernible even from afar. "Don't tell the king!" he cried in an equally rich voice, swinging his hips, his leather forearm cuffs. The mane of hair hid his face, revealed it again. He too was hirsute, although less so than his burly companion. He compensated for this lack with lustrous, mocha-coloured skin. Tom and company guessed it was likely very smooth to the touch, as was his black beard.

The dancers wore facemasks around their necks, not over their mouths. On closer inspection, Tom saw they were multicoloured. Stylistic, not functional. A shorter, Chinese guy, pleasantly stout, and leather-capped, pirouetted around the duo.

"Where you headed?" the capped fellow, whom Tom had addressed, yelled up, barely audible. The ferry was getting too far away, turning away from the three friends. The man gave a palm rub-down of his barrel chest, hidden behind a layer of hair.

"Swizzles!" Tom hollered over the music and distance, adding, "Woo-hoo!" He was unsure if they heard him.

The crowd of dancers, now all looking up, hoorayed in return.

They must have heard something, then, he thought.

"See you on the other side of the thing," the capped one shouted, although barely audible.

His fellow dancer yelled up at them but the ferry drifted completely out of earshot and the partygoers waved farewell.

"I think he said, 'Go, Hairs!'" Dave said.

"'No Hairs?'" Tom guessed.

"Ah," they said together, united in a sudden deduction: "Go, bears!"

"Geez, someone was hitting on you," Reece told Tom with a baleful gaze. "What else is new?"

"Yeah, what is with you?" Dave asked.

"Some things haven't changed during isolation," Reece drawled. "You're like the Captain Jack Harkness of the queer circuit." He was gesturing widely with the joint, as though it were in a cigarette holder and he a southern belle.

Tom bore a grin that, even through his rangy goatee, could break a heart or split firewood with its charm. Tourists always used to ask Tom for directions. No matter where the friends went. And they had been through it all together. Some tourists even asked Tom what was the best route to his bedroom.

Dave leaned into Tom, took an exaggerated sniff. "Is it the *manly musk* coming from that merkin on your chin?" Dave was not as active in Aikijujitsu and Karate as he was in his twenties, but for someone in his late thirties, he was limber. Chuckling, he easily dodged Tom's swipe.

Dave sidled up beside Reece and Tom again, closer together than they would have before the pandemic, but not as close as in their university days, after they'd met one another at a LGBT mixer.

"Remember that pick-up line you used sophomore year?" Tom asked Dave.

"'Hi! My name is Dave and I'm ...'"

"'...Chinese and queer.'" Dave cringed.

Reece rolled his eyes. "Unlike myself, being black and bi. Gentlemen, as you are aware, I consider that pick-up line some good, old-fashioned bullshit that I would never, ever, deign to say. Draw your own conclusions."

"My conclusion is that we're all far more classy than then," Dave countered.

Reece and Tom understood this as a reference to being in their early thirties. Each had a relatively stable career that somehow weathered the pandemic. Tom even had his own private practice, an office on the posh stretch of Somerset Avenue.

They pushed off the railing turned away from the river and headed down the path that descended to the foot of the bridge and into Ottawa. Below, on the left, a seldom-used path led up from under the bridge. Parliament stood to the right, or west, stoic and stony. The National Gallery's glassy tower stood leftward, to the east. Across from it loomed the U.S. Embassy in all the militant glory of a highly fenced perimeter. Reece once referred to it as Mordor, and had once dared a one-night stand to venture into the embassy and be a modern-day Frodo by dropping a doublets into the diplomatic washroom.

"So, if those are the Dancing Princesses, what are we?" Tom asked.

Reece slapped him on the back. "The Three Billy Goats Gruff, of course."

They all began to laugh, a marvelous thing almost-forgotten during the pandemic. They watched the people teeming in the streets of the Byward Market, from the gallery onward, the vast colours of not only the rainbow, from the populace of a city of nearly a million unleashed to go for coffee, or ice cream, for a drink, for a date or a hook-up, for a meal on a patio with friends in a country wise enough to not only legalize cannabis but also sodomy and marriage.

"Tell me, what's so funny, fellas?"

They heard the voice but couldn't place it at first. Until, one by one, they looked to the path under the bridge. Someone stood half-hidden, the border of shadow and light showing little more than a toothy grin and ripped jeans, boots old and scuffed but almost brutal in their thickness and stains.

"Celebrating freedom again?" the stranger asked.

The friends all exchanged a knowing glance.

"You know him?" Reece whispered. "I don't."

Tom and Dave shook their heads. "No," they answered in unison.

Eyeing the stranger, Tom was reminded of the bridge's uneasy history of hate-crimes. In the late 1980's, during that summer when he discovered the mystery of wet dreams, a waiter heading home from work was accosted by three young men, who had followed him through the night-time cruising area of Major's Hill Park, mistakenly assuming he was gay. The waiter was attacked and briefly held over the edge of the bridge by his ankles before being dropped into the water. "I like your shoes," reported on endless newscasts, quickly became the cruel taunt every bully used in middle school the rest of that year. Tom, months before a growth spurt, heard it as he was tripped or shoved against lockers.

"And yourself?" Tom asked, taking point as the tallest.

Reece extinguished his handiwork during his friends' momentary hesitation.

The stranger drew closer. "Is this where all the fags hang out?" He stared at Reece. "Fag, as in joint?" Again, that grin. "That's what the British call a dart. And you're all fags, right?"

Dave stiffened and, out of reflex, drew closer to Tom. Once, in university, while the friends were leaving a Byward Market bar, some drunken jock had begun screaming at Dave, before hurling him against a wall in the nearby alleyway. Thankfully Tom was just behind him and intervened. The walk back to their shared apartment had been taciturn one rather than the usual nocturnal joust of who had caught the most hithercome stares from locals.

"Oh, we get it," Tom said, stepping in front of his friends. "You're hilarious."

The stranger's boots scuffed the pavement. The leather vest and ripped denim were a nod to rough style but could not disguise his considerable, furry girth. He looked like he would be at home lurking on the edge of a leather bar's dance floor or a Mr. Leather competition, albeit the kind of contestant who wouldn't put in the work and would still expect to win the title.

"What do we have here?" The man's grin was either flirtatious or menacing. "The three billy goats gruff, eh?"

A pause. He looked at Reece. "The snob."

Reece's cheeks flushed. "Opinions vary."

He glanced at Dave. "A runt."

Dave narrowed his eyes at the speaker.

And then the stranger addressed Tom. "Oh, and the refugee from Goldilocks: one of the bears."

Reece began heading away from the man. The others followed downhill.

"Leaving so soon? See you on the other side, then!"

The friends walked abreast and, coincidentally, in order of size; Dave on the left, Reece and Tom on the right. Cars passed in the adjacent lanes on their right. Someone honked as they passed by.

"Anyone know what *that* was about?" Dave asked, obviously referring to the asshole under the bridge.

"No clue," Tom said.

The friends attempted to shake off the encounter with the, for lack of a better term, troll. For a moment, they only had their quiet thoughts. Ahead of them lay Ottawa, and the sea of people. Tom, Reece and Dave had walked these streets countless times before, pre-pandemic. Now those days seemed distant and halcyon, as though they took those late alcohol-and-drug-fuelled late nights for granted. But the pals were out again, in the open air, having crossed the divide and each of them was as fresh as the spring weather, randy for adventure in all its shapes and sizes after some much time cooped up, trying to arrange weird online hook-ups or date when they could. They were ready for just about anything, troll be damned.

Tom, at least, felt fit to burst. At last, he spoke. "To the Swizz', then."

"I concur," Reece offered.

"Hi, I'm gay and I'm ..."

"Shaddup, Dave," Tom and Reece replied together.

SWIZZLES, A BASEMENT BAR, STILL held old-school appeal, the kind of place closeted civil servants secretly frequented in the 1960's or 1970's, fearful of losing their jobs if they were outed against their will. It was nestled under a passable Chinese restaurant, and accessible by a side alley letting onto a concrete staircase, worn by years of grit and grime, that descended to the bar. A parking lot lay on one side, the whole works surrounded by blocks of government office buildings.

Dave, Reece and Tom approached the stairs, the head of which was, as tradition dictated, flanked by smokers. The local air was perfumed by darts and joints and vapes, oh my.

Tom's phone buzzed on his back pocket. He checked a text message. "Guys, I need a minute. It's Cindy."

"Is your sister still living with those two bitches?" Dave asked.

Reece groaned. "I cannot believe anyone in their right mind would stay with wicked roommates always trying to steal your strang and making the place a sty—"

"—and making you clean up after them," Dave finished.

"She was," Tom said, "but she finally met the right woman at some sort of banquet thing—I guess she left the case for her phone there and her new friend returned it?—and got her own place. Turns out that the new girlfriend is some sort of duchess."

"Good on her," Dave replied.

"You guys go ahead," Tom added, dialing his sister. "I'll need a minute." He wandered down the block.

Meanwhile, the smoker on the right, a vivacious blonde, eyed Reece through her halo of smoke. "Mr. Blais, as I live and breathe," Dixie Landers gasped under her cascade of blonde hair, resplendent bosom displayed in a low-cut top. Not only were the local establishments nearly bursting. "My prince has arrived. I would say 'has come' but that would be presumptuous, Your Highness, my darling."

She turned to the three sizeable gents she was chatting with, two across from her, and one beside her. Not leather-men, but all stout and well-dressed. "Fellows, I'll catch you inside."

They could not hide their disappointment. Halfway down the staircase, the last one turned back. He bore a cherubic face and handlebar moustache but no hair, beaming mischievously at her. "Just don't let me catch you sleeping in my bed again."

Dixie's face reddened like lava. She turned to Dave and Reece with a huff of breath. "What? I ended up crashing at their place recently. I was partying. So first I raided their fridge, then I crashed in his bed. Made them all brunch, though, darling, to make up for it." She waited a perfectly-timed beat. "Not jealous, are you?" She batted her eyelashes at Reece. "I have to pay to replace the bed now," Dixie added with a wink. "Some bears like to do more than cuddle, you know."

Reece turned to Dave with an imploring look.

"Uh … I'll meet you inside?" Dave passed through the gamut of remaining smokers and headed down.

At the open door, an imposing bouncer watched his progress. Dave immediately recognized him.

"If it isn't you," Dave declared. He almost added "*the troll from under the bridge*", but he really wanted to go inside.

The guy was larger up close, likely taller than Tom. Certainly wider. The smile was the same as before, one that demanded of everyone: Friend or foe?

"How did you get here so fast?" Dave asked.

"Told you I was going to work." The bouncer glanced inside, then at Dave, in an up-and-down assessment so deliberate, it could have been in slow motion. "It's quiet, though." He moved closer, smelling slightly of coconut oil, of sweet deodorant, maybe Irish Spring, but also a trace of musky sweat. "Wanna go in the back with me? I could just eat you up."

Back in college, one of his professors, a thick, bespectacled man Dave referred to as the Duke, would often treat him to coffee and advice. Dave still remembered much of it, including: *You can't fall asleep at the wheel if you bite down on it.* And *everyone flirts with the bouncer to get into a bar, but no one goes home with him.*

"Thanks, but no thanks."

The bouncer searched Dave's eyes. "Oh, come on, now. A sweet thing like you. I could gobble you right up." And then his gaze lowered until he stopped at Dave's crotch.

"Sorry—not interested. Besides, my friend is, uh, bigger, shall we say?"

"Bigger, eh?" The bouncer's stubbly smirk was not unpleasant. It was his approach, more of a crash landing, really, that needed refining. Maybe Reece could give him some tips?

"Sure is," Dave said, and glanced behind him. At the top, Dixie and Reece were still talking.

"He's very stylish," Dave continued. "Likes a martini or a glass of wine, never beer. Doesn't own a shred of denim. The kind of guy who wears dress pants while around the campfire. Also likes haute cuisine around the campfire."

This was all true.

"Alright," the bouncer said at last. "The cover is five bucks."

"Thought it was three."

The bouncer shrugged. "It's *discretionary*. As in, you can think of it as a tip."

Dave groaned and paid. Inside Swizzle's, he went right to the bar along the back wall, and ordered the house red for Reece, a micro-brewery India pale ale with far too many hops for Tom, and a vodka and lime for himself.

Back at the top of the stairs, Reece hugged Dixie and jauntily climbed down, pausing only when he met the bouncer's eye with an uneasy grin.

"Cover's five bucks, but could be free for you," the bouncer said.

"How does that work?" Reece actually had a good idea how things worked, whether in Ottawa or New York City or San Francisco or London. Human nature was ever so reliable: wherever you went, politics and sex following you everywhere you grazed, despite your best intentions.

"Well ..." The bouncer leaned a meaty forearm against the door jamb, the sounds of a mediocre karaoke cover of the Red Hot Chili Peppers' "Under the Bridge" floating out from inside. "I am hoping for a bit of tail, and I bet you can swing that ass real pretty."

"Is that so?"

Reece wondered how long this guy had worked the door? Two years? Ten? He looked like a prisoner, gone to seed, and now released from months of solitary confinement. But weren't all of them like that? Freed from the pandemic, and trying to remember how to cruise again?

And this guy was rusty. And blatant. "I like your sense of style," he said as he came close to brushing a palm along Reece's collar. "No label polo shirt ... beige slacks. Nice. Only, I'd get those messy right off the bat, by kneeling on the ground."

"I'm afraid they're staying on," Reece answered.

"Dahling!" Dixie Landers hollered down, her six-foot-two figure looming even more impressively from the top of the decades'-old stairwell. "I'll be down in a minute. There will be shots!"

"Absolutely," Reece replied with a nod and a confident wink. He turned to the bouncer. "As you can see, my dance card is full."

"Don't waste all this ... I'd love to just eat you up."

"Not sure if I'm the meal for you," Reece replied. "However, my other friend is the real dish of the night."

"Oh?" The bouncer drew closer, close enough that Reece could spot a patch of hairs, perhaps bristles, on his neck that the razor had missed.

"Oh, yes. A bear who loves to bare it all. We're talking just the right shape ... handles on the sides just where you want to grab, beefy pecs, and a pelt that gets sweaty but tastes like honey."

The bouncer looked up, saw Tom appear at the top step. "Glorious flannel," the bouncer whispered.

Tom did indeed own the customary, Canadian plaid, red and white like the flag (with some black thrown in for variety, Reece supposed). Reece also suspected Tom's boxers were flannel, likely white with a garish maple leaf right in the front. Tom was smiling and nodding at Dixie, who whispered in his ear, to which Tom guffawed. The clutch of smokers was orbiting around him, planets around a sun, drawn in by his charisma. The bouncer's observant face belied his growing interest.

"And do I need to add that he's so well-endowed that his Prince Albert always makes the sweetest 'clink' on the porcelain."

The bouncer's eyes widened. He licked his lips and added, almost as an afterthought, "Alright. Go on in, then."

Reece smiled as he stepped inside the bar.

When Tom landed on the bottom step, he was startled by the troll blocking his way into the fabled Swizzles.

Apart from the troll's profound belly, they stood roughly the same width, and height. Each was astonished that they were at eye-level.

"I remember you. From the bridge."

"Guilty as charged," the bouncer answered with a sweep of his arm, revealing some ink along the elbow that might have read, *No one's ever really ready.*

"And now you lurk ... here."

"Only on Wednesdays, Fridays, and Halloween." He pulled at his beard. "Which makes me wonder, are you my trick or treat tonight, handsome?"

Tom rolled his eyes. "I guess your middle name is not *Consent.*"

"Maybe I'm tired of just lurking around the edges of life. And now I just want to eat it all up."

"And I'm not on the menu," Tom replied.

The troll blocked the door. "Then you can't afford the cover charge."

Tom raised his palms in surrender. "Okay, okay." He waited a beat. "Your approach is not helping get in my pants, you know?"

"My approach?"

"All that gnashing of teeth. What's your name?"

The troll blinked. "It's Tony."

Where was Reece to make an Anthony Trollope joke? "Well, Tony, I'll tell you a secret." Tom wiggled his finger for the troll to step closer.

"Some guys, we have this fantasy that we would just die to finally do with a hot ... real ... fox."

"I can be a fox," Tony the troll muttered.

Tom breathed in deep and whispered right into an ear thick with tufts of hair. "I've always wanted to ..."

"Yeah?" The bouncer rubbed at the front of his pants as if there were a genie in that lamp tucked behind the zipper.

"Walk into some stranger's apartment, go right into his bedroom, and just ... prostate myself there. In his den. And just spend the night as his sex slave."

"Yeah?"

"Your apartment clean, Tony?"

The troll blinked, swallowed. "Nah, my mom calls it a cave. I think I haven't changed the sheets since Paul Martin—"

Tom reached past the troll's leather vest and pinched a very hard, thorny nipple. "Then why are you still here? You go run home to that cave and make it nice for me. And I'm going to drink some liquid courage to get up the nerve to walk in there," Tom suddenly snapped his jaws nary an inch from the troll's lips, "and let you be a beast."

Tony nodded, his tongue almost hanging out of his mouth. He muttered something that could have been a time or an address, and then, adjusting his pants, ran up the stairs, almost knocking Dixie over, as he moved out of sight.

Tom greeted his friends with a wide grin and outstretched arms and accepted a hug and then his ale.

"How did you get past the guy at the door?" Dave asked. "I hope you didn't have to palm him around the corner."

"Sorry to throw you to the wolves," Reece said.

"If I could outlast a vicious virus, some troll doesn't stand a chance to take me out."

A crowd of men filled the space between the tables, ordered drinks, danced, or stood around inspecting the scenery. Glitter pervaded the men, magically so. The Dancing Princesses, or Ottawa Knights, had arrived in all their muscular, stout, leather-clad glory.

Someone down the bar noticed Tom shrugging, leaned in to get better look. He of the leather cap, vest, and wide chest. A welcome sight. The dancer he liked from the ferry.

"We get to roam whatever fields we want, friends," Reece said, raising his tulip-shaped wine glass.

"To roam wherever we want," Dave and Tom echoed resoundingly.

They clanked their glasses together and drank.

The Ferry Fairy down the bar stood to his full height. Tom decided, from the thudding of his heart, the rush in his limbs, the swelling in his groan, the denim uncomfortably restricting, that he more than liked what he saw. It was like looking at a Tom of Finland drawing come to life, from the robust moustache, flush cheeks, dark features and broad shoulders. The man, with a nod of his square jaw, raised his pint of IPA to Tom.

Tom raised his glass in return.

The man pushed off the bar and made his way over.

"My prince," he called sweetly over the ambient noise.

Tom's friends took the cue to go off dancing. The bar was filling up. Gay Party Time was the hour. Swizzles swelled to life in all its colourful glory. Tom was not one for bleating, but growling, so he did.

A man with lustrous hair wiped his bangs from his face and shimmied up to Dave, as another dancer tipped his leather cap before pirouetting around Dave in what could only be a trademarked move. Joy filled Tom's heart at the sight.

"Your Highness …." Tom's princess from the ferry sang. Lust brought a ruddy glow to the fanciful fellow's brow as he stood facing Tom.

It was obvious, even to Tom who bore misgivings about happy ever-afters that, on this fierce note of hope, tonight would have a happy beginning.

THE RED BEAR OF NORROWAY

JOHN LINWOOD GRANT

1

T HERE WAS ONCE A QUEEN, a mighty queen, with lands which stretched from mountains tall to the salt-sea shores. Her realm prospered; her people were fair and fine, and swords lay quiet in their sheaths. Besides the produce of field and tree, the market stalls held silks from Araby and sweet spices from the Eastern Isles, and none went in need. And though she clutched the small sorrow that her husband had passed away, she had three strong sons to brighten her days.

These sons were well-favoured, each in his own way. Erys, one hour the eldest, was a quiet man with a mind of spun steel, and saw always to the realm's safety and defence, having no care for himself or the passing of his hours. Andrys, his twin, was blessed with a most nimble form; he was master of dancing revelries, the favoured child of the land's many troupes, spreading the love of art to every corner of the land. And last there came the youngest by a year, named Justinian for his father's father.

Justinian was neither as sharp as Erys nor lively as Andrys, but he held in his stout breast a heart that his mother loved, for it was a heart of dreams, of wonder at the passing seasons, and the whispers of both the North and South Winds. Of all three sons, Justinian had the broadest shoulders, the greatest girth, and the healthiest appetite—in these, he most resembled his mother and the line of kings and queens from olden days.

For many years the queen kept her sons close, but at last she gathered them in her hall, where shafts of sunlight gave the lie to shadows of stone, and she spoke of life.

"My dears, you are of an age, and more, to make your own way—to seek your own fates. Tell me what you would have, what you would become."

Erys raised his head, and his eyes of silvered grey were narrow in calculation. "Mother, I care naught for bedchamber nor bold adventure. Let me remain, and see each border safe, each and every bothy free from danger. I shall be seneschal for you, and govern these matters, that you may ease your burden of the crown."

The queen was pleased, for she loved Erys, and knew that his mind served only the realm's needs. That her son was lacking in passions of the flesh was well-known, yet he would be content in his chosen life. She readily agreed to his request.

Andrys, whose eyes were dark with the dance, traced the cracks of stone floor with one boot. "I would marry, mother, for I seek the Lady Aisha as a bride. She is most graceful. We have cut a gavotte these many nights, and she favours me."

Again, the queen was pleased, for the fair Aisha had the fires of Araby in her veins; she brought strength, beauty and wisdom to the court. Moreover, she was a horse-archer of uncommon skill, and could lend her support to Erys should adversity arise—the land was not over-gifted with warriors. And so she smiled, and once more agreed.

"And you, Justinian?" she asked.

The queen's youngest son seemed troubled. Tall and wide enough to be two men made as one, he had eyes flecked with the same golden glint as his tight-bound mane and thriving beard. He glanced at his brothers, and their eager faces urged him on.

Thus he spoke in his deep, even voice. "Mother, each night for a month, the same dream has visited me. In this dream, I stand in a great mead-hall, such as those of the Northern peoples, and brooding there on an oaken throne sits a man whose like I have never seen in all our realm. My heart pounds at the sight of him, and I know him to be the one whose favour I would gain. Whose favour I *must* gain."

His mother sat back, her expression one of wonder. "Is this a *geas* on you, placed by some sorcerer?"

Justinian shook his head. "It is ... it is a thing of the heart, of that I am sure."

"And do you know this stranger's name?"

Her son looked away, his broad cheeks each with a spot of red upon them. "You will think me foolish, or mad."

"I can judge neither, my son, unless you tell me."

Justinian met her gaze at last. "I believe—I would swear—that it is the Red Bear of Norroway I see in my slumbers.

Now the queen held silent for a moment. Erys nodded thoughtfully; Andrys only smiled with affection.

"'I will not lie in maidens' arms; another one must have my charms,'" said Andrys, reciting a verse of his own making, and he reached over to pat his younger brother on the back. "Oft we have wondered when you would settle on one man's embrace—but here you set yourself a hard challenge, dear Justinian."

And that was the truth of it, for the Red Bear of Norroway was widely known to be a soul ensorcelled. None in the Southlands knew how the doom had come about, but this fabled prince of the North was perforce a mighty and terrible bear by day, and only a man by night. Many said that he was a dark burden on his own people, though for certain no reiver or rival lord would threaten those lands, fearing the beast's strength and temper.

"So. A challenge indeed. You will need to be brave, which I know you are," said Erys at last. "And yet you must also be sharp of wit, to win such a prize—if it is even possible. Know that my counsel will always be yours, and with faith, perhaps you might yet catch your bear."

"And my counsel also, such as it is" said Andrys.

Seeing no dispute between her sons, the queen clapped her hands once in agreement. She knew that dreams had power, and besides, she was wise enough to see that forbidding Justinian this pursuit would leave him a wounded and haunted bear himself. Better that he attempted what he had set himself, for good or ill, and made his own wyrd.

"The heart must be its own master, my dear. If Norroway is where it bids you, then you have my blessing. Let your dreams be your guide, and see what comes."

JUSTINIAN LAY DOWN CLOTHED THAT night, too excited to undress. He swathed himself in goose-feather quilts, and let the dark enfold him. At first, he dreamed of spiced wine and pomegranates; of roast fowl and various glistening sauces, but at last these faded, along with the grumbling of his stomach. He turned under the quilts, asleep but restless, until at last his fancy brought him once more to the magnificent—if chilly—mead-hall.

There, on a fine and intricate wooden throne, sat a figure with long copper-red hair and a beard of the like, his clothes of leather and linen in the manner of the Northmen. In truth, the man was less substantial than those who normally caught Justinian's eye, but there was a noble melancholy about that downcast face which fascinated him. Of this prince's age, it might have been that he was a half-dozen years older than the Southlander.

It had been Justinian's intent to learn more through such dreams, and plan his journey north, but such was not be, for to his astonishment, this night he could feel the rush-strewn floor beneath his feet, and smell the low peat fire. He had been transported, body and soul, to cold Norroway!

The figure looked up, startled, and one hand strayed to an ornate sword hilt. "You!"

Justinian blinked, trying to gather his wits. "You know me, sir?"

"I have dreamed your form, your face, these last weeks, and knew not why. That you should stand before me, however, is a mystery. I am Leif Thurlasson, the prince of these parts, and do not recall bidding you to my hall; should such a meeting in the flesh be for well or woe, I will soon learn."

The young man bowed. "O prince, Your Highness, I have travelled pale nightmare and sweet night-fantasy, and there I have seen you there also, each night for a moon. I know not how I am here, nor did I mean to stand before you without permission."

Not for the first time, he wished that he had his brother Andrys' gift with words.

"I am called Justinian, and what you are named in these sad days I have from the talk of learned and well-travelled men, for I deem you to be the Red Bear of Norroway."

The prince growled. "I have that misfortune, though once I was free of care, and known as Leif of the Broad Spear. Now am I wary of strangers who come to my door, and if you know of me, then you must also know that none will risk my temper by day, or my sorrow by night."

"None in Norroway perhaps," said Justinian, setting his shoulders square with resolve. "But the men of the Southlands are bold."

"Is that so?" Leif Thurlasson looked the young man over, and must have found no outward fault, for he nodded. "Ah well, I should remember my duties as a host, I suppose." He gestured to a simple but solid-looking stool by the throne. "Will you take mead with me? No—wine, I should have said, should I not, if you are from the Southlands? I believe we have some, though it may be vinegar by now."

He clapped his hands, and a youth in russet linen came from the shadows. At his master's instruction, he brought horn goblets and a dusty bottle which swilled with a liquid dark as blood.

"I would drink the sourest vinegar if it were from your cups, my prince," murmured Justinian, sitting where he had been bid. He would not have drawn himself back into his bedchamber, even if he could, for his heart pounded to be so close to this man.

"Tell me then of these dreams, and spare no detail," demanded Leif Thurlasson.

Other servitors came within the quarter hour, and with them came smoking meats, and thick rye bread, and strange cheeses, accompanied by more bottles from the prince's cellars—deep tawny draughts that drove away the cold. The two men talked long into the night, and if there was caution on one side, and over-eagerness on the other, they found no answer to this strange transportation.

Thus were met Justinian and the Red Bear of Norroway.

2

NEITHER WELCOME NOR UNWELCOME, JUSTINIAN was given leave to remain in the holding, save that he should make no mischief. Assenting gladly, the young man made it his task to learn more of the place, and he who ruled it.

Striding from the spread nets of the fisher-folk by the shore to the huts of the trappers in mountain's shadow, he soon learned the way of things—for all that the prince's people were stalwart and healthy, this was a troubled realm.

People were generous in most matters, but guarded and soon busy about other matters should the Red Bear itself be mentioned. The tales had spoken truly of the prince's doom—from dawn until dusk the beast known as the Red Bear left the mead-hall and roamed the forests thereabouts, and all were aware that this was Leif, once of the Broad Spear, his shape and mind transformed into a thing from whom his people shrank.

It was a wonder, this creature, standing greater than any bear should be, with dark eyes deep-set above a fanged and fearsome snout and claws which might rend a longboat. The beast was ill-tempered but not intent on harm, as long as it was left alone.

Villages were forewarned whenever their prince was abroad by day, and heavy wooden shutters served to dull his interest in the folk within.

At first Justinian merely watched and waited as the beast ripped salmon from the streams, or drove that bulk through the most tangled briars. It did in truth seem to be no more that a creature of the forest.

As for the nights, Leif Thurlasson had long dismissed those shield-men who would have shared his high table, telling them they were better breaking bread with their families, and so the two men would drink and talk alone. Sometimes they spoke of their respective lands, at other times of idle matters in which neither had real interest, and Justinian's voice was the most oft heard. The prince had always regret for the lost day, and as he sank into his cups, melancholy gripped him.

Only when pressed on the Red Bear did Leif show passion, turning a hurtful glare on his guest. He would say little of the curse upon him, save that it was unwillingly gained—and undeserved. When pressed as to why nothing had been done about this burden, Leif only muttered that soothsayers and wise ones had been consulted many times, but none had been able to lift or even soften the curse.

"You have had a worthless dream, and a wasted journey," the prince would say, and the young man could not persuade him otherwise.

As the days passed, Justinian grew more, not less, determined to win over the prince. He had the courage and foolishness of youth, believing that he alone could change this dire wyrd—and why else would that miraculous transportation have brought him to Norroway? There were fair-faced men aplenty in his mother's lands if the pleasures of the bedchamber were all he sought. His heart still beat with that love he had heard of in the tales of old, and was he not fit to grasp such a rare prize?

Seeing that his words had thus far held little power for Leif the man, Justinian decided to cleave to the beast more closely, following it in its wanderings. For it came to him that he might seek to befriend the prince in this form, and thus work his way into that tortured breast.

The first time he came close earned him a deep growl, and he let it be; the second time it rose to its full height and stared with hot red eyes until the young man again backed away.

His third attempt was the greatest folly, for he came across it while it was clawing honey from a rotten tree, and reminded of the mead which the prince loved, Justinian thought to go closer and to speak softly.

"This sweetness we might share, and remember the feast-table where we talk without anger. For, my dear Leif, I know that you are beneath that doom-forged form."

The bear twisted round, its gaze on the daring young man.

The wild cuff that came drove Justinian to the ground, and there was blood in plenty mixed with the honey upon those claws. The young man's last sight before he swooned was of the Red Bear blundering away, bellowing ....

Charcoal burners from the settlement found Justinian some hours later, sprawled beneath the pines, and fortunate that they did. His tunic was ripped asunder, his shoulder bruised and bleeding heavily from deep and open gouges; making a hasty litter, they carried him back to his chamber the mead-hall, even as the first grey fringe of evening touched the woods.

There he lay in a daze, lamenting his failure more than his wounds, as his torn shoulder was washed and bound. But when the servitors had left him, he saw a pale-faced figure in the shadow of the doorway.

"Oh, my Southlands friend," cried Leif. "You must leave this place, leave me, before worse befalls. You are bold, yes, and brave, but whatever these dreams meant, staying near me will be the end of you."

Justinian propped himself up on his good arm.

"Better I perish by the claws of day," he gasped, "than abandon my prince of the night."

Then the Red Bear of Norroway wept, and kneeling by the bedside, poured drink for both of them. He cradled the young man's head with one arm, and let dark wine trickle between Justinian's lips.

"Do not ask for more favour than I dare give. I cannot … I cannot love, I am fated to remain thus, a curmudgeon of a beast whilst the sun is high; a lost soul under the moon's gaze."

Justinian's heart gave him the strength to smile, despite the pain.

"Than you dare give? Then you might not spurn me, were this curse lifted?"

Leif Thurlasson hesitated, and his lips quivered as if they might remember pleasure.

"You must rest," he said, turning his face away.

WHATEVER HE MIGHT LACK IN cunning or oratory, Justinian steered true to his course. This saw him up from his sickbed before he was fully healed, and by that Freya's Day (as they counted the days there) he was yet again wandering among the pines, trailing the Red Bear. On such things, the opinion of the holding was now divided—some folk admired the young man's honest determination and affection for their prince; others saw another sorry chapter in the making, and wondered how many men it would take to build a pyre for such a bulky fellow.

Thus it went for two weeks and more, with Leif's people sworn not to mention Justinian's activities to their lord. Each morn the young man gave the beast his scent and made it more accustomed to—though not perhaps pleased by—his presence. If it did not welcome him, it no longer struck out in anger, and confined itself to sullen grumbling.

And when dusk fell, he would engage Leif the man in talk again, stealing fine phrases as he remembered from his brother Andrys, telling of Erys' deeds in care of their mother's realm. Of their mother he spoke, and of their late father.

In turn, Leif Thurlasson softened somewhat, speaking of his boyhood, and how his parents had been lost a-viking, leaving him with this princedom. At times a rare smile was shared, and one evening, when the young man had been in Norroway for a moon and more, a darker tale was admitted to the mead-hall. Leif finally consented to speak of the sly one who had placed the curse, a traveller from far away who had come to the Northlands late one winter.

"Ovelamieli was the name he gave, and I was merely Leif, new to ruling others. He spoke with sense at first, as a wise-man might, but there seemed other layers to his words; I felt his fair face might be more a mask. Ever more uneasy, I began to suspect him to be a warlock. The longer he stayed, the more he sought my affection and the more I said to him, 'Nay' ...." The prince's voice faltered. "When I spurned him openly before others, he uncovered his true sails—I would be his or no one's, he hissed. That night, in my own hall, he laid the curse of the Red Bear upon me."

"An evil, evil deed—and clearly a man to match it, this Ovelamieli."

Leif sighed. "Do you wonder that I was cautious when another stranger came to my door?"

Justinian spread his hand across the other man's, and it was not brushed away.

"With the first cock's crow of each day," continued Leif, "I must take up the bear's pelt which Ovelamieli had first gifted me, and I cannot stop myself. I can do it no harm; my faithful servitors have tried to drag it far away, but when they do I fall near to dying, and the pelt is always back by midnight. If it is locked in the strongest iron-bound chest, still it finds its way out and near to me once more. Such is the warlock's power and the strength of the *geas* he has placed."

"This seems too cruel. Can nothing be done?"

"I have told you—neither seer nor cunning-man has ever brought an answer to that. I must be what I have been made. I wonder that you can stand it, dear to me though you are becoming. My sunlight hours are a blur, but I know I came close to brute anger again today."

"But you did not do it. I must be with man and beast—I can do no less!"

"Oh, you sweet fool," murmured Leif, and their fingers intertwined ....

NOT THREE DAYS AFTER THAT, with Justinian's wounds much mended and too many glances between them to ignore, they found their way to the bedchamber for the first time, and there they gloried in each other's bodies. Nor was Justinian disappointed; Leif Thurlasson had tenderness, but, at times, he also possessed the earthy passions of the beast whose name he bore—and he wielded a 'broad spear' indeed.

This change was a joy to the young man, but always in the far corner of the bedchamber lay the huge russet pelt that the prince must don when morning came, the pelt which would transform him into a creature of instinct and base urges.

One night after pleasure they lay abed, and drew in the scents of fresh, clean sweat and cedarwood which filled the chamber. Leif ran his hand down Justinian's body, exploring the dense curls upon that massive breast.

"You have something hid behind that fair brow. I sense it."

Justinian hesitated, his fingers tangled in the other's hair. "It is nothing. I was thinking idly, and realised that … I miss my family, so far away. I have not spoken to my mother, my brothers, for such a long time, and the seas are so wide …."

"Oh." The prince sat up. "I did not dare say before, but I am minded there is a way—dreams have bound us, and dreams are surely to our hand in this. Only lie in bed at night and think hard on your family just before you sleep. Imagine yourself stood with them, and so you will be."

"But then I will be apart from you, and—"

"Do the same in your bed at home, and imagine your troubled prince in that same manner. If you want to be with me, you will return."

The next night, Justinian went to an empty chamber and lay down on musty furs, his family in his mind. Within moments of closing his eyes, he felt a shudder run through his body, and found himself wrapped once more in goose-feather quilts. It was morning, and he was in his mother's keep.

Rushing into the great hall, he saw his brother Andrys and the queen breaking their fast at the long oak table. Such was his excitement that he gabbled as he grabbed at platters of food.

"Rye bread is … very heavy," he said, tearing into a sweet white loaf. "And they don't have the fruit we … oh, he really does become an actual bear. And he wants me, but …" He swallowed a mouthful, took a deep breath. "Where's Erys? Is he well?"

"Erys is riding the eastern borders," said the queen. "We are hoping to open up some new mines—your brother believes there is silver there."

"Oh. Did you miss me? What did you think had—"

"We guessed where you had gone." Andrys stood up and hugged him. "Idiot. You could have left a note."

Justinian sat down, restrained himself from filling his mouth again, and told them the whole of it, from the evening of the dream which took him to the Red Bear of Norroway. They marvelled at his tale, being cheered that he had found someone for whom he cared, and sad at the curse laid upon Leif Thurlasson.

"How long will you stay here?" asked the queen. "So many will be pleased to see you again, and Erys will return before the new moon."

Justinian shook his head, his appetite lost. "I do not know, mother. I love Leif Thurlasson, and I must seek out if any in our realm know of a way to relieve my prince's curse."

And after a morning with his kin, this he did. He saddled up his faithful grey, a solid stallion who bore Justinian's bulk with ease, and rode to many a town and village, up into the hills, and down to the slanted houses of the fisher-folk. He talked to the witch-men of the hills, who burned rats' entrails to read the smoke, and to the star-women of the great towns, who read the night sky. He spoke to the seer of his sister-in-law, Aisha, an old man who had travelled more roads than might be found on the Earth. But none had answers—there had been no skin-changer, by choice or doom, in the land for centuries, and Aisha's seer said that the Northern warlocks had bitter ways which were closed to even him.

Dejected, Justinian let the grey stallion bring him back to his mother's keep, for his brother Erys would soon return. In Enrys's chambers of state, he found a thin fellow of some thirty winters, who was going through bundles of manuscripts.

"My lord," said the man, bowing. "Your brother is delayed. I am Gullscope, one of his aides—is there aught I can help you with?"

So sad was Justinian feeling that he poured out the tale of the curse, though with less of his heart contained in the telling.

"A tragedy indeed," said the man at the end. "Although ...."

"You know something?"

Gullscope hesitated. "It is only, my lord, that your brother keeps many scrolls of antiquity, and I believe I saw once a reference to such a curse—a young sea-captain ...."

"A bear-shifter?"

"No, not quite, my lord. In that tale, the victim was trapped as a bull-seal by day and a man by night. But I dare say the principle is much the same."

"And was there some way to be freed of that burden?" asked Justinian, eager.

"I would have to find the scroll, and—"

"Do that, I beg you," said Justinian, and swept away in awkward passion.

Later that same day, after dogs were at their hearths and men in their cups, Gullscope came to Justinian's quarters. The young aide shuffled, his eyes lowered.

"The old tongues are hard to read, my lord," said Gullscope in his thin tones, "but they tell that a friend of the sea-captain stole into his room one night, and took the pelt to burn it—for the deed cannot be known nor done by the one ensorcelled. A man cannot act against his own curse."

"And ...."

"Thereafter, the man was hale and untroubled, for all the evil resided within the pelt; the shore-witch who formed the doom was thwarted, and died soon after."

Justinian had little to cling to but this strand of hope. "You believe that if I did this, Leif Thurlasson might be freed?"

"Who can be sure, my lord? Not all old tales are wholly true, and ...."

But other words were lost on the air, for Justinian was away to the queen.

"Dearest mother, I must haste away, back to the mead-hall of Norroway. I beg you give my love to my brothers, and take twice that for yourself."

The old woman looked down at the son whose favours most mirrored her in her own youth, with tousled, corn-gold hair and those same, gold-flecked eyes that marked the ancient line.

"You will be uncle soon, for an heir has been born to Andrys and Aisha. Is this prince truly your heart's desire? A duchy would still be yours."

Justinian's head bowed to his mother's knee. "The realm does not tremble in the night, nor bead itself with tears; if it is not mine to free my prince from his doom, then who else will?"

Then the queen knew her son's great heart was truly set, and she reached to the chest of rosewood and brass which stood always by her seat of state.

"Justinian, take then these tokens which have lain forgotten, unneeded in our peace."

And she drew out, one by one, treasures of the line—a knife of black obsidian from the burning isles; a silver brooch, shaped as a tumbling rook, and last, the finest spider-silk, wound upon a bobbin.

"You will know their use when you have need, though I pray you do not. Go well, my son."

The purple of sunset brushed the mountains as Justinian took himself to his bed, and in the embrace of his quilts, held his mother's gifts close to his breast. He had supped deep of the ruby wine, and eaten three men's meals— the first for pleasure, the second to be sure that his belly did not complain— and the third to be sure of sleep, which was not long in coming ....

True to Leif's word, when Justinian awoke, he lay in the small, musty chamber from whence he had come, back in Norroway. The cock had not yet crowed; the household drowsed. Unable to hold back, he rushed to the bedchamber of Leif Thurlasson, treading barefoot so as not to wake the prince. In the corner, under a shuttered window, lay the hated pelt, a thick, shaggy mass of reddish fur and hide.

Justinian took it up and bore it out of the mead-hall, bore it to the fire-pit where sometimes oxen were roasted. A pot of coals glowed by the pit, and it was no hard matter to get a small blaze going. It went against his nature to act without speaking to his love, but if Gullscope were correct, the deed must be done without the cursed one being aware, lest it rebound on him.

"Let my prince be freed," he murmured, and threw the pelt upon the fire.

The flames which came were thick and oily, and they came so quick that Justinian was filled with wonder—this was no simple blaze. The thick fur charred and spat; the heavy hide beneath embraced its fate with unnatural speed ....

"No!" cried a figure from the door of the hall. Wrapped only in a linen sheet, Leif Thurlasson ran forward and made to drag the pelt from the fire, but the smoke billowed and choked him, driving him back.

"My prince, I—"

"Fool of a man!" Leif wiped tear-filled eyes. "Now you have completed the curse—as the Red Bear, I could at least keep my place here. Without the pelt, I am thralled to the warlock, and have no choice but to go to him and share his bed forever."

And Justinian, stunned, watched as the man he loved ran off into the growing dawn, as fleet as the hill-goat or the wild deer ....

DARK WERE THE DAYS WHICH followed. The holding woke in wonder at what had occurred, and those around Justinian were split between sorrow and relief—for they had love for their prince, but feared him also. Some spoke of sending to one of the Kings of Norroway, that another might order the settlement; others held that Justinian should carry the burden of rule, being as near a consort to the Red Bear of Norroway as they might ever have.

"For you have lost us our prince, and thus owe us duty; besides, you are well-favoured by many here," said a one-eyed elder.

"I have done a terrible thing, for love, and shown I have not the wisdom to rule," said Justinian, wracked with regret. Seeing that they still waited for his word, he caught at what his brother Erys might say. "Form you a council of those sound in judgement, and not too young. Let them be your voice. For I have proved that youth's passion, untempered, is folly!"

Inside the hall, they served him mead and slabs of roasted sheep; mushrooms, gathered from the forest and baked, and the thick dark bread of their land. He would not touch a morsel, but sat in sorrowful thought. Each hour he called for one or other from the older men and women, to ask where the warlock might be found, and sought word from the cunning-folk of the prince's land, but only at dusk did one come who gave slender hope.

"East of the sun and west of the moon, far beyond the pastures and the lands we know," said a wizened ancient, his large head almost too heavy to be held aloft. "He who caused the Red Bear of Norroway came from there, and I heard him speak, in those days when he sought to catch the prince in his arms. He talked as those who dwell between our people and the Finns; moreover, his magicks sang of Finnish cunning."

The old man had little else to offer, but said that the way was hard—perhaps too hard for a man of Justinian's youth, girth and appetite, one who had lived comfortably in fine halls all his life.

"Then I must die upon that trail," said Justinian without anger, for the man's words were not unwarranted.

He slept, turning uneasy in the bed that he had shared with Leif

Thurlasson, and in the morning, he ate well once more. The people saw his face was set, and they brought him a huge hide cloak against the cold; dried fruits and strips of deer, and with them the prince's spear and harness for combat.

"I am no warrior," said Justinian, refusing weapons and armour. A staff of yew he did accept, to help where the footing was poor, and in this way he set himself upon the path to find his prince ....

3

THERE WERE EASY DAYS AT first—his stride was long, and he had muscle as well as girth. Farmsteads and small villages gladly gave him sustenance when they knew his purpose; those who might have wished the prince to take a wife instead were consoled by knowledge of Justinian's fair and kindly nature. They felt they could have done far worse—"Better a lord of good heart, than a lady with cold ambition," had been said more than once in the time Leif and Justinian had been together.

But winter was not far ahead, and with each league he came to lands less farmed and with fewer and fewer roads or tracks. One beldam in a cottage thought she had seen a lean figure stride past, unspeaking, a week before; two snot-nosed children thought the same, but none could have named the man. This was no longer the princedom of the Red Bear of Norroway.

Justinian did not relent. He learned to forage, and paid coin for what folk could spare, pushing himself ever eastwards and higher. Hills gloomed around him; birds stared, unsure at the purpose of the great figure who passed them without glancing. And at last he came to a lone farmstead, the only chimney in all the land around him. The air was harsh, the fields mostly stones and wiry grass, and only a lone rook moved, its head tilted as it watched him approach the farm.

"Ho the household!" he called, standing near the open door.

After some moments, a cautious face appeared above a lean body.

"We have nothing to steal," said the man, doleful.

"I am no thief," said Justinian. "But if you have peat or logs a-burning, I would lie quiet by your hearth."

The farmer assented, and let him enter. At a rickety table sat a thin-faced girl with downcast eyes.

"My daughter cannot speak," said the farmer. "A warlock stole her words, a week and more past now."

Justinian started. "A warlock?"

"Aye, one who visited unasked for. Gyttha must have angered him or showed him fear—thus he served her, in return."

"Of what did he speak?"

"I do not know. I was returning with logs, and caught only the shadow of him as he swirled past me and went ever east. I fear ... I fear my child will not speak again in this life."

Troubled, Justinian asked the farmer if he had seen such a man as the prince, but he had not.

"My daughter may have, but none shall ever know."

Justinian's reply was lost to the harsh caw of the rook outside, and he went to the doorway. Now there were three black birds, perched on a broken fence, and each was looking at him ....

From within his meagre pack, he brought out the silver brooch of a rook that his mother had given him. Without knowing quite why, he went to the mute girl, and pinned the brooch in her shawl. Wide eyes, she wondered at his act.

"All creatures should have a voice," he said. "Try to speak."

She parted her lips, but all they heard was the caw of a rook outside.

"Go on," he encouraged her.

A cough, a caw from the yard—and then a word from her lips.

"Father!"

The farmer ran to her side, nodding that she try again, and Justinian saw that more of the birds had gathered around the farm, not four, not five, but dozens. With each opening of the girl's mouth, a rook cawed, and gave her back a word.

Home. Hearth. Grass. Sheep. Arm. Stranger. Warlock ....

"He came at dawn," said the girl, stroking her mended throat with pleasure. "I asked idly if he knew the man who had passed the day before, the sorrow-eyed one who strode towards the wild places. He said it was not my business, and when I asked more—for I did not like him—he raised his hand and snapped his fingers.

"'Questions are knives, in others' lives,' he said, and pressed his thumb to my neck. 'No more questions for you, girl.' And then he left, and I could not form the smallest word ... until now."

The farmer and his daughter brought roots from their stores, and salted meat, setting these in a cauldron on the fire and insisting that Justinian eat until he could eat no more. Over many helpings of the stew, he told them of his search for the missing prince.

"The sad man must have been the one you seek," said the girl. "But my lord, he trod the path to stony Trolldal, where only death lies."

They both urged that he go back, but Justinian would hear none of it. He was only seven, perhaps eight days behind, and he set his face for the narrow gorge they had called Trolldal.

Now, Justinian was no hillsman, and these were not the gentle slopes where he had ridden in his youth. Such trees as stood were wind-slanted and bare of leaf or fruit; even the grass found little comfort on the rocky scree. Cliffs of dull grey stone rose on either side of the way, stealing the light and leading him—along a dry stream-bed—into a gloomy ravine. Not bird, nor beast, nor smallest insect moved in the silence around him, and he knew fear—but his heart remembered Leif Thurlasson in his arms; the scent of his lover was on the clothes he wore.

"Bright is the day we die with honour," he said, without entirely being enthused by the saying, and stepped forth into the ravine.

Each step echoed; he would have been bolder had he not seen that sometimes what crunched beneath his boots was not loose rock but the bleached remains of men. A broken skull lay here; a shattered leg-bone there. His only comfort was that none of these were fresh, and he trudged on for an hour and more, until at last he saw a glimmer of daylight from the far end of the gorge.

And then there came another sound, a heavy, grinding which did not delight the ears. Justinian held up his staff in readiness, but he was not ready in his mind for what gathered shape ahead—a troll, and a troll such as only his distant ancestors had fought. It seemed to haul itself from the rock face, looming over Justinian, and it stank of death. Its eyes were wide and sickly green; its mouth a savage cut across its ash-coloured face.

"I would pass without harm to any!" called out Justinian, but the troll spread its arms from wall to wall to make its intention obvious.

A slight youth or maiden might have dodged beneath those arms; Justinian was neither, and so he charged, driving the end of his staff at the creature's eyes and hoping his weight might make it stumble. The troll, surprised, gave ground a pace; it lashed out and scarred the ravine wall with its claws. Justinian pressed himself to a shallow cleft, but that was no true shelter, and all seemed ill. He thought of the knife his mother had given him but, strange to his own mind, he brought out the bobbin from his pack instead.

As the troll lunged, the little spindle danced from his hands and described its own curious movements in the air, the spider-silk gleaming silver as it unreeled. It tangled first between the troll's talons, then down its lanky arms, and at last from ugly head to crooked feet, wrapping all in a gossamer stronger than iron chains, until the thing could scarce move.

When the creature's angry bellows subsided, Justinian came forward.

"I seek a comely, sorrow-eyed prince, and the warlock who has bound him. Tell me if they passed, and whence they went."

The troll ground its yellow teeth, but said nothing.

"Very well," said Justinian and, taking hold of an end of spider-silk, he pulled with all his might, dragging the bound troll towards the end of the ravine, nearer and nearer the light.

At this the creature moaned, for the touch of the sun would finish it.

"The warlock has me thralled," it cried, "and I must bend my knee to him and his."

"Neither knee nor any part of you will bend, when yonder clean sun shines on you," said Justinian, and set his shoulders to move his burden another pace.

"Enough! The man-thing has no choice; his master no mercy. Both will be found far east of Trolldal, in the warlock's hold beyond the Weeping Plain."

Justinian stopped hauling.

"With time you may free yourself," he said, "but not before I return to seal your fate, should you speak falsely."

"On my father's twisted gut I swear!" said the troll.

So Justinian left him there, and scrambled to the welcome light.

Beyond lay a flat, drear marsh, pocked with pools of foetid water.

Tussocks of thin grass stood in places; others were rank with weed and dying moss.

"The Weeping Plain," he said, low in spirits, and took up his staff to test the ground before him. It was well that he did, for there was no straight path. A boot placed here might find firm purchase; elsewhere, the staff could find no bottom to the mire. In this place and that could been seen, half-submerged, a finger-bone with ring upon it, or a rotting leather helm.

Slow and difficult was the journey, which took all of two days and more, Justinian resting an hour here, an hour there, on some meagre hillock of land between the chill pools. As his eyes could tell little of the danger, it was no worse to travel at night, the end of his staff ever poking at the footing before him.

By the third morn that followed, he trod little but noisome mud, and could see the dry, featureless land that lay beyond. Featureless, except for the single low building which crouched a league away, unattended by tree, or bush, or other sign of nature's blessing.

Justinian halted, for he had neither Andrys's wit and lore, nor Erys's cunning, and was without a plan. It came to him that warm heart and earnest will did not always win the day, yet what else did he have? So he stretched out and slept a while in a dry gully, that he might face the warlock with as much vigour as he could.

When the sun was full, he arose, and casting aside his staff of yew-wood—for its virtues were too weak to trouble the warlock—he made for the hold. The closer he came, the more he feared the place, for it was uncommon wrought, and did not look clean of purpose. A stone's throw, and he could see how the split pines were made fast with human hair and yellowed dead men's nails; the doorposts were of bones bound in dark patterns, and there was no door.

"Ho the household! I would have word with the master here."

"Come in, come in, and be welcome," replied a reedy voice—one which Justinian seemed to recognise.

He stepped into the light of tapers and oily candles, which revealed a single chamber barely high enough for Justinian to stand. His first gasp was at the sight of Leif Thurlasson, huddled in misery at the back of the hold, by a wide and soiled bed; his second was when he saw the man who sat on a stool in the middle of the chamber.

"Gullscope!"

"It is a name I use from time to time," agreed the warlock. "I had word of your travels home, and in your brother Erys's absence, I guessed that you would need counsel."

"False counsel! You are also the cur Ovelamieli; you knew that if I burned the pelt, Leif Thurlasson would be yours."

"Of course. I trusted that your blundering would deliver."

All Justinian's woes seemed met together, and his folly complete.

The warlock stood up. "Yet I am pleased to see you, still full of figure and fine despite your journey. For I tire of this wretch, who is thin and without spirit these days. I see the golden curls upon your big chest, the rich tangle of your beard, and find that you might suit me well. My bed is eager; my appetites deep, and you will last many a moon."

"Do what you will to me," said Justinian, sinking to his knees, "only free my prince. Let him return to his people, to mend and prosper without my foolishness."

The warlock shrugged. "As you wish, so shall it be—but I am no child to be gulled like you. I will bind you, until I am assured your word is good."

"Very well. You shall have me, for I count myself worthless now. But the prince—"

"Pah. A small matter." The warlock snapped his fingers, and Leif Thurlasson rose to his feet. "Go you now," commanded the warlock, "and find your mead-hall, tarrying not until you have it in sight. By black thread and broken reed, I release you."

And the prince staggered out through the empty doorway, his face towards the west; in his wordless passage, he showed no recognition of his Southlands lover, which tore Justinian's heart the deeper.

The warlock grinned, and kinder grins were seen in graves. He snapped his fingers again, and thick ropes wound from the corners of the chamber, twisting around Justinian's ankles and his wrists. The touch of them brought a shiver of disgust, and he knew they were no common ropes.

"No steel can cut, nor fire burn, these bindings," laughed the warlock. "You will grow used to them, and when you grow used to me, I may command them back into their dens. If not, there are parts of you unbound that will bring me amusement in the days to come."

Thus was Justinian subject to the warlock's whims. Ofttimes the sorcerer was far from his hold, making mischief in this land or another. One day was he Gullscope; another was he Peterkin, or Malvolt, or even Sweet Peggy, so easy did he move from guise to guise. And on certain cold nights the man would return, and take pleasures with Justinian's body, delighting that his new captive was full of form, caressing the golden hair on every limb and in every secret place ....

The ropes which bound Justinian had their own ways, giving him lease to attend to most needs, but they would tighten fit to break bone should he offer threat or stray beyond the warlock's doorway. The blade used to carve his meat would not mark them, nor could his teeth split a single fibre from their coils. True to the warlock's word, when Justinian braved the fire and held his bound wrists over the flames, all that came were pain and blisters; the ropes remained unmarked.

His only comfort, in pain or unwanted pleasure, was to know that he had freed the Red Bear of Norroway, that his prince was safe, and might— in time—recover from the warlock's wickedness and Justinian's folly ....

TWO MOONS HAD PASSED; HIS captor was away in the land of the Finns, but would soon return, and Justinian's will was low. The sun in the warlock's land was without vigour, but the captive would drag himself to doorway and stare longingly to the west. Not the least discomfort of his prison was the rank smell within, and the scuttling noises from the shadowed corners.

On one drear morning, he sat silent between the pillars of bone, when he heard a harsh caw, and saw a single rook tumbling and swooping in the air. For a heartbeat he remembered his journey, and in the next, he saw a tall figure striding the earth towards the hold, coming from the Weeping Plain. Too tall for the warlock, surely? Half Justinian's great heart hoped for the prince to have come; the other half wished his lover safe and far away.

Leif Thurlasson it was, for good or ill. Gaunt and fell-looking, he walked with a long spear rested on his shoulder, halting as he espied Justinian in the doorway.

"Better I die at warlock's hands, than live loveless in my empty hall," said Leif before Justinian could even rise.

"Avaunt!" the captive cried out, torn between love and fear. "Go back, dear soul! The foeman is on his way, and we have naught that can give him pause."

Lief ran forward, and kissed Justinian tenderly upon the lips, stroked the golden hair.

"What has he done to you?"

"I am bound hard to this hold, and cannot leave. My prince, if failing you and freeing you are equal measure, then nothing is owed. Go back to your mead-hall and your people, and forget."

"Neither can I do," said Leif taking out his sword.

He slashed at the ropes; he stabbed the point between their strands; he hauled with all his might. There was no yielding.

Again the lone rook croaked its warning.

"The warlock is near," gasped Justinian—yet the bird's call drew his thoughts back to the brooch he had used in that time of need. "Wait—my pack is by the bed within. There is a knife there ...."

The prince swept past, and was soon back with the obsidian knife of Justinian's mother.

"No steel can cut these bindings, the warlock said." Justinian gazed upon the glistening black stone blade, edged like sudden night. "And no steel is in your hand."

Sure enough, the ropes might have been soft flax beneath the obsidian; almost was it that they parted and fled, rather than let it touch them. Eager hands pulled the last of the strands away, and Justinian was free.

"He is come," said Justinian, seeing a swift movement over the prince's shoulder. "But I am fearless when we are shoulder to shoulder, even to our ending."

There in the bone doorway they stood, and looked hard on Gullscope and his furrowed brows.

"Two pretty birds, eh?" The warlock's lips formed a narrow smile. "No matter. This time I shall keep you both, I think—one for the bed and one to scour the pans."

The prince hefted his spear and stabbed forward, yet a mere whisper from Ovelamieli shattered it, casting the fragments aside.

Justinian groaned, too worn to think of what else he could do.

"I am not made," said the warlock, "to be taken by the weapons of men—or by those of women, if you think yourself clever." He lifted one thin hand to snap his fingers and work some evil ....

"Clever enough," said the prince, "to turn your ways upon you. As you gave, so shall you be given," and drew from his tunic a singed and ragged piece of hide, with coarse red hair upon it. "Not all was fully burned—nor is a doom so ill when it is chosen."

And he thrust the hide between his lips.

In an instant his gaunt form filled, grew, and in Leif's place stood the Red Bear of Norroway, more terrible than a troll, more vengeful than a thwarted love. The warlock froze at the change, his snapping fingers stilled by shock, and that pause was plenty; he had neither Finnish cunning nor stolen glamour enough to escape the two huge paws which clapped sudden to his skull, claws sinking to the bone ....

Spine parted, sinew snapped, and the head of Gullscope bade an unexpected farewell to the body which had borne it. Over and over in the air it went, and when it fell it was but a misshapen lump of rock, like any other boulder thereabouts.

The Red Bear of Norroway bellowed, and turned to where Justinian stood, black blade now in his hand.

"Would you still have me in your arms?" growled the bear.

"Oh, I would, my prince."

And letting the knife fall, Justinian charged full into the embrace of the coppery beast. Such love and urgency was there in that charge, that the piece of hide shot out of the prince's mouth.

Instantly did the form in Justinian's arms shudder and change, but to their wonder, Leif of the Broad Spear was no longer the massive bear that had been there a moment before, nor was he the gaunt and troubled man that had been its shadow. Instead, he stood fine and proud, his long red hair shining, his beard a proud mane at his jaw, and his chest as wide as Justinian's.

"Well now," said the younger of the lovers, "This doom I like. More of a prince than ever to hold in the cold nights."

Leif marvelled at this new form, caught twixt shaggy beast and noble man. "I shall not complain," he grinned. "Though we may need a sturdier bed."

Justinian nodded. "I shall ask that such be my troth-gift from my mother, when we tell her of our triumph."

And he laughed full loud until his belly shook.

"But for now, 'I need not look for maidens' arms; another one has shown his charms.'"

So IT WAS THAT, WHEN the Red Bear of Norroway and his lover took ship to the Southlands and stood in the great hall of Justinian's line, none could question that Justinian's heart had chosen as it must. Naysayers could not be found, for those few skulked in meanness in their homes and battened on petty thoughts.

"The Red Bear and the Gold," announced the heralds, and in brightness were the two lovers hand-fasted. This joyful deed was done before the eyes of Andrys, his dark-eyed Aisha and their new son; of Erys wise in his governance, and of the queen, who had no complaint that the Northlands were now her ally.

Besides, she too had a generous nature. She had heard that Leif yet had an unwed aunt in Norroway, a fine, big woman who was said to be seeking warmer climes—and possibly a goose-feather quilt to share ....

SOMETHING OLD, SOMETHING NEW, SOMETHING BORROWED, SOMETHING BLUE

JONATHAN HARPER

1

How I remember that first night on the train, face pressed against the glass, watching the silhouettes of trees, their knifey branches, their skeletal frames, whisk by in the dark as I felt nothing but dread. There was an ever-constant feeling of danger or warning, a notion I could not fully understand. Back then, I was a timid boy, one who was easily intimidated by his own shadow, having relied (perhaps too much) on the protection of his older sister. Amelia, sat across from me in our private car, dressed in her new traveling suit, feigning sleep. That night, I felt such a kinship with her. I knew she also felt the dread. Her body was so tightly knitted together that she appeared ready for a brawl.

But I had no idea why she would be so nervous. She had already married the Duke, had already consummated their relationship in our parent's sullen bed, had already sold off our property and shed all the trappings of our previous home. Amelia was the stronger sibling, a brazen woman, a tough woman, one with the will to survive.

As the train rolled on through the night, I could find no sleep as I felt my grasp on our old life lose shape. I already missed my old village, despite its faults and disappointments. By the morning, we would arrive and be delivered into the hands of the Duke and begin our new life under his roof. What I feared the most was not knowing what awaited us at the end of the journey or how we would eventually be changed by it.

WE CAME FROM A HUMBLE beginning, typical for a story like this. Our mother, a strong-willed farmer, and our father, a stoic former soldier, were long dead. They had taught us well: how to churn the butter, how to pluck a chicken, the best price for grain and how to sell just enough to keep money in our pockets and bread in our bellies.

I should say that I was never meant to be a farmer. I did not have the constitution for it. I was a small boy, a lithe boy, a *sensitive child* as my mother often proclaimed. And my father, bless him, agreed and did all he could to ease me into the demands of such labor. Thankfully, Amelia possessed the raw strength I never had. She was a sturdy girl, obstinately pretty with a keen eye. When I think of our childhood, I remember those happy mornings saddled next to my mother, helping her sew and to prepare the broth, while Amelia joined my father in the fields. It was she who learned how to shoot our father's pistol, how to drink harsh liquor, how to laugh at a bruise. So, when we were finally on our own, we both knew she was to be master of our house.

Fate continued to test us after our parents departed this world. Our father's pension was not as plentiful as we had originally believed and after overspending on farm hands one season, we were unable to afford them the next. Then, two of our fields soured as if the land itself was rejecting our stewardship. We survived off Amelia's brawn and determination, working until we would collapse in an exhausted heap and still it was never enough.

This all changed when the Duke entered our lives.

After years of training, my sister had developed a reputation for her skills with our father's old military pistol. She could draw quicker than a field vole could dive in its burrow and with a closed eye she could shoot the cap off a bottle from a field's length away. Every summer, at the county fair, people would crowd in wooden stands to see her shoot. She always wore our mother's high-collared dress, her hair pulled back in a single braid, and drew her pistol with lightning reflex, shattering clay doves in rapid succession to the applause of many.

The Marvelous Amelia, they called her. The Pistol Maven, the Lady Sharpshooter with the Eagle Eye. This was how the Duke found her.

He was an older man, a sturdy rugged man with grim patriarchal stature and a surly black beard that shimmered with a hint of blue when the light struck it so. I was sixteen that summer when he came to town, having arrived on his honeymoon, escorting a beautiful black-haired woman, near exotic in her dark features and exaggerated hand gestures. Word around town claimed she was an opera singer, one of great standing in far-away cities.

But my eye had been on the Duke since I first caught sight of him in the open market. They perused the many stands and drank in our tavern. He admired our township with the scrutinous eye of a man enjoying caged beasts in a zoo, while his wife perused little trinkets, what she called, "darling folk art." And I followed them through the market, observing the Duke almost hungrily. I had felt compelled to do so, felt it in my gut, starting as a spark until it ignited into full infatuation, as if his mere presence nourished me.

It was the opera singer who noticed me first, who suddenly lavished me with compliments of the fairgrounds and asked me about my life in this humble little village. "What a darling little Ganymede," she told her husband. "Can we keep him, Your Grace?"

As if I were a pet, a little companion dog to follow her about and rest on her lap. For a moment, I was almost amenable to the idea.

There was the same glint of curiosity in the Duke's eye as he asked what I wanted. But what was I to say? My infatuation had come on so suddenly that I had hardly the time to interpret these feelings. I only wanted to be near him, to catch another glimpse of the blue in his beard. In my frustration, I rambled on about my sister, that she was a performer and they would enjoy her art. I escorted them to the stands and when Amelia took her first aimed shot, the Duke laughed and applauded, and I felt proud that I had somehow brought him joy.

His wife daintily applauded before she pulled him away, for she was tired of the fair. She left, twiddling her fingers at me. It was the last time I ever saw her.

A year later, the Duke returned a widower. Rumor circulated throughout the fairgrounds and we descended upon it like hens to grain. She had died in childbirth, some said, or by sudden illness. It was unclear.

But the Duke had been sighted loitering about the market and it was all the town could talk about.

Our farm was hemorrhaging money by then, and in my dim youthful hope, I wondered if the Duke had come to rescue us. My chest rising with delight as if it were full of clouds, I darted out through the crowd searching for him. When found his bulking stature was draped in black, and he stared openly at me with a grim concentration. It was different than the first time. Grief had left him hard as stone. Still, I once again led him to the stands where my sister performed and watched him gaze upon her work with the focus of the devil.

A week later, they were married.

2

OUR TRAIN RIDE WOULD TAKE us to him, to our new home on the other side of the country by the sea. He needed a week's time, he said, to prepare his manor for a new bride. And the week had gone by in a such frenzy that I could hardly believe I was sitting in this cushioned train car with ample space, dressed in a coat that was more costly than the entire farmhouse. I should have savored in this newfound luxury, but it was an arduous journey, and I still could not comprehend the world we were entering.

A little distance makes one reminisce fondly over their previous circumstances. I realized I would actually miss the reaping of grain and our yearly jaunts to the summer festival and watching my sister shoot in front of a dazzled crowd. I would actually miss the simple folk and their politeness— even if they had never been my friends, they were pleasantly familiar.

A sense of dread had taken hold. For as much as I desired the Duke, I also feared him, his stern, harsh demeanor and the loneliness his manor would offer. It was well after midnight, Amelia finally asleep, when I decided to spend my time wandering about the cars. Trains are phallic places: long and hollow. I paced in an endless loop, until I caught the eye of one of the night attendants.

The porter was a strange man, thick-bellied with a crooked mustache, subtly flamboyant in the way he grinned every time I passed. He said he recognized me, as if I was someone of prominence now, and after meager conversation, he offered me a touch of brandy to help pass the time. We sat in an empty compartment, one reserved for the night staff to linger away the longest hours. I cannot remember what we talked about, but I cannot forget the crude taste of the liquor, the feverish heat of the compartment. And the porter's hands: how he fumbled through the buttons of my shirt. Thanks to the benefit of years, I know the tumbling loss of balance, the texture of his mouth, unlocked something intangible within me. And when we were finished, he kissed me softly on the cheek and cradled me gently against his furry chest. I must have felt as if I had entered Heaven. Eventually, I left the compartment, retracing my steps to my sister's car, where she stirred slightly, feigning sleep, as a small smile crept upon her lips as if she had known all along this night would be temporal for us both.

I HAD ASKED HER ONCE, and only once, if she truly loved the Duke. This was the morning of their wedding, with us standing in the small vestibule of our town's chapel, Amelia draped in her makeshift wedding gown. How I adored my sister, but how at that moment, I despised her. She had the Duke, and I had nothing.

"He will be good for us," she replied with such sincerity.

What she could not know was that I had spied on them the night before, that I heard the Duke express such displeasure at the thought of me living with them, how he thought it was my place to stay and manage our family's farm, and how Amelia boldly declared she would never abandon me, that their marriage was contingent upon my presence.

"I will always look out for you," my sister said in her soothing tone, as if cooing a cholic babe, and I resented it. All of it. No one wishes to be seen as feeble. No one prides themselves in being either bride-price or burden.

IT WAS MID-MORNING WHEN THE train finally lumbered and stalled and came to a halt. As we gathered our pitiful luggage, my eyes kept darting in search of the porter but he was nowhere to be found. Part of me imagined he would emerge at the last moment and embrace me tightly, offering to let me stay aboard as his steward so the two of us could continue traveling together. A juvenile fantasy, this I know, but I was so inexperienced in the ways of the world.

3

WE TRAVELED BY CARRIAGE, PASSING through dismal towns and fields, until we could smell the salt of the sea. Situated near the cliffs, the Duke's manor was bloated and bulging, perhaps once a simple house but successive, competing owners over the years had erected ever-more ungainly rooms and walls and eaves. One small crack in the foundation and the whole structure could crumble apart and tumble down into the open mouth of the ocean waters below. Awaiting us on the grand steps, the Duke stood with his entourage of servants flanking him in a long militant formation, a full artillery row of housemaids and groomsmen, all dressed in black. They bowed and curtsied, though their eyes creased suspiciously at. Amelia and myself were tired and disheveled from overnight travel. Only as the Duke gently kissed Amelia's hand did they temper their grimacing faces. It was real, the act told them; this was the new lady of the house.

Once ushered inside, I found myself pulled by the wrist and into the bosom of servants, escorted through the majestic foyer and up the grand staircase to what would be my quarters: a large bedroom, roughly the size of our cottage back home, with two windows overlooking the sea. I was bathed and dressed by these strangers, who I kept pushing away in hopes of some privacy, but their grip was relentless in preparing me for the afternoon. I emerged in a stifling shirt and jacket and led down to the parlor, made to sit on a chaise lounge where a small tray of coffee and tea sandwiches awaited me. I had marveled at the intricate patterns on the plates. My first encounter with real china! My cup was trimmed in gold leaves to match the saucer. To merely sip from its rim was a fretful act—how could I bear witness to such an elegant and fragile thing as it toppled from my clumsy fingers and shattered apart?

Looking equally frazzled, Amelia was escorted into the room. She wore a draped champagne-colored dress that had obviously been thrust upon her, as she kept adjusting the fabric in agitated fashion and shooing away the lady's maid who hovered by her side. For nearly an hour, we sat in silence nibbling at our sandwiches—for how could we talk openly when her maid leered over us?

Finally, the Duke emerged with a stern formality to his entrance. He glared at us for a moment.

"When I enter, it is custom for you to stand," he said, and we did as he poured himself a cup of coffee and sipped. "It's cold," he grumbled.

A butler materialized to collect the silver urn and returned promptly with another.

Only once the Duke had settled into a few sips did his mood improve somewhat.

"I should say welcome to your new home," he said as he turned to Amelia, giving her the faintest of smiles. "I'm sure you are tired from your journey, but there is much to do. We must get you acquainted with the staff and your new responsibilities in running the household."

Then, he turned to me with an uneasy look in his eyes. "And you will also require some tutoring. You have much to learn about the expectations of your station here."

I nodded, making eye contact at first only to drop my head submissively, for I felt paralyzed by his penetrating gaze. I'm sure he appreciated my submission.

Our moment was interrupted by yet another maid, who came holding our father's pistol wrapped in a piece of linen and placed it in the Duke's hands.

Amelia straightened in her seat. "I was not aware anyone would go through my things," she said.

"Fear not, my dear. We keep such objects locked up for good reason."

"But what if I want it? What if I'd like to go shooting?"

The Duke laughed. "Then all you need do is request one of the servants or myself, for that matter, to fetch it for you. Or, if you'd prefer, you can try one of our hunting rifles, though it is some time 'til pheasant season." And then, as if to discourage any further conversation, he added, "We keep such things locked up when they are not in use." And to seal off the matter, he rose from his chair and began our tour of the house.

The manor was impossibly large, a central house with two wings, each full of rooms and passages, some of them practically hidden from view so servants could effortlessly move undetected. We were introduced to various entertaining rooms: the parlor, the drawing room (which should not be confused with the morning room), and the formal ballroom designed for large parties in contrast to the library specifically designated for only the family and elite guests. The lower levels contained a large overbearing kitchen and larders, along with a fathomless wine cellar and the butler's office. The upper level of the two wings contained endless rows of unused guestrooms, suites, and nurseries. Some rooms had remained closed off for so long that even the Duke could not remember their purpose and did not bother unlocking the door. At first, the tour was overwhelming, as I felt we were being led through a decorative labyrinth and one false step would have me lost among the corridors.

Our last stop was the west-wing gallery a poorly lit rectangular chamber that existed almost as an afterthought, with plenty of old stonework suggesting it was an original section of the home with little renovation. Despite being an interior room with no windows, we could still sense the presence of the nearby sea, and the narrow rug was so faded and moth-eaten that it did little to absorb the cold rising from the tiles. Drapes of cobwebs existed in every corner. Both sides of the gallery featured rows of framed portraits, each canvas dating back through the generations of the manor's inhabitants. The Duke droned on about his various ancestors, mentioning that our portrait would soon be added to the collection.

And then he lingered over the last in the row, a portrait of the voluptuous opera singer dressed in a long scarlet gown, posed serenely next to the Duke with his stoic eyes and blue beard. I had anticipated it but not its sibling, a canvas with the Duke standing with a humble blonde woman dressed in a powder blue dress that was frightfully ill-fitting. And next to it was yet another: the Duke looking impossibly young, his face covered in blue stubble, proudly standing next to a short boxy woman in a silver dress, her eyes bulging in delight. I stood there, methodically examining each portrait until the Duke was suddenly beside me, placing a hand on my shoulder (My heart! It felt like it would leap out of my chest!).

"Yes. I have loved and lost more than the most men will do in their entire lifetimes," he said almost distantly. "This house has seen much grief."

"There will be happier times, Your Grace," Amelia said, though I could hear the uncertainty in her voice.

The last thing I should mention of the gallery was the lone door at the far end, one in such perfect harmony with the stone around it that a careless wanderer might pass by without ever noticing it. It was made of thick wood planks and rusted brass trimmings, and was far too heavy for an interior door. Curiosity compelled me to approach, and when I made the effort of pulling on the handle, I found it locked.

"That area is not for you," the Duke said. And with that, he led us out of the gallery and off to the banquet hall for supper.

4

WE HAD ONE WEEK IN the manor, one week to orient ourselves to our new life, and the Duke ensured that our time was well-managed. Those first few days passed in a dizzy intoxicating spell that left me disoriented. Each morning, I awoke before dawn as some unseen servant was lighting the hearth in my quarters. I would fight off the sluggish residue of sleep before a groomsman ushered me out of bed to bathe as a breakfast tray was laid out for me. I rarely had time to finish my meal before I was again collected to be poked and prodded by tailors assigned to make me suitable clothes; an hour-long tutorial followed with the elderly groomsman so I would understand how to speak and eat with etiquette, to know the difference between the cocktail fork from the fish fork, followed by the relentless quizzing on the names and histories of the neighboring aristocratic households. Then, to the music room, where I received my daily lessons on the piano, for if I could not engage in conversation, I must be able to entertain guests in some other way. Every day at noon, our lunch was served in the drawing room, where we ate from silver trays coupled with a tasty treat of port wine to warm the belly, followed by a walk along the cliffs overlooking the sea. Then, we were forced to dress in our formal attire and sat in front of the grand salon's mantle while a tired-looking artisan began the long and tedious process of our portrait: the three of us standing together in a horrid hushed silence. An entire day of being jostled between instruction and activity would go by, and I was quite relieved that we received no visitors. But then in the afternoon, when there was no obligation, I would find myself alone with nothing to do but count down the remaining hours until dinner.

EACH EVENING, THE THREE OF us ate alone in the cavernous banquet hall, hovering over an obsidian stone table. By the end of our meals, we retired to the library for whiskey as the servants appeared to bid us farewell for the night. Where they went, I did not know, but they left in unison from the property not to be seen again until the next morning. And it was there, in the library where the evenings grew most grueling, that Amelia was expected to retire earlier than the men of the house, and she would strangely obey, leaving us alone. It was the only time when the Duke would acknowledge me directly, offering me books that I could barely read and forcing upon me glasses of sharp whiskey that I could barely drink. Those nights were my most conflicted. I felt hungry for him, starving even. Yet when I caught his eye, he gave me a menacing glare, judging me harshly until my mind flooded with the sense of trespass.

5

THERE WAS ONLY ONE RULE in the house: that lock doors remain undisturbed. And the only door I found locked against me existed in the back of west-wing gallery.

6

IN THE DWINDLING AFTERNOONS, WHEN I was left on my own, I learned quickly that I was quite adept at moving about unnoticed.

WHEN YOU ARE YOUNG AND inconsequential, it is like existing under a cloak of invisibility. I spied on the servants in their own workspaces, sometimes following them throughout the narrows access halls, and marveled at how

52

long it took them to notice my presence. Once, I surprised the head butler in his pantry and the poor old man thrust upon me his own stash of sweetened oat cakes as if to bribe me into silence ... but silence over what? Another time, I wandered into the Duke's private study, observing him peruse his papers, ashing a cigarillo, before I was clasped by the wrist by some maid and forced out. Often, when I was someplace I ought not to be, I was gently escorted back to an appropriate room where I would be more "comfortable", as they put it. I ended up back in that bloody parlor so many times I began to resent the room altogether.

One such afternoon alone in the manor, I made my way down to the cellars into the kitchen, where I startled the poor chef, who erupted into boisterous laughter. I liked him immediately. He was a jolly, pot-bellied man with a red beard, and unlike all the others, actually welcomed me into his domain. Maurice was his name. Jolly Mr. Maurice. He was a new hire, he explained, and currently the only chef at hand without even the benefit of a scullery maid to assist him, something he did not seem to mind except that the kitchen was rather lonely throughout the day.

By mid-week, I gave up my haunting the other servants in favor of heading directly to the kitchen where Maurice had tea waiting for me, anxious for any gossip I had acquired and eager to share his own. We never broached any topics of sensitivity, but we did talk at length about our own lives as I began to assist him with dinner preparation. I figured as time went on, this would be a way for me to make myself useful. That, and there were moments when I caught that glint in his eye that was reminiscent of the train porter's. I even let my hand brush against his during one of his cooking instructions and we grinned at each other.

But when I leaned into him, simply to feel that brief connection, he quickly retracted and created space between us.

"Sir, we must be careful not to get too comfortable with each other," Maurice said. "After all, you are technically one of my employers."

I buckled and felt my face flush bright red. Embarrassment overtook me so that I excused myself as quickly as I could to get dressed for dinner.

I still thought of it later that night in the library, long after Amelia had gone to bed, and I was alone with the Duke. We drank our whiskey and pretended to read and observed each other in a wordless confrontation. I daresay, with my nerves, I drank too much, and when the hearth embers began to fade, I found I could not lift myself from my chair, having almost fallen sideways into the side table.

A haughty laugh erupted from the Duke—a swollen belly laugh, which only increased my frustration, so that when he reached for my arm, I shrank away.

"Don't help me!" I yelled, my voice cracking with some undeveloped will of masculinity, enough to startle him into a backstep. And, horrified by my own insolence, I slurred out, "I must do this myself."

If the Duke took offense, he did not show it, but instead hooked his arms around me and pulled me to my feet where I fell deeply into the heat of his robes, the curve of his belly, and to steady myself, I wrapped my arms around him. This was first time since the train I felt that same urge and anticipation.

If not for the drink, I would have gushed into a flood of apologies and excused myself out. But, in that moment, I found myself helpless, and the Duke was well aware of my state. He escorted me up to my room in genteel fashion and began to undress me with the tenderness of any trained servant. But he did not leave. I can remember my head against his chest, the rhythm of his heartbeat, the musk of his undergarments, the slow creak of my bed, the curvatures of ceiling medallions above us, and our collective sigh of relief when we were finished. And then, he was gone, as if the manor house had swallowed him up.

I tried to tell Maurice about it the next day. My mind had been so foggy, delirious with drink, that I still questioned what had actually happened. Yet, I found myself unable to articulate the experience and Maurice, as if sensing a deep confession, hushed me with a slice of cake, his eyes showing temperance.

Later that afternoon, I walked the halls alone and settled in the west-wing gallery. The locked door stood sentinel. It beckoned me and I shuddered.

7

AT THE WEEK'S CLOSE, THE portrait was finally completed. Amelia appeared pale and distant. I looked nothing but an imposter, a farm boy masquerading in a gentleman's suit. The Duke was his bold self, painted to be the very emblem of all he projected. As I stared at the finished product, I thought solemnly about my act of infidelity with the Duke and wondered if Amelia was suspicious.

THAT EVENING, WE FOUND OURSELVES alone in the banquet hall, formally standing until the master of the house was seated. When the Duke arrived, he was not dressed in his formal dinner attire, but his traveling clothes. Even Amelia gave him a confused look.

"I have received a telegram from my accountants back in the city," the Duke said. "I have urgent matters to attend to of the most sensible nature and must leave tonight."

It was Amelia who spoke with her usual confidence. "Then I shall pack my things. I can be ready within half an hour." My stomach plummeted and then rose again—the thought of being alone in the manor with Maurice felt like an unearned prize.

"No, my dear," Duke replied. "These are financial matters I would rather close and be done with altogether.

I would rather expedite this process on my own. And I should not be gone long, a few days at most."

He looked at me.

"And I think you two should have some time together. I'm afraid my life here is a quiet one, perhaps not suitable for a growing family, so perhaps you both can spend this time plotting on how we can all reemerge in the public life ...."

The way he looked at me gave me shame. I despised him now; yet I still desired him. I did not know what to do with these feelings.

"There is one last thing," the Duke finally said, almost absentmindedly, and produced from his pocket a brass ring full of keys. "While I'm gone, I entrust to you my keys, as this house is as much yours as it is mine and you shall have full control of its access."

So many keys, one for each lock in the entire house. Huge oval-headed keys, silver keys with crooked teeth, tiny square keys for lock boxes, some of them old, rusted, almost Baroque. He singled each one out to explain its function. There were keys to the front doors, the spare bedrooms, the china cabinets, the keys to his office ... the list went on. The final key was smooth and fragile, as if carved from bone. For a moment, he looked ready to remove it from the ring and swallow it whole, but he left it there.

Amelia observed everything with her keen eye, but did not say a word, so I did it for her.

"Your Grace, what is the last one for?" I asked.

The Duke narrowed his eyes. "Nothing to be concerned with." An oddly-placed smile crept upon his lips as he placed the key ring firmly in Amelia's hand and helped her fingers envelope it. "That final key is to a room at the end of west-wing gallery, just a private study I keep in an older part of the house. To you, it would be a stuffy bore, but for me, it is my one secret place, the sole chamber I can sit in on my own, for those rare moments a man requires solitude, and can pretend he is not married."

"Call it a bachelor's chamber, if you will," he said with a chuckle. "We must all be allowed one secret." He gave me a narrowed-eyed wink.

Then, he fixed his gaze upon his bride, my sister. "You may use any key in the house. Use, touch, play with anything you like ... but that last key, I beg you not to touch. That room is mine alone, and this is all I ask of you."

The valet entered like clockwork and announced the carriage was ready. The Duke was leaving already, giving his farewells and within moments we stood outside on the front steps, bundled in our coats, watching his carriage depart down the winding road. But my mind drifted to the keys, or specifically the final key to the final room in the west wing.

The evening lowered its shroud upon the manor with a cooling touch. Servants appeared in their odd processional to clear our plates and start the library hearth and within moments, they were bidding us goodnight, anxious to be away to their own homes. And still, my mind remained singularly focused on the key. By now, I knew the Duke kept secrets and if we were to survive here with some semblance of happiness, I felt strongly that we should know them.

In the library, after Maurice had bid us goodnight and we were finally alone, Amelia sipped her whiskey and said, "Thank goodness they're all gone."

I was worried that there would silence, that the week had created a deep wedge that separated us further, but this was not the case. We talked pleasantly for a while, though I knew my sister well enough to know when she was concealing her unhappiness.

"Why would you marry a man you barely knew?" I finally asked.

"Because I understand sacrifice," she said. "Come on. I hate this room—let's walk."

We moved through the darkened manor by candlelight, crossing through the rooms and remarking on how we would repurpose them. Amelia would occasionally remark on some tiny feature that reminded her of home, of the farm, and the yearly fair. But my mind was settled on the locked door as much as the keyring in her hand.

I led her there, or at least she allowed me to, through the many painted rooms, until we stood in the west-wing gallery with its long rows of family portraits standing sentinel to greet us. Our portrait was now at the end, our morose faces staring in solidarity with those who had come before us.

I knew I would come here the moment it was possible. As I moved to the back door, Amelia paused. "We should not be here. It was his only rule."

"Then let's break it," I said. "And maybe he'll send us home."

I took the keys from her hand and strangely enough, she did not resist. The bone key slid into the lock as quick as a hot knife through butter. And I twisted it and turned with the care of a lover as the lock clicked and the heavy door pushed open.

8

IT WAS A VESTIBULE THAT opened to a lone staircase, unlit, descending into darkness. I was drawn into its spell, hypnotized by the dark, feeling pulled by invisible strings. I held my candle close and moved downward and the stairs ran deep, deep into the bowels of the manor, further down than the basement kitchens and the larders, until I entered a room of medieval stature. Once my eyes adjusted to the dark, the horror became as clear as mid-day. Instruments of torture, long racks with cords and wheels, shackles fit into the walls, shelves holding vials and metal instruments, the kind that cut and cleave and pierce, surrounded me. My eyes went to the solid image of the metal case, almost a coffin, erect—I recognized it only from old tales—the iron maiden.

The dim light allowed only one or two details of focus at a time and I was overwhelmed, and uncertain where I stepped and what truly lay within arm's reach. But the iron maiden captivated me most, almost whispering to me, begging me to investigate it further. With trembling fingers, I pried it open and thrust my candle through the crevice.

It was the body of a woman, almost perfectly preserved, impaled not by one but a hundred dreaded spikes, having long bled out, her gown stained in rust and blood. Her face was instantly recognizable: the opera singer, the previous wife. I should have screamed or fallen back. I have always been a fragile boy, and though I had witnessed death before, never with such violence. Even in the dulled glossiness of her pale eyes, there was the unrecognizable shock, a sign that she had not believed this could happen to her. My fascination briefly turned clinical. Her skin was spongy and cold to touch. How long did it take to die in such a monstrous contraption? Had she been dressed up in silk in preparation for this act?

The other wives were not hard to find.

The second wife lay out on a table, draped in what could only be a withered bedsheet, her body preserved, perhaps embalmed, the red, cauterized slit across her neck stitched back together, one final kindness.

Unlike the first wife, less care had been taken with her. I recognized her only by the withered, rat-eaten dress strewn upon what I suspected was her skeleton.

The first wife, had she been an experiment? Had she been an accident? I asked these questions to no one in particular, because I assumed I was alone in what could only be the hellmouth of the Duke's estate.

"We should not be here," Amelia said.

I had no idea how long she stood beside me, but there she was.

She held no sign of fear in her voice, no tremble in her step. Her hands calmly cradled the candleholder, her brow creased in observation. She made a short tour of the room, enough to know what fate had befallen her predecessors, before clutching me by the wrist. "We need to go now."

And so we did. We dashed back up the narrow staircase with such speed that our candles flickered and almost extinguished, and soon we had resealed the door, locking it tight behind us. And then, we ran through the halls to the main foyer, Amelia clutching my hand with such a grip that my wrist might have shattered beneath it. But I paused there.

"Come on, there's no time to dawdle," she commanded. "To my room we must go. There are jewels there. Rings, bracelets, necklaces, all heirlooms from the Duke, all gifts that could be sold."

"We can leave tonight," Amelia said, "even if we have to walk the treacherous road until dawn."

"I need to get some things, too," I said as I pulled away from her. "Trust me." And I rushed off through the house.

When I returned, I found her in her room, hastily stuffing everything she could into her suitcase with grim determination. "Are you almost ready?" she asked.

"Almost."

But our plotting was interrupted by the loud gong of the dinner bell and we froze in place.

"Maurice?" I wondered aloud, but knew instantly that we could not be that fortunate. For Maurice was already gone for the night, sleeping snugly in his own home, and besides, for an entire week, the gong had never rung once.

It sounded again, casting its evil echo throughout the house followed by a hideous laughter.

The Duke.

He was already back, or else he had never left. And then, I wondered if this entire night had been well choreographed, a simply-plotted play with a rushed last act.

Amelia and I stared at each other morbidly, before the gong rung a third time.

The Duke was summoning us.

"I will go," I said.

"Of course not. We will face him together."

But I knew I was the one who had opened the door, that I had already betrayed my sister in so many ways. And whatever should happen next, I knew that I was the weaker of the two and where I would fall, she might still survive. Perhaps, after such a brief tepid life, I was ready to be brave and that such bravery did not mean great feats, but to simply act in the way that is necessary.

"I'll go down first," I said and thrust my things into her hands. "This will buy you some time. Trust me, please."

And with that, I left her standing there and turned down the hall with a solemn determination to meet my fate head-on or off ... whatever the Duke intended.

He waited in the central foyer, still in his traveling clothes, a large saber strapped to his side, his beard a cruel blue in the pale light. He was smiling, a menacing wide-mouthed smile, the kind that showed the whites of his teeth, his eyes lit with demonic jubilance. I knew now that he was a fiend himself, or under the control of one, that there was nothing human left within him.

"One night between the two of you," he said. "I'm so pleased with this experiment. The last one took four months to cross the threshold."

I had reached the end of the stairs, still in possession of the key ring. "Amelia is innocent," I said in a whimper.

"My bride is no more innocent than you and those who came before her." His smile wide, serpentine. I suspected a forked tongue. "Come here," he said, and an extended a hand.

"Are you taking me down to the torture chamber?"

The Duke's grin did not bend. "It is usually reserved for the women, but for you, I feel I could make an exception. Would you like that?"

"If you will it," I said, my heart racing in my chest.

I did as I was told. I went to him, the way I would go to anyone, to feel the embrace of a lover and a murderer and to not know the difference between the two.

He left his saber at his side and took my hand, caressing it sweetly.

The first tear budded in my eye, and yet I could not wipe it away when he was so tenderly stroking my palm. And for a moment, I wondered if he would actually spare me.

Such gruff hands fitted so tenderly around my neck.

"The chamber?" I muttered, and the Duke shook his head. I wondered if he'd do me the courtesy of snapping my neck in one swift motion, or if I would smother there under his blue beard. His smile remained demonic. As his fingers began to tighten, I wondered if that cruel mouth could widen and unhinge and attempt to swallow me whole.

But the end did not come.

There was movement in the background and the Duke froze, his eyes tracing the lines of the staircase to the descending figure of Amelia, dressed in her traveler's coat, her face hard-lined. And the Duke looked back at me with the first trace of fear.

For it was at this moment when he must have realized that I, too, had a keen eye. An eye for details, an eye for numbers, and wits to remember them. And when you underestimate a person and reduce their worth, you overlook the fact that they move quite undetected, that they observe and remember such things like where you keep a trusted pistol and the combination to the lock. For during that brief time of separation from my sister, I had moved effortlessly through the hidden servant passages, collected our father's gun, and delivered it to Amelia.

And he too must have realized that there was time enough to load the chamber.

Amelia called to the Duke once so that he raised his head in abject horror as she took aim. One shot fired. One shot was all that was needed.

I felt the spray of blood and brains coat my face, as the split skull of the Duke balked in a silent howl.

The whole manor was alive with its sound.

9

ONCE ALL THE LEGAL MATTERS were finalized and the bodies properly buried, we made plans to leave the manor forever. Amelia inherited all. I will not detail the following weeks for they were tiresome. Extended family and society members appeared in droves with palms out, demanding their share of the fortune and Amelia appeased them as best she could. We kept very little from the manor, for it was difficult to fall in love with treasures that were never yours to begin with, but we managed a few crates and pieces of furniture, and a modest amount of money that would last us the rest of our lives. We sold or donated the rest until we came upon the west-wing gallery one final time and a historian offered to take the portraits for the sake of prosperity. Our own portrait we would have preferred to burn in a magnificent blaze but were content enough with leaving it for academia to add it to the records of history.

In the end, the manor was closed up and sold and Amelia used the proceeds to let the servants go with full pensions so they could start anew elsewhere, without fear of scandal.

All except one. Maurice, our wonderful cook, another lost soul among the wreckage. When I informed him that we were leaving, I asked if he wanted to come with us.

And surprisingly, he did.

The three of us returned to our small town, able to repurchase our farmhouse and hire the appropriate farmhands to tend our fields. We were welcomed back with open arms and sly looks and plenty of gossip, for Amelia was now a young widow with considerable funds. Suitors arrived with great urgency, coming and going with the yearly cycle of the summer fair. But she never re-married. She was a different creature now, hardened yet still gentle, with her keen eye that could shoot the smirk off a man's face from a mile away.

I used some of our assets to open in town a proper tea house, a modest little building that I stocked with ceramics and silver from the old manor. Maurice served as the cook, and happily baked confections that drew in visitors from across the county: happy women who came to admire the golden leaves on the china, who came to eat and gossip while their husbands and children ate their fill. And each night, Maurice and I retired to our little apartment above the shop, eager to forget the horrors that originally brought us together.

We grew old and plump. We prospered.

SNOW MELT AND ROSE BLOOM

JOHN T. FULLER

NOT SO LONG AGO AND in a place not far from here, in a clearing at the edge of the forest stood a cottage. Many people might call it small, but the correct word would be cosy. It nestled in the glade like a pip in an apple, the trees reaching over to shield it from the busy, brutal world outside. Every summer, flowers blossomed in the yellow thatch, and in the rambling front garden that did not need nor desire a fence two rose bushes bloomed—one white, one red.

The woman who lived in the house should probably have known there was something about those roses, from the way they flowered all year round, no matter the weather. However, Mama Anna was a pragmatic soul, and so accustomed to magic that she never gave it a thought. She tended to her garden and she played her guitar, she baked biscuits for her friends and told stories to the animals of the forest. She painted pictures that she sold at the local market, and she was happy. Sometimes she'd leave the forest to go out into the world travelling, which she enjoyed very much, but she always missed her peaceful little home and liked best when she could return there. "Because missing something makes you grateful to have it back," Mama Anna would muse. Often, she'd leave the forest for just long enough to see bands in the nearby city, and meet new people there. It was one of those outings that led to the twins.

"I think his name was Walt, or was it Albert?" She told Delia the fox. "No, it was Walt, I'm sure of it. Like Walt Whitman." She smiled, broadly and rubbed her round belly. "TreeFlower were playing, it was such a trip. And I came home with this beautiful gift."

Delia twitched her tail, and scooted into the blackberry thicket that hugged the house.

Mama Anna gave her a little wave goodbye. Beside her, the roses seemed to wave, too. A breeze shook the blushing bushes, petals falling to the ground like confetti.

Mama Anna said, "I wish for a child as white as snow. I wish for a child as red as blood."

The sun shone, bright and leaf-latticed. Birds clamoured in the branches above. And the sleepy heads of the roses nodded, as if they understood.

With the passing years, Mama Anna's gold hair turned silver, but she lived on contentedly in her cosy cottage in the forest, with the animals and her music and her sons, Walt and Whit.

The twins were born only seconds apart, but from the moment that Whit yelled hello to the world, it couldn't have been clearer how different they were. Whilst both boys were happy and kind, raised that way by their mother, and they got along as well as any brothers could, the resemblance ended there. Walt was slender and delicate like Mama Anna, with blond curls so pale they were almost white: he quickly earned the nickname "Snow." He was quiet and thoughtful and given over to music and poetry, writing odes to the singing woods as soon as he was old enough to speak. Whit, though, looked nothing like his mother or brother. Bold and loud, he could build or break anything with his big, square hands and his laughter echoed always around the house. "You have your father's colour," Mama Anna would tell him, smiling. That colour was fiery: pale skin dappled with freckles, and coppery hair that meant his nickname could be nothing but 'Red'.

There was never a question that the forest was their home. Fearless and bright, as children, the twins camped outside night after night, wrapped in the knowledge that the animals were their friends and the boys could never come to harm, and that in the morning Mama Anna would have breakfast waiting for them when they wandered home again.

One winter evening when the twins were twenty one, there came a booming knock at the door.

"It's late for visitors," Snow said, looking up from his book.

Mama Anna waved a hand. She didn't hold much stock in timekeeping. "Go see who it is!"

"I'll go," Red said. He clambered up from the couch.

The wind was a howling hound down the chimney, making the fire dance wildly. When he lifted the latch and pulled open the door, in blew a whip of snow like a twirling cloak, before any of them could see who their visitor was.

"It's a bear," shouted Red. He sounded more excited than afraid, as he turned to Mama Anna and Snow. "Don't worry, I'll protect you—it won't hurt anyone!"

And, with that, he widened his stance and put up his fists.

Mama Anna put down her macramé and shook her head. "No, no—nobody's getting hurt. Let him in, poor thing, he's half froze!"

"Come in, friend, and warm yourself by the fire," she called out to the bear.

To the astonishment of the twins, the bear replied, in a deep but quite human voice, "Thank you, Mama Anna. I mean no harm. I'm just cold."

Red stood back, as the bear lumbered into the cottage. Where he trod, the floorboards creaked and he left big puddles that seemed to look more like footprints than paw prints. He sat before the fire, taking up the entire hearth, and curled around himself like a huge dog, while the fire melted the mantle of snow from his shoulders and his fur steamed.

Red hung his head. Then he raised his voice and addressed their visitor. "I'm sorry for trying to fight you," he said, with a sheepish smile, then he dropped down to sit on the rug next to the bear.

"That's alright." The bear opened one sleepy eye to look at him. "I protect the things I love, too."

EVERY NIGHT THAT WINTER, THE bear came and knocked on the door, and Red let him in to sleep in front of the fire. It didn't take very long for him to become almost part of the family. It was nice to have some new company in the cosy cottage. The bear told them all about his life in the forest: where to find the entrance to secret caverns underground, and where the best berries grew. When it got later, he wove them wild tales of the forest and of magic, of fairies and goblins and treasures lost and found. Mama Anna told stories of the bands she'd seen play and the people she knew. Snow and Red had heard them all before, but the bear's delight made them seem new all over again. Snow played guitar for them and talked about his girlfriend, Marie, who had green eyes and yellow hair and was his sun and stars and rolling ocean. When it was Red's turn to speak, he fell unusually quiet.

"What's wrong, baby?" Mama Anna asked: Red was never quiet.

Snow knew his brother well. He reached out to pat one hefty shoulder. "Don't worry, man. One day your prince will come."

WINTER MELTED INTO SPRING. ON the morning that Red saw the first green spears of snowdrops poking through the snow, their friend the bear left the cosy cottage for the final time.

"Don't go," said Red, when the bear told them he must. Of the three of them in the Ruskin family, Red was the one who had grown closest to the bear, staying up until the small hours every morning, talking about trifles and dreams and wishes.

The bear blinked at him, solemnly. "I wish I could stay, but I must leave. I am bound to guard a great treasure from the wicked goblins who live in this forest and would try to steal it. Nothing must cause me to leave my post."

"But ..." Snow hesitated, as though he was loath to point it out. "You've left your post already, by visiting us every night this winter?"

The bear shook his huge, shaggy head. "In winter, the ground freezes and the goblins stay sheltered in their caves below. As soon as it thaws, they dig their way out." He paused on his way to the door, looking back at the family, although it seemed like he addressed Red alone. "Next winter, I'll come back. I promise."

Red smiled, but he felt all scrambled up inside. He would miss the bear's company and his stories like missing a part of his heart. Sadly, he lifted the latch and pulled back the bolt. But when the bear went through and ran off into the forest, a bit of his pelt caught on the catch and pulled away as if it was a fur coat, revealing a brief glint of silver beneath.

IT HAD BEEN A WEEK. Spring unrolled like a patchwork quilt, embroidering the hedgerows with primrose, and fat pansies and waxy crocus laced across the cottage lawn.

"Red, are you okay?"

Red straightened up and wiped his brow with his shirt sleeve, resting the head of his axe on his boot. He looked at his brother. "Yeah. I'm fine."

"It's just …" Snow nodded at the pile of chopped firewood that heaped up all around him like a fortress wall. "You've chopped enough to last us 'til next winter."

Red huffed, which was not like him. He wasn't okay. He'd been moping for seven days. "You're right. Maybe we should go for a walk."

"That's the spirit."

"We could collect some more firewood."

Snow sighed.

Despite his gloomy mood, Red's spirits seemed to lift the deeper into the forest he and Snow wandered. Winter walks were fewer and shorter and both brothers missed the outdoors when they were kept shut up inside.

Whilst they walked, they talked. "Tell me truly, though," Snow asked. "What's wrong?"

Red heaved a sigh. "Nothing, really. I mean." He swiped idly at a passing dead branch with his axe blade. "You have Marie, and I'm so happy for you …." He didn't need to say any more: Snow nodded in understanding.

"You'll meet someone. You will."

"I know." Red frowned. "I meet plenty of men in the city, and lots of them are very good looking and really nice, but they're just never the one, you know? I don't want a fling. I want someone to fall in love with. Someone I can talk to for hours, and tell all my hopes to. Someone who'll be my best friend as well as sleeping with me." His frown became a rueful smile. "It's funny: I usually feel even lonelier in the winter when we can't go out as much, but this past year, when the bear visited every night, I didn't feel lonely at all."

"You miss him."

Red sighed again. "I think maybe he was my best friend. Why can't I just meet a man with a personality like that?" He paused, to glance at his brother. "I never told you, did I? A weird thing happened as the bear was leaving."

"What weird thing?"

Red tilted his head, musing. "As he went out of the front door, some of his fur caught on the latch and it sort of … pulled back. And underneath it was silver, like metal."

Snow rounded on him, blocking the path in front of them, his eyes wide. "You know what that means, don't you?"

"No, I don't," Red said, patiently. "If I knew, I wouldn't have asked you." He thought for a moment, and his mouth dropped open. "Do you think he's a robot bear?"

His brother punched him lightly in the arm. "I've heard stories like this before. The bear was certainly a bewitched prince!"

Red raised his thick eyebrows.

"No, listen. A handsome prince, all clad in silver, and under a spell. A spell cast by a wicked witch, to turn him into a bear." He eyed Red's dubious face with an expression of exasperation. "How many talking animals have you met?"

"Mama talks to the animals all the time."

"Yes, but they don't usually talk back, do they?"

Red had to concede that point: he nodded, slowly.

Snow continued, "So, the witch turns the handsome prince into a bear—"

"Why?"

"Well, I don't know, do I? We should find him and ask!"

Red pulled a face. "I'm not so sure that's a good idea. I mean, he might actually be a bear. It would be a bit rude to go asking him if he was a cursed prince. It might hurt his feelings."

But Snow was adamant, and Red was rarely one to argue with his brother, and so they carried on, into the forest, searching for the bear.

When it was past three, and they'd eaten all of their food, and it was certainly time to turn back and be home for dinner, they stopped for a rest.

"Alright," Snow sighed. "We can look again tomorrow."

"Before we go back." Red nodded toward a large, fallen tree that was blocking the path. "Might as well take some more firewood while we're here."

However, when they approached it, they began to hear some very strange sounds, of grunts and growls and muttered swearing.

"What the fart are you staring at, lamp-lighter?"

An irate goblin was standing on the log, shaking his fists at them. He was dressed in a brown velvet suit and long, black boots. He had ears like a rabbit and tusks like a pig. His eyes were glaring red, his wrinkled skin green as clover leaves, and the hair and beard that trailed clear six feet behind him were whiter than Snow's curls.

"Hey," said Red, with a little wave.

"What the coccyx!" bellowed the goblin.

Red winced.

"Well, don't just stand there, corn-starcher, make yourself useful and get me free!"

Peering closer, the brothers could see that the end of the goblin's trailing beard was caught in a split in the tree trunk.

"How did you manage that?" Red asked.

The goblin's green face turned a shade brighter in rage. "Master-thatcher! I was cutting some wood for a modest fire. I don't require so much as you folks—so wasteful! Look at you—the amount you eat!"

Red glanced down at his ample belly and narrowed his eyes at the goblin.

"But when I split the trunk, the edges sprang back and caught the end of my beautiful beard. And now you two prongs are here to laugh at my misfortune, on top of everything!"

"We're not laughing at you," Snow said. He approached cautiously, inspecting the split in the trunk.

"We want to help you," Red agreed, bending down to try and pry the fissure apart. But it was no good. Even with Red's tough hands on the job, his strength wasn't a match for a big old oak. And even with Snow's nimble fingers at work, he couldn't tease the goblin's hair from the grasp of the tree.

"It's only the very ends," said Snow, consolingly. "It'll hurt you if you try to yank it out. Just think of it as a trim."

"Do what you must" the goblin spat.

And Red raised his axe and chopped off the tip of the goblin's beard, freeing him from the split oak.

"There," Snow said. "It looks fine! Neater, even. All nice and straight."

Now that he was free, the goblin seemed more irate than ever. "Fishing crates!" he screamed. He jumped down and gathered up his fallen axe, and a heavy bag that clinked when he hefted it: beneath the buckled flap, Red glimpsed the glint of gold. "How dare you cut off a piece of my wonderful beard? I wish you nothing but ill luck for all your days!"

And with that, he ran off into the trees.

"Well," said Red. "He was a dick."

Snow nodded in agreement.

They lingered in the clearing just long enough for Red to chop some firewood and bundle it up to carry: after their altercation with the goblin, even Red wasn't really in the mood for logging. "It's getting late," Red said. "Mama will wonder where we are."

Snow nodded. "Let's walk back by the stream. It's quicker."

THE SPRING RETURNED TO RED'S step as they followed the melody of the stream. In winter it sometimes froze, even though it was fast-flowing, and in summer it sometimes dried up. But now, in spring, the water was in full surge, musical and jolly, its banks fringed with flowers.

"Oh no," said Snow.

Red followed his gaze to further down the bank, where an all-too familiar figure in brown was hopping towards the water.

"Hey," shouted Red. "The bank's right there! Stop, or you'll fall in!"

The goblin's barrage of curses broke the peace of the waterway. "Bendy fools! You again!"

Several birds erupted, panicking, from the undergrowth.

"I know where the flapping bank is. Do you think I'm doing this on purpose?"

Looking closer, the twins saw that the tip of his trailing beard was tangled up in a fishing line being towed upstream by a not overly large, but very determined fish.

Red exchanged a perplexed glance with his brother.

"Dig your heels in and sit down; it's just a fish," Red advised. "It might tug you off balance, but it's not strong enough to pull you in if you're sitting down."

Grumbling, the goblin went down on the bank like a dropped sack of beets. He jutted his chin forward, howling in outrage. "It's worse! It's worse! You stupid bedspread! Oh, it hurts, it hurts."

"Wait there," Red shouted. He scrambled down the bank, wading up to his knees in the stream until he reached the goblin struggling on the opposite side. "Here, I've got you."

He tried to pull at the fishing line, but it was too thin to get a grip on, so he held onto the end of the goblin's beard as gently as he was able, pulling it up to take away the strain.

The goblin howled all the louder. "Unhand me, you terrible clump! Your dirty hands are besmirching my beard."

"If I unhand you, you'll fall into the stream," Red said, placidly. He called back up to Snow, "Dude, do you have any scissors on you?"

"Scissors? What!" The goblin's eyes leaked fire. Then they looked in danger of popping right out of his skull at the sight of the little army knife Snow handed down to his brother, miniature scissors unfolded. "Keep those things away from my beautiful beard! You mean to disfigure me! Frock!"

"Chill, mate." Red tried to wrangle the tiny blades with one big hand, the other still full of squirming goblin. "I'm only going to cut the fishing line."

And with that, Red snipped the line, the tension broke, and the goblin fell backwards up the bank.

The goblin stood up, shakily, brushing himself down. He was vibrating like a whistling kettle ready to boil.

The twins exchanged a nervous glance.

"You pieces of shed! Look at what you did! My fine suit is all covered in mud! My fishing line is quite ruined and now I shall have no dinner, because of you!"

Scrambling up the bank, he paused only to rummage in a patch of dropwort to retrieve another large, hessian bag—the gleam of pearls visible within—before running off into the trees once more.

"You're welcome," Snow called after him.

THE GOING WAS SLOWER AFTER that, with every step punctuated by the squelch of Red's wet boots.

"I don't know why you helped him," Snow said. "He was the worst."

Red shrugged, and shook some weed off one foot. "Even horrible people don't deserve to fall in streams," he said, although he didn't sound entirely convinced.

By the time they reached the little path that led home, the shadows were starting to lengthen, the trees bending down to whisper. Above, the branches crowded with unseen birds, trilling and warbling in unison. Both men jumped at the sound of an almighty squawk that was definitely not a bird.

"What on earth was that?" Snow asked; but Red was already running soggily down the path towards the source of the noise.

There was a bird, although it wasn't the bird who was making the noise.

"You again," Snow said, when he caught them up.

Flapping frantically, a gigantic buzzard was trying to fly back into the canopy, the goblin caught firmly in its claws. Thrashing his legs, the goblin squealed and bellowed, as Red held firmly onto the hem of his velvet coat.

"Let go!" Red called. Snow noticed then that the goblin was clutching the buzzard as hard as the buzzard was hanging onto the back of his coat.

"If I let go, I'll fall, shot-glass!"

"I'll catch you," Red said. "Just let go." Spotting his brother, he shouted, "Come and help."

With both of them holding tight to his coat tails and tugging, finally the goblin lost his grip. With a ripping of fabric, he fell out of the clutches of the buzzard's fierce talons, and landed harmlessly in Red's strong arms.

"Ugh," the goblin spat, struggling more frantically to be free of Red's grip than when the buzzard was abducting him. "Set me down, you pike!"

Red did so, gladly, taking a step back as the little creature puffed up with rage once again.

"How dare you! Look at what you have done! My fine coat; it's ruined! First my beard and now my suit—why do you carts torment me so?"

"Sorry about your coat, man," Red said. "But you were about to be bird-feed. We had to help you."

"Well next time," the goblin spat, "don't bother." Turning, he dragged a cloth sack out from behind a tree trunk, hefted it onto his tattered shoulder, and stormed off along the path.

BY THIS TIME, RED AND Snow were quite exhausted and more than ready to be home. They trudged on in silence, until, not far from the cottage in the clearing, they saw a most unexpected sight.

"Bear!" called Red joyfully, but then faltered in his tracks even as he made to run towards their friend.

"You flagging pests again!" the goblin exclaimed, cowering against a stone, cornered by the bear. The bag of jewels he had been carrying spilled a rainbow of light across the rocks: the goblin glanced down at it and licked his lips.

"Dear bear," he said, in a wheedling tone. "See, those two who have come along—they are a far finer meal for you than a slender waif such as myself. Just let me take my jewels and be gone and you can eat them both up!"

"I think not," the bear spoke.

The goblin flinched, paling in fright, at the words.

"What, didn't you recognise me?" the bear asked. "You thought I was a bear of the forest?"

"Please!" moaned the goblin, now turned a greenish shade of grey. "Have mercy! Spare my life and take them instead."

"I have a counter-offer," the bear said in a terrible tone. "Return those jewels you stole from me, lift the curse you placed upon me, and then I might think of sparing you."

At this extraordinary exchange, the brothers, speechless, shared a glance.

Snow mouthed, 'I told you so.'

"You're lying," whined the goblin. "How do I know you won't just kill me anyway?"

"You don't know. But," The bear raised a paw bigger than the goblin's head, "you have a much better chance against me as a man than me as a beast."

The goblin screeched in rage. He made a strange little gesture of his hands, and there was a great eruption of blue smoke.

Red and Snow covered their faces and staggered back. When they dared open their eyes again, the smoke had cleared. There was no trace of the goblin, who had escaped under cover of the spell. Instead, there, surrounded by a fallen pelt of fur, stood a man.

"Hey," said Red, stunned.

"Hi," said the man, in the bear's voice. He sounded strangely shy. "I'm sorry. I'm not a prince."

"I can see that," said Red, in a tone that sounded as far from disappointed as could be.

The man was short and stocky, with shoulders as broad as an oak tree's trunk, and a big, curving belly. He was dressed in the greens and tans of a forester, and his brown arms were sculpted by hard work. His hair was thick and black and curled past his shoulders, and his beard was even thicker and blacker. In his belt, there gleamed a silver axe.

"What's your name?" Red asked. "You never would tell us."

"I was bewitched to never say my name, or anything that could reveal me as a cursed man," the forester said. "Several years ago, the king hired me to guard a cache of treasure he had hidden in the forest. One evening, I caught that goblin trying to steal from it. He was so angry when I cornered him and demanded that he return what he'd stolen. He said he would 'turn me into the beast that I am.'" The forester let out a little laugh.

"I don't think he was banking on that beast being a bear. Even so—I was so confused by being a bear at first, that he was able to steal the treasure anyway. When I recovered my wits and got used to my new shape, I swore I would get the treasure back and try to break the curse he placed on me. And then, I met you."

He smiled at Red, a wide, brilliant smile with a gap between his front teeth.

"My name is Arthur. But you can call me Art."

Red smiled back, even wider.

THE SUN HAD SET BY the time the three of them finally made their way back to the little cottage in the clearing. Snow set down the sack of pearls he'd been hefting, and ran to the front door to call Mama Anna.

"I'm sorry you had to leave all that wood you'd cut behind, to help me carry these," Art said as he and Red added to the pile the four sacks—brimfull of jewels—that they been carrying between them. He looked at him, almost shyly, and patted the axe at his belt. "Maybe I can come back and help you cut some more?"

Red gazed at the man who was a bear. "I'd like that."

There in the starlight, Art was the most beautiful man he had ever seen, with his dark curls and his black eyes and his barrel chest. "I feel like I know you already."

Art smiled, and Red could have sworn a few more stars lit up above them. "Of course you do. We talked all winter. It was still me, even though I looked so different."

He took a hesitant step forward. "I've never known anyone as well as I know you."

"Right now, I don't feel much like talking," Red said, quietly.

His heart galloped as he stepped forward, too, both of them leaning in until their lips met in the middle. Red gave a different kind of sigh, as their arms slipped around one another almost of their own accord.

Art's lips were plump, soft amidst the brush of his beard. His mouth was warm and wet. It made Red feel dizzy, a shivery sort of throb blooming at every pulse point: in his temples and his throat, in his belly and between his legs.

When they drew apart, he blinked, staring in adoration. "I thought that might be weird. You know, with you having been a bear when I met you and everything. But it just feels like I've fallen in love with my best friend."

Art's eyes looked kind of shimmery. Damp. He said, "You've just made me the happiest bear in the world, Whit Ruskin."

WHEN SUMMER CAME, TURNING THE blue of the sky up to full volume, Snow left the cosy cottage in the clearing to move in with Marie in her flat in the city, with earnest promises that they would both visit often.

"Well," said Mama Anna with a smile, to Art, who had been staying with them while he recovered fully from the curse. "Seeing as there's one less in the house, it would be silly if you didn't stay for good."

Art, who'd become very fond of Mama Anna too, moved into the cottage with her and Red.

The king, very grateful to have his treasure returned, had listened with concern to Art's terrible tale. Then he back-paid all of Art's wages he'd accrued whilst being a bear, with added compensation for being attacked on the job and a bonus for retrieving the jewels. It was more than enough, over the next year, for the two of them to build themselves a second cosy cottage in the clearing, facing Mama Anna's. Between the households, their two gardens met as one (for they did not need nor desire a fence) with the twin rose bushes at centre.

"We should plant some roses, too," Red said, one evening, looking into Art's dark eyes.

Art nodded, and kissed his forehead.

Art and Red planted two more rose bushes across from the white and red. The yellow roses flowered as vivid as sunshine and the reds as dark as velvet and almost black. Summer brightened and blazed. The garden rejoiced, the roses growing into an archway, the right size for two people to walk through hand in hand. Yellow, white, red, and black intertwined, all blooming, no matter the season.

THE THREE LITTLE PRIGS
M. YUAN-INNES

OF COURSE I KNOW THE Wolff guy.

He's the reason I've got my bullwhip 24/7.

What, I never told you about him?

He's a massive guy—I mean enormous, in every sense of the word—with enough hair to keep both of us warm in winter. But totally broke, could hardly afford the boat trip over, y'know what I mean?

So, who should he run into but my youngest brother, Hamlet?

Yeah, you've never met Ham. He's this skinny vegetarian artist with straw-blond hair. Ham refuses to come to the city. He claims that real art is being made underground anywhere but NYC or LA. Really, that means Ham's stuck in flyover country, writing letters for Amnesty International and crying over starving children in between classes at a no-name college.

The only fun Ham gets is swimming laps. He swims like a seal, and he's almost as hairless, except for the mop on top of his head. He says that doing laps inspires his art. He climbs out of the water and works on his "pieces."

Here's a pic of his latest one, made out of square hay bales. He calls it "Tiny House."

I don't get it, either.

Anyway, my seal of a brother runs into Wolff at the Y. Now, I bet that Ham barely comes up to Wolff's armpit and is about as thick around as one of Wolff's thighs. If Wolff attacked him, Ham's biggest defense would be making a sculpture out of Wolff's chest hair.

You'd think my little bro would squeal and sprint the other way. Instead, he feels sorry for this "displaced person" and adopts him. Food, rent—the whole shebang. Moves this Wolff right into his house.

Well, I ripped Hamlet a new one when I heard about it. He's a poor college student, and he's letting some huge, scruffy Wolff mooch off of him? Dad taught us better than that.

I tell my other brother, Smokey, to get Wolff the hell away from our little bro. Smokey lives in the sticks outside Detroit, it's closer for him, so he goes.

Smokey's just like you remember. Same haircut and jeans since 2012, got married to David right after earning a B.A. Bought some horrible log cabin fixer-upper and keeps asking me to "come out to the cottage." Still working in insurance and tweeting jokes about policy coverage. Smokey's idea of a good time is swapping Instant Pot recipes.

Yeah, I guess you could call him stick-in-the-mud, but he's reliable. Like a Volvo. So, I send Smokey down to evict the Wolff.

And he does, but only because Wolff ends up crashing with Smokey.

I know. I never thought Smoke'd do anything but David at six a.m. on Sundays, but Smokey ends up blowing up his house with Wolff while his husband's off on a business trip—probably getting his own business done—but the point is, the Wolff's now huffing and puffing with my middle brother.

Smokey calls in sick for work, he forgets to walk the poodle, he stops donating money to the Log Cabin Republicans, which is how I knew my bro's truly fallen off the deep end.

I had to drop the enemy a line.

Wolff,

You've been porking my brothers. Well, I'm the one built like a brick house. I run a hedge fund. I live in East Midtown. You want taste, the real deal, come to NYC.

I text a selfie, dressed in my open bathrobe, standing in front of my apartment's view, though you can only see part of my face. Just a tease.

One week later, the Tuesday after Labor Day, I'm on my phone, closing a deal after-hours as I duck into my building on Vanderbilt Avenue.

I nod at the doorman, who's dwarfed by a giant, black-haired man at the front desk.

The giant doesn't speak. His presence is enough, a human mountain. He's trimmed his black beard to a neat point. He's stout, filling up a dress shirt and tight jeans. He's rolled up the sleeves so that I can see there's plenty of hair running along his biceps. I can imagine those wiry hairs scrubbing my bare skin.

Instead, I turn away so I can continue my phone negotiation.

The doorman hands a piece of ID back to the giant and says, his voice trembling slightly, "Who are you here to visit, sir?"

"Kevin." The giant's voice rumbles through the faux industrial brick lobby, raising goose bumps under my Dolce and Gabbana suit.

I shake myself and speak into my phone, saying, "That's unacceptable," as I march toward the elevator. There is no need to feel hypnotized simply because some lupercal guy has uttered my name.

I can still hear the doorman doing his best to interrogate the giant. "We have more than one guest named Kevin, sir. Do you have an apartment number, or would you like to call him and let him know that you've arrived?"

"He's expecting me." Wolff's voice echoes through the lobby, growing louder as he follows me toward the stainless steel elevator, where the operator has already pressed the button for me.

"You can't go in there," says the doorman.

I can hear the heels of Wolff's boots striking the terrazzo floor behind me.

"I said, don't go in there!" The doorman raises his voice and chases him across the lobby.

Wolff has my number. He probably looked me up before he came and recognized my face, if he hadn't figured out the family resemblance. He could call me instead of storming my building.

This is a power play. It always is.

The elevator dings. The steel doors glide open, and the operator gestures me inside, but his eyes travel upward, behind me, to stare at the giant.

I swivel around, phone still in hand.

The big, bad Wolff advances upon me. His eyes pin me like a predator's. I remember Rasputin's legendary, hypnotic eyes, and I know why my brothers fell before him.

I can hear Wolff's slow, even breaths. He grins at me, a lazy, toothy grin that communicates his intentions. He has no need to rush. This is a game for him.

"Come in, sir!" The elevator operator wants to shut the elevator doors behind me, but I'm blocking them. I can't move.

Meanwhile, Wolff grins down at me. "Let me in."

He's so close that I could stroke the bristles of his beard and let him nip my finger. I can feel his hot, damp breath on my face; I imagine those arms clamping around me.

This is the kind of man who would eat you up for breakfast, and leave you saying thank you. I have to close my eyes.

I hear the doorman say, "I'm telling you one more time, sir, leave the premises immediately, or I'm calling the police!"

It sounds like the elevator operator's already dialing on his phone.

My eyes snap open, and I hold my left palm out to both of them. "It's okay, Nick. Jerry. I got this."

Meanwhile, I cut off my phone call. That deal can wait.

Wolff grins at me with his colossal white teeth. His immense hands remind me of baseball mitts. The broadness of his chest makes me think of a grizzly bear standing up on its hind legs to roar at me.

But his eyes. The eyes shining—those eyes tell the whole story.

"Get a hotel," I tell Wolff. My voice sounds steady, if a little high-pitched. "Text me when you're ready."

Forty minutes later, I meet the Wolff in an ice-white penthouse. Before he says hello, I kick the steel door closed and pop open my briefcase.

Five seconds later, my whip cracks through the air.

He backs up, wary. He's bigger than me. He knows he could wrestle the whip away from me.

If he could get close enough.

I ignore the strong, male scent of him. I grip the leather handle, grounding myself, watching him feint to my left.

This time, the whip smacks his hand. His breath hisses between his teeth.

I catch my breath. That's the kind of noise he'd make in bed. I can't lie, I want to know what it's like to have this man work me over. He knows it and I know it.

If it weren't for my brothers, I'd lay my whip down and let him have at it.

But I think of Ham's straw art, that I don't even understand. I think of how Smokey's face used to shine when he served Instant Pot lemon chicken with Basil at Thanksgiving.

I proceed to whip the Wolff. I work him over until his screams of pleasure echo off the soundproofed walls. I keep working until I'm afraid the whip will slip out of my sweaty palms, but I don't dare take off my suit jacket. I've got to stay 100 percent dominant, 100 percent of the time.

And when I throw down the leather dog collar I brought, I don't even need to demand he put it on. He volunteers, and he's eager to see what other surprises I have in my briefcase.

All guys like him are alike. They think they are this big daddy. They talk the talk. *Hey baby, I'm so hot, I'm gonna blow your house down.*

But I can tell. I've got him hooked now. He couldn't get it up the regular way if the Rockettes went down on him.

I gotta admit, he's got me hooked too. That's why you haven't seen me lately. There's something about him. Even when he's not around, I can almost taste him.

That's why I keep him on a such a short leash. If you go down to the Port Authority Bus Terminal, that's him with the sign, "Will blow you for food."

The police keep busting him, but I love how Wolff keeps coming back to me. With his tongue hanging out, begging for more.

A GIANT PROBLEM
CHARLES PAYSEUR

BEN INHALED DEEPLY, DRAWING THE smells of his castle over his palate, allowing him to—

He gagged.

"Fee-fi-fo-*fuck!*" he bellowed. "I smell the blood of ..."

His gaze darted about the room. The knickknacks on the mantle were moved or knocked over; one tiny wooden penguin was splintered on the stone floor far below. There was a telltale indent on the softest pillow on the couch. There were small bites taken out of the bread sitting out on the great counter and—he nearly gagged again—*tiny finger trails* through the butter.

"A human! Ugh!"

How the hell did they even get in? His castle, built in the clouds far above the human realms, was supposed to be impossible for humans to reach. That fact, above all others, had sold him when the estate agent had shown it to him. The castle inside the active volcano had been tempting as well, for the same reason, but Ben didn't much care to live inside a sauna all day, every day.

But there was no mistaking the signs or the smell. Humans. Great. Ben went to the wash basin to wash his hands and stopped just shy of putting his hands in the cool water. What if ...

Images of a human using the basin as a bath assaulted his mind. Filth and disease sloughing off a tiny, naked body making mockery of the beautiful and burly appeal of a giant. He slouched, hands hovering, unable to dispel the fear and disgust building in him.

He threw out the wash water, the bread, the butter, and anything else the human might have contaminated that he couldn't have cleaned. He brought more well water to give the castle a thorough washing when he saw movement out of the corner of his eye. Low to the ground. Fast. He dropped the bucket he was carrying and ran outside, slamming the door behind him. Not only had a fucking human been in his house, *it was still there.*

And nope. Nope nope nope nope.

He walked to the edge of his cloud, held a hand to either side of his mouth, and called for an exterminator.

HE WAS STILL WAITING OUTSIDE when a rainbow streaked through the clear blue sky, connecting his home to the wider world. Magical creatures got around in various ways. If you had wings, you just flew. For the rest, though, either you had some sort of pegasus you got around on or you counted on the network of rainbow bridges that could be called to connect any two places. It was how Ben went off to the larger settlements when he needed supplies, and now it was also how the exterminator opted to arrive.

Ben's breath hitched.

Some people slanderously claimed that all giants look alike, though few ever saw two in one place. Giants were, as a rule, solitary creatures, their castle or other homes in remote mountains or deep in the earth. Yes, they tended toward the very large and hirsute. Most sported beards. But Ben was hardly the biggest of giants. Yes, the earth trembled under his boots, but his beard was short-cropped, his hair similarly neat, and he tried his best to walk softly when he could. Not like the giant walking toward him over the glossy rainbowed surface of the bridge!

He moved with the deliberate power of a glacier, one hand thumbed into a work belt, the other swinging lazily at his side. He wore jeans and a muted flannel shirt he'd rolled up over forearms that looked almost too thick to be contained, and bushy with dark hair. More hair poked out from between the top two open buttons of his shirt, leading up to a full beard.

This beard showcased a devilish grin under eyes sparkling behind thick-framed glasses. A trapper hat with its flaps up revealed what might have been a receding hairline, and he seemed to radiate a sense of stability and strength, like a sexy mountain that had just grown legs and sauntered over.

"You call for an exterminator?" the man called as he reached the cloud bank of Ben's home.

"Yes, Daddy," Ben whispered.

"Excuse me?"

Ben's eyes shot wide, mind racing to cover his mouth's poor attempt to hide his attraction.

"I mean, yes ... Danny?" Ben said, cringing. "Is ... is that your name? You ... uh ... look like a person I know. Named Danny."

Smooth. The exterminator pursed his lips and took a moment looking Ben up and down.

Ben squirmed internally under the scrutiny, but willed himself still. Finally, the man's gaze returned to Ben's face, and he gave a roguish wink.

"I think I'd let you call me anything you'd like," he said, "but my name's Drake. I understand you have a problem?"

So many problems, Ben stopped himself from saying. A bed that was woefully empty. A fully stocked kitchen with no one to cook for. An ass that just wouldn't quit.

"Humans," Ben said. "Or maybe just one. I didn't stick around to count. I just can't stand the creatures!"

"Humans," Drake said, slowly, almost a question. "And you didn't just find them and grind their bones to make your bread?"

Ben rubbed the back of his head. Normally it wasn't a deal breaker, but he knew he wasn't exactly normal by giant standards.

"I'm a vegetarian," Ben admitted.

"Ah, well," Drake said with a shrug. "Does that mean—"

"I'd prefer live capture if possible. Hopefully nothing ... painful for them."

Drake looked from Ben to the house, then gave a fleeting glance back toward the rainbow bridge before he stomped his foot and dismissed his conveyance.

"That's fine by me," he said, grinning again and giving Ben another wink. "I'm always up for a challenge."

Ben sat on the recliner, feet well off the floor, just in case. He scanned the room, from the blanket chest to the small collection of folded paper birds on the side table. So far there were no signs of the tiny invaders.

Drake was fiddling with a small black box in the kitchen.

"So you live here by yourself?" Drake asked.

The question might have been innocent, but Ben certainly hoped it wasn't merely politeness. A thousand thoughts bubbled inside him. Almost all the giants Ben knew kept to themselves, dwelling in cavernous homes and covetously guard whatever treasures they had accrued on vacations. "Just me and Tyson."

Drake shot him a glance, brow furrowed, eyes narrow behind his thick frames.

Jealous, Ben hoped.

"My goose," Ben explained, even as a chill worked its way down his spine. His goose, who was still in her large cage in the bedroom. Who was probably none too pleased about still being locked up despite Ben's arrival. Who was altogether too quiet.

"Your goose ... named Tyson," Drake said, the firm edges of his expression softening back to humor. "Of course."

"I should check on her. You'll be okay here?"

Drake nodded as Ben took a deep breath and put his feet down slowly to the floor, then hurried on tiptoes toward the bedroom.

Please let there not be humans, please let there not be humans, please no— The mantra replayed in his head as he reached the door and opened it, hand tight on the knob in case he had to wrench it shut. But there was no sign of a human, no scurry of tiny shoes on stone. But neither was there the indignant honk of Tyson, which wasn't a good sign.

The cage took up most of the space on top of his dresser. Tyson wasn't exactly giant-sized, though she was large for a goose, a bit bigger than his fist. Most giants who kept pets had animals that had been magically altered to make them proportional to their people. But Tyson was a rescue, plucked from the court of a wicked king who had cruelly enchanted the poor creature to lay eggs made of gold. Ben had put a stop to that (part of his activism work to end animal abuse), and found that, though she was a cussing little devil, he could hear a bit of love in her honks.

Crossing the room, his fears were realized when he saw the door of Tyson's cage hanging open. Had a human been *in his bedroom?* Was he going to have to burn the whole place to the ground? And did one of them steal Tyson?

Then came a honk. Ben jerked his toward the noise, and saw movement toward his open closet door. With only a slight hesitation, he rushed after it. "Tyson?" Ben asked, reaching for the small lantern he kept inside the door. With a practiced flick, it caught, and Ben froze.

It's not that Ben had never been around humans. He would venture down into their lands occasionally—normally to free some magical cow from a cruel farmer or maybe to sink a few whaling ships while they were still in port. But he was always careful, because, well, humans were small. Tall ones maybe came up to the top of his boot. The one standing wide-eyed in the middle of his closet wasn't a tall one. Maybe still an adolescent, or perhaps just short, almost as long as the tip of Ben's middle finger, and somehow that only made the creature creepier.

Ben took a half-step back, unable to tear his gaze away from the small human, who seemed to sense his hesitation. Was it smiling? What the fuck? "H-help," Ben said, unable to raise more than a whisper.

The human seemed to relax, gave a small stretch, and began walking boldly in Ben's direction.

"Dra—"

But before Ben could call out for help, there was a new noise from deeper in the closet. An angry hiss. And then a violent eruption of feathers and honking as Tyson streaked out from the shadows and into the pendulous light cast by the lantern. The grin on the human's face dissolved into terror as the unwanted visitor bolted directly past Ben, who cringed but managed not to hurl himself out of the room.

He kept his feet planted, knees locked. He couldn't banish the thought of what it would be like to accidentally step on a human. The mess! The guilt! He shuddered, but recovered in time to reach down and pick up Tyson before she could follow the human out of the closet. She bit him, of course. Swearing, he moved her quickly back to her cage and bundled her in. She bit him again for good measure and then honked at him.

"Sorry about this," he said, "but until this is taken care of, I need you out of the way. Can't have whatever Drake's doing accidentally hurt you, okay?"

She honked and tilted her head to the side.

"Drake's the very sexy exterminator who's helping to fix our human problem."

She hissed.

"Don't be jealous just because you're not getting any right now. We'll take you to the pond in a few days, and you can get as frisky as you like."

A final honk, and she squatted and pooped, wiggling her tail feathers derisively.

Ben rolled his eyes and turned to the door—to find that Drake was standing there, leaning against the frame, a lazy smile on his face.

"Oh, hi," Ben said. Shit. How long had he been standing there?

"Well, this very sexy exterminator is about ready," Drake said, and Ben felt his face heat up as if he were living in that volcano. "I saw it scurry out and underneath the couch, so this will be a good test."

DRAKE REPOSITIONED THE BLACK BOX again.

"What's in that, anyway?" Ben asked. He was trying not to think that just across the room, there was a human underneath his couch. He stared at the dust ruffle, imagining their little eyes staring back from the thin shadow where the fabric parted. His palms itched with the desire to bleach everything.

"The latest in humane human deterrence." Drake popped the lid off the box and motioned Ben to peek inside.

Ben did so cautiously, half afraid that there would be some sort of tiny magical tiger that would leap out and attack whatever was closest. Not that it would be humane, but maybe it would only retrieve the humans and deposit them alive outside somewhere. However, the box didn't contain anything so mobile. Instead, Ben saw what looked like a harp. Big by human standards, it would still barely fill a giant's hand. Small knobs on the outside of the box appeared to connect to the delicate workings of the harp, allowing it to be manipulated easily without having to use forceps and magnifying lenses.

Ben thought of a soothing harp lullaby, and his eyelids felt heavy just imagining it. "Is it supposed to ... put them to sleep? So that we can gather them up and remove them?"

Drake grinned. "Even better," he said, then replaced the lid and flicked a switch on the outside of the box.

Noise filled the castle. Intense, shuddering noise, like the box contained an earthquake of music and riot.

Ben gave a squawk, hands flying to cover his ears.

The kitchen, the entire castle, bounced from the deep bass and almost electric rhythm of the box.

"It's magic," Drake yelled over the ... Ben would have been generous and call it music. "Should be enough that any humans can't stand it."

As if to underscore his point, movement from the couch brought all their attention to the small figure darting out and toward the door, which they had left open.

Ben whooped as he noticed the human, too, was covering his ears. Another minute, and the human was out, and Ben was locking everything.

It was almost bittersweet that it had worked so well, so fast. On the one hand, it meant Ben could clean, and his daily routine could settle down, and he could put this all behind him. On the other hand, it meant ... all of that. That Drake would leave. That Ben would go back to being all by himself. That he'd be left as he was, too afraid to go out anywhere he might meet another giant, where he might do more than dream about being wrapped in strong arms, heavy and warm.

As he walked back to the kitchen, he waited for Drake to turn the harp off, but the exterminator made no move to do so.

"Don't you need to turn that off?" Ben asked.

Drake shook his head. "For best results, it should be left on for a day or so."

Ben tried to force a smile, but probably only managed a grimace. A whole day of this? And yet maybe it meant he'd get to see a bit more of Drake. Maybe *a lot* more.

"What am I supposed to do?" he asked. "I can't exactly sleep with this going on."

Drake shrugged. "I've got some ear plugs if you want them. Though I'd recommend staying the night somewhere else."

Ben felt something warm and fragile beat inside his chest. A chill followed sensations hot and hopeful and bordering on desperate. Everything inside him told him to run, to flee, to protect himself. There was no way this would end well. Giants were solitary, and even if he got a momentary release from that isolation, giants weren't the settling-down types. And hoping for it, either reprieve from his loneliness, or more, just might kill him.

"Perhaps with a very sexy exterminator," Drake continued, "after you take him out for a celebratory meal and drink?"

Ben's mouth was a kingdom cursed with a hundred years of drought. He wanted so badly to say *yes*, to believe this was happening. He wanted to ... he took a deep breath.

"Well, I mean, i-if that's something you—"

"You'll have to speak up," Drake shouted over the noise. "I can't hear you."

Ben pursed his lips and glared. Arrogant, sexy bastard. He was enjoying this. Ben bit his lip, tried to channel his inner Tyson.

"Would you like to go out for dinner?" he said, loudly enough to be heard. "A-and afterward, would it be okay if I stayed the night at your place? And can my goose come with?"

There was no way that Tyson was going to tolerate being left alone with the racket for an entire day. It would be animal cruelty.

Drake broke into a rumbling laugh. "I would *love* to have dinner with you. And I'm sure I can find *somewhere* for you and your goose to sleep. I don't live in a castle, but I think you'll find what I have acceptable."

A HYDRA BAND PLAYED SOFT jazz as jinn flitted around the room, indistinguishable from the cigarette smoke and sizzling steam off the steaks brought out from the kitchen by teams of sweaty incubi. Ben ordered asparagus and pasta with a wine reduction sauce, while Drake ate something he'd ordered in French and that looked heavy on mushrooms. It had been an age since Ben had gone out like this. He smiled to hide his nerves as Drake rumbled about some of the more interesting cases he'd worked.

The plates were a bit small, though. The club, while catering to non-human clientele, obviously wasn't used to seeing giants out and about. A makeshift table had been erected in the back of the room, where the hastily-reinforced chairs still strained under their weight. The harpy manager kept stealing looks at them, a huge fake grin plastered on her face, as if all she could do was calculate how much damage their insurance would cover.

"The worst are the elves!" Drake said, slapping the table and earning them a worried look from half the room. "They always think they're doing *good*. Some hapless retiree starts finding his home full of clogs, or dolls, or toy boats. They can try to sell them, sure, might even make a bob or two. But to the elves, that's basically a contract, and now they're owed for services rendered. Plus interest. And they're even smaller than humans! I swear I have to go into places with tweezers sometimes."

Ben's laughter was genuine, though his mind was divided between trying to enjoy Drake and worrying about his home. The human was probably alone and had just been walking around, looking for things to take. Probably opened Tyson's cage upon noticing the golden eggs.

Just one human, and Ben was ready to wash the entire place out with lava. Or maybe he was just trying to distract himself from thinking about what might happen next with Drake. What happened when the immediate problem was over and there was no reason for them to see each other again? Drake seemed to be having fun, seemed *interested* in all the right ways. But was this a one-night stand? Did it have to be?

"So, why extermination?" Ben asked. He needed to stop obsessing and get lost in the moment, but he also needed to know more about the man across from him.

Drake's eyes crinkled at the corners. "I could say that it's because I get to meet hot men in desperate need of me," he said, and the heat in Ben's face inched upward. "And that *is* a nice perk of the job, don't get me wrong. I guess I like a bit that it's so, well, unusual for a giant. But I can't stand being locked up in one place for long. And I like the problem-solving. I'm a tinkerer. I like working with my hands."

And his grin grew a bit as he said that.

The meal passed quickly, and the wine flowed. Their conversation wandered like a sheep without a shepherd, but it never got lost. And then they were on their feet and headed toward the floor near the stage. The manager looked ready to have a heart attack, but she didn't stop them, just cleared out everyone she could get to move. The giants had to crouch a bit under the vaulted ceilings, but they danced, neither really leading or following, just getting used to their bodies close, their hands finding shoulders, waists.

Ben let himself lean forward against the powerful expanse of Drake's chest. He had never been on a real date. A part of him was terrified he was doing it wrong, that he didn't know how. Perhaps, despite all his pining and his hopes, Drake was secretly laughing at his inexperience. But when he looked into Drake's eyes, he didn't see cruelty. He saw a heat that must have reflected in Ben as well.

The rest of the bar seemed to hold their collective breath, waiting for something to go wrong—giants were not known for their restraint when dancing, or their grace. But that didn't mean they didn't have any. They danced, close, while the hydras played and the night's possibilities beckoned.

By the time they got back to Drake's place, though, most of their grace was spent and their restraint abandoned like a prophesied baby on a woodcutter's doorstep. They stumbled through the apartment. Drake's lips like fire, his hands managing to deftly unbutton Ben's shirt without just ripping the damn thing off. Ben's fears and uncertainties were still present but muted by the wine and the need for this, the immediacy of Drake's hands and body. The rest he'd just deal with tomorrow.

They aimed for the bedroom, entangled and panting, pausing at the closed door only long enough to throw it wide and—

A trumpeting ball of feathers erupted at face height, and Drake swore as Ben, pants already halfway down his legs, got caught trying to back away and tumbled to the floor.

"Bloody hell!" Drake shouted as the vengeful poultry landed, pivoted, and launched herself at his chest.

Ben managed to pull up his pants and stand, reaching to catch Tyson before she could hurt herself or either of them.

Hissing, she twisted out of his grasp to crash on a nearby table.

Before she could recover, Drake grabbed Ben and half ran, half fell back into the vacated bedroom, shutting the door behind them. A second later came a thud and more angry honking as Tyson attacked the door from the other side.

"I think she might be upset from all the stress today," Ben said.

"You think?" Drake's eyes were wide, though there was still a fire burning in them when he looked at Ben.

They were just inches apart, bodies heaving, clothes still hanging off them. Ben bit his bottom lip. They had made it to the bedroom, after all. As if sensing his thoughts, Drake leaned in.

A new crash broke the moment, and in the apartment beyond, there was a shattering of glass and further irate honking.

Drake grimaced. "I guess that means we probably can't …."

Ben wanted to close the distance between them. He leaned just a bit closer. Maybe, if they were quick ….

A louder crash this time, and both men winced. No, if Tyson kept this up, she would probably destroy Drake's apartment and accidentally injure herself.

Ben sighed and pulled away.

"I guess not," he said, then took a deep breath. "That is, if you value your stuff."

"Hard call." Drake glanced down Ben's body. "Really *hard* call."

They both shared a look full of frustrated longing. Then they squared their shoulders, and got ready to open the door.

BEN DABBED TENDERLY AT HIS still-swollen lip and almost felt guilty as he left the pet boarding house. Both for Tyson, who was only being her usual self, and for the boarders, who would soon learn exactly what that meant. But Drake's smile, waiting for him outside and gilded by the rising sun, was enough to banish anything but keen anticipation for the time when they were back at Drake's place. Well, there was also the fresh worry that this was all somehow too good to be true and couldn't last.

They summoned a rainbow bridge and walked in companionable silence. They could hear noise first—the screech that seemed ripped from the throat of a siren who'd just stubbed her toe. A dull bass throb built as they approached. It almost sounded louder than Ben remembered. But at least he'd have his house back. At least, could daily life return to normal?

Ben squinted as they reached the cloudy shore of his home. From inside the house, there were strange bright lights. Was the door open a crack? Hadn't he closed that? And what the hell were all those little squares littering the clouds leading to the house?

Drake, apparently full of the same questions, strode forward and picked one of the things up. They were tiny, but as Drake returned, Ben could tell they were paper of some kind. Blank on one side, and with inked designs or words on the other.

"Uh oh," Drake said.

"What is it?" Ben asked, stepping forward and immediately stepping back as a tiny figure emerged from the cracked door. Human. Staggering. Collapsing to its knees on the stone stoop. Vomiting. Eww.

Drake retreated as well, handing the bit of paper out for Ben to see.

Rave in the Clouds! Jack's throwing a party, and this time it's HUGE!

There was a graphic of a human on top of a mountain of food. Not technically accurate, as it was largely meats and cheeses, but the implication was clear. The humans were having a party. They were in Ben's house, eating his food and befouling his home. He didn't know if he was going to be sick as well.

The whole cloud island still rocked with noise, and Ben's gaze fixed on the windows, the strange colored lights pulsing from within. How many could there be? A dozen? Certainly the humans couldn't have organized something so large so quickly. But the bits of paper littered about gave him a sinking feeling, like his feet were dropping through the fluffy surface of the clouds.

Drake moved a short distance away, eyes on the ground. He seemed to be following a stream of the dropped papers from the door. He followed it to end the trail, and knelt, rumbling, "Well, here's where the problem started."

Ben joined him and saw that there was a small hole in the cloud. This hole was lined with green. Peering through, he saw an enormous vine stretching all the way from the base of his clouds to the surface below.

"Magic beans." Drake shook his head. "I've seen this before. Should have guessed, what with your setup."

"Can't we just, you know, pull it up or something?"

"Wouldn't do much good at this point," Drake said. "You'd just strand however many are inside. At least we'll be able to cut off their route of re-entry when we get them to leave, though."

"And how do we do that?"

Ben mused about just abandoning it all and going to live in the arctic where humans didn't typically have parties. That idea almost seemed more manageable than dealing with whatever was happening inside his house.

"Lethal measures still out?" Drake asked.

Ben nodded.

"Then I have a few options. We could try an offensive odor, like heavy garlic or something similar. But that would probably linger well after the humans fled. We could produce smoke enough to make them believe the castle was on fire. That normally convinces them to leave, though it might also lead to some tramplings. Similarly, we could try to flood them out. Your place is stone and would be relatively easy to clean up or dry out afterward, but there'd probably still be some damage."

All the options sounded terrible, but Ben held back from saying so. He didn't want a smelly home, nor did he want to risk actually setting it on fire. Slowly he moved closer to the castle, to the large front window. If he was going to make the call, he needed to know exactly what he was dealing with. He needed to see, even though his stomach rebelled at the idea. He made it to the window, swallowed, and went on his tip-toes to peer in—

Hundreds of humans cavorted in a pounding mass across the floor. They were dancing, grinding, tearing apart his bread, smearing butter on each other, raiding his pantry, pulling food into piles to frolic in. Ben couldn't hold it back any longer and retched onto the clouds, losing his breakfast and the last of his indecision.

Drake laid a comforting hand on his back, patting him softly.

"We flood them," Ben said when he was well enough. In his mind he saw a wave washing the humans away, carrying them out of the house, and then a great waterfall sweeping them back down to Earth.

UNFORTUNATELY, FLOODING A CASTLE IN the sky was a bit more difficult to execute than it was to imagine. They rigged a siphon from the well through the window in the washroom, which the humans hadn't managed to open. Taking a deep breath, Ben jumped and pulled himself up as Drake pushed from behind. It was almost a shame to move away from the firm hands on his ass, but Ben managed to clear the window sill and drop himself into the washroom. He turned and pulled Drake in with him. The noise was even louder inside the house, cut with the sound of so many stomping feet just beyond the door, though maybe that was Ben's imagination fixating on the waves of humans so near and so numerous.

Drake pulled his end of the siphon and knelt in front of the door. Wrapping his mouth around it, he sucked, his body heaving with the effort.

Ben couldn't restrain a smirk, and he felt himself warm at the sight.

Drake noticed and shook his head. "You want a turn?" he asked.

Ben stuck out the tip of his tongue and then pulled it quickly back into his mouth. "Not exactly what I'm interested in getting in my mouth. And besides, you're doing such a *good* job."

Drake narrowed his eyes but got back to work, alternately sucking and breathing.

Ben watched as the water inched farther and farther down the long tube, until finally it reached the end. Water streamed forth, and Drake coughed. He sputtered as it ran down his chin and through his beard. He quickly shoved it into the space under the door.

Ben's heart leaped. That would show those humans! Let them run! What would be a tiny puddle to him would be a raging river to them. A lake that they could drown in. A danger that would spread until it took them all.

"And now, to see how it worked," Ben said.

He barely cracked the door open, hoping the humans had pressing concerns with the sudden, gushing water. He smiled, thinking of their panicked retreat. Through the gap in the door, just enough for him to see through, though, he did not see the frightened and running shapes of humans trying to get away. It was the joyous shouting and cavorting of humans running *toward* the water. They bounded into it, only to be swept back. Humans rode the lead edge of the wave, which unfortunately spread out not too far from the washroom door.

"Oh, for fuck's sake," Ben said. "They're *enjoying it*."

Drake nudged his way forward, and Ben was only too happy to stop looking at the tiny joyous faces as they played in the water, a fountain to them.

"Ah, well," Drake said. "Fuck."

Ben wanted to bash his head against a wall. "Do *any* of them look scared?"

Drake squinted. "A few of them are backing away from the water, but it might be that they don't want to get their clothes wet. Or they haven't had enough of that big cask of ale you had in the pantry."

Ben closed his eyes, trying not to cry. Nothing about this was working the way it should. He wanted to give up, maybe even run away.

"We're going to have to try and scare them out," Drake said.

Ben furrowed his brow. "Fucking *how?* If the threat of an imminent flood just makes them think they're at the beach, what more can we do? Maybe we should just let them have their party and hope they wear themselves out af—"

"We could threaten to eat them," Drake said, and it took a minute to realize that he was being serious.

"I'm a vegetarian!"

"But they don't know that! To them you're an enormous, terrifying giant. So am I. If we go out there and snarl at them, maybe threaten to eat a few of their limbs, there's no way they're sticking around."

Ben opened his mouth to object further, then paused. Closed his mouth. Fucking hell, it just might work. Here was an entire castle of freeloaders caught red-handed, eating his food and wrecking his home. They'd be devastated by the guilt alone. And if that didn't convince them to tidy up and leave, the prospect of being ground into flour might.

"Fine," he said.

BEN TOOK A DEEP BREATH. He had to psyche himself up a bit, imagine himself as a rampaging monster capable of biting a human in half. The thought made him wince. Okay, well maybe not that far. He was up to giving them a stern talking-to, though. He looked back at Drake, who stood ready, nodding at him.

He pulled the door open.

The humans beyond, playing in the flowing water, paused in their revelry and looked up. He could see their wide eyes as he stopped over them, stomping hard enough to shake the whole castle, though careful not to crush any of them. He made a show of barreling out into the main room, of puffing out his chest, of roaring. Behind him, he could hear Drake do the same. Two terrifying giants and a few hundred humans.

The room was packed with them, and for a moment they all shared his gaze, transfixed perhaps by his confusion, by his size. He hadn't stepped on any, but it was a close thing. They all stood poised until they realized that he might eat them all. They panicked and ran screaming. Maybe ...

He took a deep breath, ready to bluff and pretend to be the evil ogre they probably thought him.

But one of them stepped forward from the mass. And he looked familiar. The original human, the one he'd seen in the closet. That same smile on his face, like he didn't have a fear in the world. The tiny person took another step toward him, and Ben's resolve crumbled.

He stepped back.

The human ran at him, and Ben started, retreated, looked for a way out. But they were surrounded. The harp inside the box continued to play. As if the little person's advance broke their spell of fear, the other humans reacted. They pointed and laughed. Anger boiled through him. He reached for the box, but the same damnable human darted to cut him off, and again Ben backed off.

Behind him, he could practically feel Drake restraining himself from just stepping forward and booting the bastard through the wall. But Ben didn't want to resort to violence. He felt tears well up in his eyes. It wasn't fair. He tried his best to be nice, to be peaceful, to protect animals from those who would abuse them. But this human! This fucking human.

He reached again for the box. Maybe if the noise stopped, the humans would stop.

They had already recovered from their horror at seeing giants. It was as if they could tell that Ben was afraid of them. Perhaps they knew he couldn't stand the thought of grabbing them and throwing them from his house or listening to their bones snap if he squeezed them. They danced. They laughed. And they made a wall between him and the box. He balked, stepped back, and nearly bowled into Drake, who caught him and held him at arm's length.

"Are you okay?" Drake asked.

Possible answers raced through Ben's mind. Doubts. Fears. Ben could see his every missed opportunity, every time that he had stopped himself from pursuing something he wanted, and retreated. He saw the future: Drake waiting, at the end of all this, for Ben to ask him back out to dinner and Ben just failing. He could anticipate the lonely nights when he was too reluctant to go out and try to meet someone. He could imagine himself complaining to Tyson that giants were just too reclusive, too hard to find, when really he wasn't even trying.

The humans spread around him. Ben could tell from their expressions that the humans knew he was a coward. Not that being soft was wrong. Not that caring about not hurting them made him less of a giant. But he was *afraid* of hurting them and of being hurt by them. And he was letting that fear stop him when this was *his home*. His castle. And they were trespassing, and if he backed down now, they'd only keep coming back. And he'd always be running.

Ben drew in a deep breath and let it go.

"I'm fine," he said, and he turned back to the human. The man. So small. And Ben knew what to do.

He stepped forward. The man seemed to feel the air shift and hesitated as Ben stepped forward again. Then the man advanced, and it took everything in Ben not to recoil. But he didn't. Instead, he bent down and reached for the man, whose eyes went large enough that Ben could clearly make out the whites. Ben encircled the man with his hand and plucked him up like he was putting Tyson back in her cage. Not tight enough to hurt, but tight enough to contain.

Finally daunted, the rest of the humans edged backward as Ben carefully stepped to the side table and his collection of folded paper birds. He picked out a large crane and moved to the window. The man in his grasp struggled but could do little as Ben placed him on the crane's back and, opening the window, sent him sailing out. There was a moment where Ben felt bad, when the man's look of shocked fear made Ben almost sorry for doing it. But then Ben remembered who was the invader, who the invaded. And he turned back to the humans still in his home. And Drake, who was wearing the most delectable of tiny smirks.

It was though some great weight lifted, and the noise finally did sound like music. Who and what were important here? Drake and his mouth, which Ben desperately wanted to kiss. He walked, and the humans edged back even more. He reached Drake and took hold of the front of his shirt, pulled him close. The exterminator's eyes had time to widen a second before Ben's lips crashed against his. Ben was tired of waiting, tired of worrying. So there were humans. Whatever. They'd better get the fuck off the bed, because Ben knew where this day was going.

Drake recovered quickly, returning the kiss, reaching behind Ben's neck to maintain the contact and prolong the kiss. Their tongues wrestled, their beards mingled. Ben started pushing Drake back, out of the main room, towards the bedroom. For once he didn't check to make sure the humans were moving out of the way. This was his house, and if they didn't want to get stepped on, they should move. Clothes were pulled off, removed, all while the two giants kissed and stumbled toward the promised softness of the bed. They splashed through the puddle still growing near the bathroom, and Ben wanted to giggle. To laugh.

They burst into the bedroom and paused long enough to slip free of their boots.

Around them, Ben was dimly aware that the humans were moving. But they were just background noise, nothing to the consuming foreground of Drake's gloriously naked chest, a forest of hair leading all directions, but especially down. Boot-free, Ben hooked a finger in the waist of his jeans and with a practiced flick undid the button.

Drake smirked.

"Impressed?" Ben asked.

"It takes more than that to impress me."

Ben knew a challenge when he heard one. He dropped to his knees and pulled on Drake's jeans hard enough to drag his boxers too, relishing the slight shock on Drake's face as his cock bounced free, already half hard. Ben wrapped his hands around Drake's thighs, squeezing his ass and making sure he couldn't pull away as he opened his mouth. Drake groaned as Ben took him into his mouth, a sound so deep and loud it dwarfed the noise of the music, of the rave. Ben sucked at the head, then pulled back with a pop. He licked his way down Drake's shaft, then took him in his mouth again, deeper this time, pushing his limits. He refused to gag as Drake thrust gently forward in response, feeling his cock push against the back of Ben's throat.

He rocked, taking Drake again and again. He could taste arousal, and he relished the needful grunts each time he pushed forward.

Then hands grabbed his shoulders and heaved him up. Suddenly Ben's mouth was covered by Drake's. The final bits of Ben's clothes were pushed free, and he was nearly picked up and thrown onto his back on the bed. Drake followed, a charging bear, and Ben knew better than to fight.

"Lube and condoms ... drawer in the nightstand," Ben managed, his body aching for Drake's touch. He'd had enough foreplay. Enough anticipation. What he wanted now—

Drake flipped him on his stomach with one heave, and Ben relished the strength of those arms that could move him so easily. He could feel the bed shift as Drake leaned toward the nightstand, but with the music, it was hard to make sense of what was happening. Music seeped into him and thrummed like his heart hammering in his chest, his body a symphony and Drake, behind him, the conductor. With the really nice wand.

He felt the cool slick of Drake's fingers get him ready like the rap of the wand on the stand. Musicians ready. Pay attention to this next bit. To— Ben cried out as Drake pressed into him, as they joined, rose, fell, their movements in time to the music inside them, to the manic need of the day, the situation. They needed something, some relief from the stress, some release from the worry and the anxiety. They drew each other in, moving in harmony, the chorus building, rising, the tension replaced by something else. Something warm and immediate, something that started where they met and worked its way up into Ben's stomach. A rushing climax that held, that held, that held until they both seemed to dissolve into the bed, into the floor, into the walls of the castle. They escaped it all, slipped free beyond the stone and clouds and came, hard, both of them breathless as they rushed back into their bodies and rocked with the power of their crescendo.

Spent, Ben rolled onto his side with a groan. The world seemed to vibrate with his beating heart, in sync with the music still blaring through the castle. Drake snuggled against his back. His awareness drifted, a haze of afterglow that he didn't want to lose. But as he lay wrapped in Drake's arms, his vision cleared, and he saw the state his room was in. The bits of food and dirt and paper. The puddle slowly expanding in from the hall. And as the music transformed back to a kind of keening noise, he swore.

"Don't suppose you know any hot cleaners who work cheap?" he asked, and was rewarded by a rumbling laugh from Drake.

"Like I'd let them anywhere near you."

And the two grudgingly got out of bed to face whatever awaited them in the rest of the house.

THE CASTLE WAS EMPTY AND, once they disconnected the siphon and stopped the harp, quiet. They checked each room plus the pantry and closets, but there wasn't a human to be seen. They had certainly left their mark in the form of a mess Ben did not want to think about cleaning, but not a single one remained.

"You think the party just, well, ended?" Ben asked.

"I think the sight of two giants doing the dirty might have been enough to make them rethink the wisdom of their venue choice." Drake was tracing the mess back to the hole where they had found the beanstalk. "Especially after you so boldly defenestrated their leader. I'll have to keep it in mind the next time I have a client who requests *nonlethal* pest control."

Ben rolled his eyes, then stiffened when he heard a strange, rhythmic sound coming from the hole. Both men leaned over and peered down the vine's expanse.

"What do you think it is?" he asked.

Before Drake could answer, though, the noised stopped and the vine lurched. The tendrils gripping the solid cloud tore free as the whole thing broke off and tumbled back towards the ground.

"I'm guessing they've decided they want no part of your cloud kingdom."

Ben didn't know whether to smile or frown. On the one hand, it meant that his problem was over. No more beanstalk, no more humans. On the other hand, though, no more humans meant no more need for an exterminator. At least in a professional capacity. And for all that he wanted to ask Drake to stay, to go out again, to get married and share co-parenting responsibilities with an ill-tempered goose (and okay, maybe that was taking things too far, too fast), he also didn't know what Drake thought about it. Was this just a job? A fling? A one-time deal? Ben felt the uncertainty churning his stomach; it felt as if the humans had all just migrated into his gut instead of fleeing back to their homes.

"So," Ben began, feeling a bit like that beanstalk tumbling through the sky, weightless but expecting the hard slap of the ground at any moment. "So I was wondering—"

"If I'm free for dinner?" Drake finished. "Oh, sorry, didn't mean to assume. I mean, maybe you were about to ask if I wanted to follow you back inside for a bit more adult fun."

Ben blushed. "N-no!" he said, then immediately, "Wait, yes. Or ...

gah! I mean, I wouldn't necessarily be against some more of ... *that*, but I *was* wondering if you wanted to get dinner. Tonight. With me. I mean, it's completely okay if you don't. But if you were free, and wanted to—"

Drake laughed, and Ben wondered if the humans far below could hear him.

"You're adorable, you know that?"

Ben stiffened, and his blush darkened.

"I'd love to go to dinner," Drake said. "My treat, seeing as how I sort of screwed up the whole 'exterminating' thing big time. There's just one thing ..."

Ben flinched, caught between hope and fear. Did he have a boyfriend he hadn't mentioned? Some sort of curse that turned him into a very sexy pumpkin under the full moon?

"Can we leave Tyson at the boarding place an extra night?" Drake asked.

Ben let go of the breath he'd been holding, and with it the last of his doubt. "We most certainly can. Though I'm totally going to tell her it was your idea, so if she tries to bite your face off the next time she sees you, you'll know why."

"I'll just have to take her to that pond you mentioned by way of apology. That way you won't be the only one in the castle getting frisky."

Ben smiled. "Then it's a date."

THE MOST LUXURIANT BEARD OF ALL

B.J. FRY

"MIRROR MIRROR, IN WHICH I peer, tell me who has the most luxuriant beard?" The king stroked his luxurious curls in front of the mirror. He'd been combing the beard, shaping it, for years. Oils and balms imported from distant lands kept it silky and charming, a contrast to his brutish reputation.

"Ah, Your Majesty, can I say you are looking more masculine than ever? And may I just add—"

The mirror shook against the wall, vibrating and distorting the king's reflection with his fear.

"—no other could compete with the amount of care and attention you pay your bristles."

The king grinned, seeing through the faint outline of the mirror's face, a prior lover long since transformed. A spell gone slightly awry.

The lover had asked for one thing when the king, a mere merchant at the time, told him they must part ways. To be together forever, but not in the traditional sense of "together". To be able to stare up at his face every morning and bid him goodnight every evening. Surely, the mirror had been only wishing for more of a relationship, but the king could not grant that, not when his future husband, a prince, had shown interest in him. No, the lover had to go.

And now, the one and true king could no longer remember his lover's name. Forever to be called upon as the mirror. A fact that became apparent as soon as the mirror had morphed into a fragile frame of glass, years ago.

"Yes, yes." The king twisted his fingers around the sideburns. "But answer the question."

"Of course, your most … magnanimous one." The mirror dragged out his words, further delaying the inevitable. For he could see, through the mist and haze of his gaze, that the image of the king's beard no longer drifted to him from the world of magic. No, a new face appeared, and with it a name he had only heard in angry tirades. The unwanted stepchild of the late king's husband.

But man, his beard really was one of awe and beauty. The mustache hair practically tickled the mirror's fancy. If only he could still feel such things.

"And …" the king prompted.

There wasn't much the mirror could do. Part of the spell that created him forced the image past his face and into the king's reflection. An image of strength, courage, and daring. Dark black curls twirled down and around the husky man's head. His dark locks swirled, encasing his face, making his pale blue eyes all the more striking. The beard highlighted his cheekbones, like belonging to a god of old, chiseled out of stone, yet rosy, to match the shiny lips that peaked out just beneath his waxed and shaped mustache. The picture was not easily achieved, but oh did it cause the mirror to tremble for an entirely different reason.

The king gasped when his stepson, Forrest Snow, was presented on the glass, whether from the shock at not seeing his own image or the awe of being presented with a truly magnificent specimen, the mirror could not be sure.

Either way, it was unlikely any good would come from this day.

THE BIRDS TWITTERED AND CHIRPED outside of Forrest Snow's window. While Forrest was not ready to leave the warm comfort of his bed, he knew that his stepfather, the king, had arranged a lesson today with the notorious huntsman and that was not something he was willing to miss. Even if it did require a certain level of perspiration and grime.

He decided on a suit meant for a prince. An undershirt of silk, a vest that tapered at his waist, highlighting his chest. He left the crown, not wanting to draw attention. But he couldn't help but brush and shape his beard. He'd always admired his stepfather's and felt like his own had grown in nicely. When he'd been younger, it was patchy and awkward, the true testament of youth. But now, as a man, the beard filled and sprouted down his face. His only saving grace was trimming and brushing it, as any man should do. He tamed the beard, but only just barely.

Obsessed with cleanliness, Forrest kept his things orderly like his father had before him. He made his bed and tidied up before leaving, a stickler for a well-kept room.

As the messenger had said, the huntsman was waiting for him in the courtyard. He wore a plaid button-down, the shirt open at the chest with a bush of hair escaping out.

Forrest caught himself staring and forced his eyes away until they landed on the ax the man was carrying.

"What are we to do today?" Forrest shouted jovially. "Chop down a tree?"

He walked over and patted the man on the back, admiring the tight muscles underneath his button-down.

The huntsman smiled shyly, his beard more like a light shadow on his face. Perhaps he was shy being this close to the prince. Forrest could not be sure.

"Something like that." The huntsman's mouth tightened. "Shall we ride together or separately, your highness?"

Now that was a lovely prospect. Forrest considered wrapping his arms around such a delectable man. Or would the huntsman ride behind him, engulfing his large body with his own? Would he smell like sweat and pine? Forrest's pants tightened. That could get embarrassing.

"Please, call me Frosty. That's what my friends call me." Forrest reached out to shake the man's hand. Not wanting to make the huntsman uncomfortable, he added, "And let's ride separately."

And so they did. Deep into the forest, beyond the kingdom's land, if Forrest was not mistaken. The trees clustered closer and closer together until the two men could no longer ride side by side, and yet still they went further. Finally, the huntsman stopped and dismounted from his horse.

Forrest followed suit.

"So, are we to chop down an oak?" Forrest asked. He opened his hand towards the huntsman. "If you hand me the ax, I can get started. Though

I'm not sure what we're to do with the wood."

The huntsman paused, the ax heavy in his hands, his shoulders slumped. Finally, he relinquished it. Perhaps a family heirloom? Forrest decided then and there he would be gentle with it. Well, as gentle as one could be when chopping down a tree.

"How's this one?" Forrest pointed at the thick trunk of the tree. The wood should burn nicely if they were to make a campfire. Would this be a survival trip? His father had always told him how he needed to become more familiar with nature.

The huntsman nodded, his mind seeming far away.

Forrest lifted the ax and swung at the bottom. He wasn't quite sure about the art of chopping, but he figured a good swing should do the trick. He set the ax down and looked at the damage as a boisterous laugh erupted from his throat.

There was barely a mark.

"I seem to be quite terrible at this." Forrest smiled at the huntsman and noticed the man was looking remarkably stoic. "Oh, come on now, it can't be that bad. Surely if you show me how?"

Forrest, his hand sore from that small bit of labor, brought the ax over to the huntsman and lifted it towards the man.

But the man just didn't seem to have the heart to grab the thing. "You are not what I had imagined."

"Oh, no one could imagine someone like me." Forrest rubbed his fingers against his beard. "I'm one of a kind."

"Yes, I'm noticing that."

The huntsman shook his head, some sort of internal debate ongoing. Would he really refuse to teach him?

Forrest straightened his face, determined to take this task seriously. "I'm sorry if I offended you in some way. I really do want to learn and become a better outdoorsman."

"No, it's not that." The huntsman sighed, defeat written all over his features. "I'm the one who should apologize."

"What for? We've only just begun. Surely I've not learned any bad habits that quickly."

The huntsman paused, his face transforming to anger. "The king has hired me to kill you." He spit the words out with a scowl. "I'm supposed to bring your beard back as proof."

"My beard?" Forrest rubbed the precious thing. He'd worked so hard on it, but if it could spare his life …

"But I cannot. It is far too lovely to be chopped off like a common garden weed. And you are far too kind to be taken from this world. No. I have a different plan! If you'll help me, we shall shave off my chest hair and present that instead. But you can never return to the castle, or your stepfather will know that you live and what I've done."

"But your chest hair, it's …" Practically a work of art, Forrest wanted to say. How could one choose between the two?

"To be honest, I've been wanting to trim it. It chafes when trapped inside my shirts and it tends to grow back quickly anyway."

The huntsman unbuttoned his top, revealing a wide furry chest. The wires of hair were just long enough to be convincing as his beard, if not the wrong color. "Don't worry, I'll dye it before returning. The king need never know."

"If it is the only way." Forrest still felt it a pity, but he helped the huntsman. It wasn't like he wanted to die.

As he was prepared to take Forrest's beard, the huntsman had more than enough supplies to shave his own chest. Since they needed to keep the hairs as long as possible, Forrest got to do the honors.

They found a river close by and wet his chest beneath the high sun. Water glistened off his skin. Forrest touched his warm torso and began the delicate procedure, rubbing the sharp blade beneath each strand of hair. He'd never been this close to another man, and was thankful for the beard hiding his face, hot from blushing. He placed the hair in the huntsman's bag amongst pieces of coal.

Forrest wanted to provide the huntsman with some gift, something to thank him for saving his life, but he could not think of anything that could repay such a debt. He knew someday, somehow, he would help someone else in need. He would be more than a spoiled prince.

As the noon sun dipped in the sky, the huntsman had to go back. The king, not anticipating an overnight stay, would be expecting his swift return. And Forrest bid him goodbye, fearing for the night ahead. Fearing for a future he did not know.

Forrest spent the night alone, cold and shivering on the ground. He tried to make a bed of leaves, but he was woefully inept at the task. Dirt and bugs and rocks pressed against his back. The stars kept him company; his mind searched for a reason why his stepfather hated him so. He understood the pride that went along with an impressive beard, but to order Forrest's death? Perhaps, as a prim stepson, he was left wanting any skills he could offer such a tyrant. For while Forrest's father offered kindness and love, all Forrest had felt of late from his stepfather was emptiness.

Morning brought with it a new day, and although his clothes were wrinkled and smudged, he felt a renewed sense of survival. He'd made it one night. He could do that again. Even if his back did ache and his stomach rumbled. He'd been saving the paltry amount of food the huntsman left him.

But after the morning sun reached high in the sky, a squirrel approached Forrest. Its beady eyes stared up at him as if asking for something. The small amount of food he did have included a handful of nuts. Forrest pulled them out, placing them on the ground near the poor woodland creature. The squirrel greedily took them, shoving nuts into his cheeks before scurrying off.

A few minutes later, it returned.

But poor Forrest had nothing more to give. "I'm sorry, little one, but I have nothing to spare. Unless you want this?" Forrest produced a small loaf, the last of his food, and placed it on the ground, his stomach growling in protest. The squirrel squeaked and, instead of gobbling the bread up, moved away from him, as if signaling for him to follow.

Grateful that his last meal was no longer under consideration, he picked up the loaf and followed, curious where the creature could want to take him. A squirrel did not make for a good forest guide, but eventually, they came upon a small cottage. As if seeing him settled, the squirrel trilled with delight and disappeared into the undergrowth.

Excitement and, dare he say hope, filled Forrest. He walked up to the front door and knocked with his big heavy fist against the wood. No one answered.

He glanced around, inspecting the area for signs of life, but found none. Although he knew it was terrible manners, and really quite shameful, he did the unthinkable and peeked inside the windows.

The room he could see was an absolute mess. Just in shambles. A complete disaster.

Fearing for the resident's life, Forrest tried the door to find it unlocked. He rushed inside, forced to duck as he entered the small cottage, and began searching for someone in trouble. He called out, fearing he would find the worst. The floor rumbled and shook beneath his feet.

Instead, he found a kitchen full of moldy dishes, a living room with clothes laid all about, covered in dust, and a bedroom with seven unmade beds. Curious. Obviously, whoever lived here had a lot going on in their lives, he decided. Based on the quality of furniture and cookware, they appeared rather well off, perhaps the benefit of combining seven incomes. As a prince in hiding, he had nothing to offer them. Therefore, as a failure of a stepson, failure as an heir to the throne, he would give them a hand in the only bit of business he ever managed to do well.

He cleaned the cottage.

Forrest couldn't think about the task as a whole, as it was a very large task for even one such as him. But he worked on each room one at a time. The clothes he piled up, preparing to wash them by hand tomorrow. The dishes needed to be soaked, if ever he was to remove all the grime. The beds were easy enough to make, if not a little short for his comfort.

As the day wore on, he grew more and more exhausted. His night on the forest floor had been not one of peace and he longed for the feathered bed at home, and of the cleanliness of a bath. Deciding that it couldn't hurt to take a nap, he chose a bed at random and lay down. His feet hung comically off the end, but he no longer cared. Forrest was too tired.

As soon as his lids closed, he felt a rough hand shake his pants.

A gruff voice spoke, "And who are you?"

Forrest sat up, a tad too fast, and rubbed the sleep from his eyes. The sun had gone down. Seven men stood before him, holding lanterns.

Embarrassed, he quickly stood up and away from the tiny beds. "I'm sorry, I'm sorry. I didn't mean to ..."

"Didn't mean to, what?" the thinnest one spoke, a scowl on his face. "Clean our house or climb into his bed?" He pointed towards the oldest member of the group.

"Well, no but yes." Forrest shook his head. "I'm doing this all wrong. First, I should introduce myself. I'm Forrest."

"Oh sure, and I'm Otter." Otter rolled his eyes and pointed to each one of the men as he spoke. "This here's Cuddle, Glutton, Chubb, Girth, and that there is Whiskers. Oh, and as I said, you're in Carnal's bed."

"No really, that's my name," Forrest sputtered. "But my friends call me Frosty."

"Like the snowman?" Cuddle asked with a smile.

"No, like …" But then Forrest remembered he dare not speak his last name, or they would know his identity. And then they would be in danger as well.

"Got it," said Girth, the largest amongst them, who nodded vigorously, succeeding in popping a button off his taut vest. "Like the snowman."

"Winter's the best time for hot toddies," said Glutton, wiping his mouth.

Carnal also wiped his own lips. "I'm always up for Todd to come around."

Whiskers stepped forward, the hair on his head graying, his namesakes darker the farther from his head they grew. "What matters is the kindness," he said. "You cleaned our home, and all of us really appreciate that. If you'd like, you're welcome to stay as long as you continue to take care of the place. We work all day, and never have time for such chores."

"I …" Forrest thought about it. He really had nowhere else to go. He could continue wandering lost in the woods, or he could stay here with these delightful fellows. They seemed friendly enough, even with the dark and caked smudges on their face. "I think I'd like that."

That night, the men showed Forrest where they kept the food and other important items. The next day, they helped build him a bed befitting his stature and to give him some privacy from the tight-knit group. He found them quite charming, in their own way.

But after that, most days they left him there alone, fending for himself and cleaning. He started to hunt, as it was not like they would be bringing home meat from the mines. He found their form of trade quite interesting. They mined for ore. One of them, typically Whiskers, would travel to trade for more supplies. He offered to take Forrest on the next trip, but Forrest just didn't have the heart to leave his new family.

Then one day, Forrest was bathing in the river, when he heard the heavy footfalls of a galloping horse. Through the tree line popped the colossal beast, its nostrils flaring, its chest panting.

"Oh my, have you gotten lost, my little lamb?" Forrest called to it. But he was even more surprised when a shape on its back shifted and he was greeted with a handsome sight.

For upon the steed was a man like no other. Wide shoulders, wicked dark eyes that devoured the soul, and a trimmed beard that remained alluring, begging to be touched. Forrest was absolutely spellbound.

The stranger dismounted, revealing his tall stature and stylish clothes. He called down to Forrest, "Are you okay?" as if the man thought to rescue him.

Forrest smiled a glorious grin. "Oh, more than fine. You're welcome to join if you'd like." Forrest wasn't sure he could handle this man without a shirt on. He licked his lips at the thought.

The man brushed his fingers through his hair. "Well actually, you see I've managed to get myself lost, and I was wondering if you could point me in the direction of home."

"I could point you to my home if you'd like." Oh, how Forrest would like that.

"Ah, that sounds very nice. I've had a terrible day, up until meeting you, and what I wouldn't give for a place to relax."

Forrest remembered what that was like, being lost and feeling hopeless. He walked to the shoreline, unsure how to proceed. If he stepped any higher, the man would be able to see more than he probably had in mind. But feeling bold and a tiny bit lonely, Forrest exited the river, his erection bouncing in the air. He felt the water drip off his wide body, and he smiled when the other man clearly appreciated all of him.

He dried off with his towel, taking longer than was probably necessary. He tried to pretend he didn't have an audience, but anyone with eyes would notice his performance. He acted brazen, like a young buck. Taking his time, he gingerly pulled on his pants and buttoned his shirt only halfway.

Inside the small cottage, the two men talked and joked together, each one "accidentally" brushing against the other, small touches on the arms, little bumps of the legs. They were giants in such a tiny space. Forrest usually felt overly large in the cabin, but with this man, he finally decided to just stretch out his legs and hold still. The other man followed suit, their thighs connecting above the knee.

He was an interesting fellow, Forrest found. Some great weight seemed to lay on the man's shoulders, some heavy burdens left there by his parents. He too understood the weight of burdens and expectations and wished to relieve the man of his hardships. But for now, all he could do was fill the man's cup with something warm and offer him food.

Day turned to night, and with it the temperature dropped. By the time the seven inhabitants of the cottage returned, the two were snuggled up on the couch, their limbs twisting together for warmth.

"What do we have here?" Otter demanded. "Another stray? See, this is what happens when you invite a stranger into your home."

"I think he's dreamy," Cuddles added.

"Is there something we could do for you?" Carnal asked the man and raised his eyebrows suggestively.

"I seemed to have gotten lost and while Frosty here is quite the outdoorsman and has been more than hospitable." The man tossed Forrest a sweet grin. "It seems he lacks the knowledge necessary to locate the nearest road."

"Ah yes, Frosty's not from around these parts," Whiskers said. "But we can help you out with that. Which way are you trying to go?"

Forrest watched with heavy sadness as Whiskers and his friend discussed how to leave this place. His stomach felt wrenched as the man announced he would leave in the morning and Forrest just couldn't bear the thought of being alone again. The seven cottage inhabitants had been more than nice to him but they just never seemed to trust him enough.

Ever the gentleman, the man insisted on sleeping on the couch, letting Forrest keep his giant bed to himself, much to Forrest's disappointment (and Carnal's).

And true to his word, the next day, his friend left. Leaving only his name as they parted. Philip.

"MIRROR MIRROR, IN WHICH I peer, tell me who has the most luxuriant beard?"

It had been weeks since the king had bothered to ask. Something about sentencing his stepson to die had changed him, the mirror felt.

When the huntsman had presented the massive collection of beard hair, the king barely spared it a glance. He placed it into a box next to the vanity, like a trophy. Yet he never came back to visit it, never opened it. And never spent more than a passing glance with the mirror .

"Why it's so wonderful to hear your voice, Your Majesty," the mirror said. "How I've missed ..."

The mirror paused when the king scowled at him impatiently. "Yes, of course, on with it."

Determined to make the king happy, the mirror focused through the haze of magic, completely and totally expecting to see the king's handsome mug staring back at him. But no, shockingly, horribly, terribly no. The king's stepson still stared back at him through the haze. Oh, what was a mirror to do?

Though he really couldn't do anything. Forced to do the king's bidding, the mirror reflected the stepson back at the king. Even he could see that the beard had grown in length but the boy had done a remarkable job at maintaining it. Wherever he was, he must have had just the right mixture as the sheen was admirable. And this coming from a mirror who had the honor of admiring the king's luscious beard daily.

"What? How can this be?" The king turned ashen; his lips slammed together. He lifted the box, opening the lid. "Then what's in here?"

Because he asked, the mirror obeyed. "That's, uh, not beard hair."

"Then what is it?" He reached inside, pulling out the thick, wiry strands. Black dust coated his fingers.

The mirror glanced through the haze and choked on a laugh. "Chest hair ... and ... "

The vision showed him, but he resisted telling the king. The huntsman feared the amount of hair was insufficient, so he had reached down and trimmed an entirely different landscape. "Pubic hair."

"This cannot be." The king threw the box on the ground.

Something inside him was at war, a battle the mirror could not comprehend.

"No, I cannot allow this. I've sacrificed too much ... I ...."

And the king stormed out, leaving the mirror alone with his thoughts about the king's reaction. Was he relieved to see his stepson's face?

Either way, the king left with a face set in resolve. The mirror could only fear for the huntsman and hope the man was smart enough to get far away after trying such a ruse.

ANOTHER WEEK PASSED, BUT WITHOUT Philip, Forrest felt lonelier than ever. He should have asked to join him. He could make a living on his own. The cottage was clean now, much easier to maintain than before. He'd even been teaching the men how to take care of themselves, instead of relying on him, and they were doing a lovely job. Girth, who always was ready with a needle and thread, had managed to hem a pair of pants all by himself, along with properly sculpting the new hairs peeking out on his face.

But that day, as Forrest was cleaning alone in the cottage, he heard a tender knocking on the door. Excitement flowed through him as he considered Philip's return. Philip knew where they lived. As long as he found that path home alright, he should be able to come back.

With a pep in his step, he ripped the door open only to come face to face with an old man. Forrest tried to keep his face from falling in disappointment. "Can I help you?"

"Yes, I seem to have gotten lost." The stranger shook with age. "Could you be a dear and point me in the direction of the road? In exchange, I'd be more than willing to share this …." The old man reached into his basket, pulling out a banana.

Having paid attention when the guys had explained the path to Philip, Forrest felt more than capable of helping this time. He offered directions before adding, "And you don't have to share your last banana. You may need that for the journey."

"That's kind of you." The elderly man arched his furry eyebrows. "I'm sure it's not easy living out here in the woods."

"No, not at first." Forrest glanced down at a wandering squirrel and smiled. "If you need to rest your legs, you're welcome to come inside."

"No, no, I have places to be." The stranger's tight smile faded to a frown. "Did you build this place yourself?"

Moss twirled and crawled up the side of the building.

Surely, Forrest thought, a man of the world would recognize the wear and tear of aged wood? "No, but I found a few friends who were willing to take me in."

"Ah, I see," the old man said, as though he didn't. "Living off the goodwill of others, as your generation tends to do."

"That's not at all—"

"Either way, I must thank you somehow," the stranger interrupted, passing the browning fruit towards Forrest. "You'll offend these old hands if you refuse."

Staring into the man's eyes, Forrest took the fruit. There was something familiar about him. An unease settled in Forrest's stomach as the man ogled the prince's beard and lips, licking his lips in response.

Forrest shrugged. If the old pervert wanted to watch him eat a banana, so be it. As long as he left afterwards. Forrest peeled the sides and thrust the entire thing into his mouth. Feeling rather proud, he smiled as he chewed. But then a heaviness started to settle on his chest.

Feeling like an anchor dragged his stomach down, he lowered himself to the floor. The last thing Forrest heard was the sigh of the old man as his eyes drifted close.

PRINCE PHILIP TRIED TO FORGET his reckless trip in the forest. He'd been young and foolish to think even he could not get lost. And yet now, all he wanted to do was return, even if he did risk getting lost again. Anything to find Frosty.

It had to be love. He didn't think it would be possible but after one night together, he was greedy for more. He'd never met a kinder man, and the fact that he was handsome just made him all the more irresistible. They were practically made for each other.

So, after many sleepless nights, he finally convinced his parents. He packed a bag and headed back out to the forest. He was determined to return with Frosty as his consort or remain with him in the cottage.

He rode into the forest as if being chased by a fire, only stopping to keep the horse from tiring. He needed to feel Frosty's warm hand against his arm. Needed the light bristle of leg hair brushing against his own. And what he wouldn't do to comb his fingers through that glorious beard.

Suddenly, riding the horse became very uncomfortable for Philip.

But how could he forget that first image of Frosty, as if a member of the fae folk had stepped out of a fairy tale and into his life? He had been lost, hungry, and scared when he heard the splash of water. And then, when he saw the liquid glistening and pooling on the man's body, he just ... he couldn't stop staring. Frosty was like no other man he'd met. So large, so hairy, and so utterly delectable. He had to have a taste.

And as he came upon the cottage, he felt pure joy. This was his moment. This time, Philip would do all of things he could only dream about. But as he drew closer, he noticed seven shortish figures bowed over a glass case. He rode up next to them, glancing down. "What's going on?"

Inside the case lay Frosty. It must've taken all of them to lift him inside. The case was rather unusual, and it took Philip a moment to realize what it truly was. A casket.

The dwarves were crying, tears streaking down their faces and into their beards if they had them. The one called Cuddle looked absolutely distraught. Of course, Philip felt the shock easing away and turning into something terrible in his chest. His heart was shattering. How could love so new and so pure already be gone from this world? It wasn't fair. It wasn't right.

Philip jumped down from the horse and walked up to the glass case. "What happened to him?"

To Philip, Forrest just looked like he was sleeping. He didn't look like he drowned, for no river could ever take out such a man. He didn't have any puncture wounds or bruises, as if from a fight. Was it illness? But how could he be so ill and the others fine?

"He's been poisoned," Glutton wailed.

Whiskers shook his head and a tuft of his beard came loose. "I knew Forrest was the king's stepson, I just figured he had good reason for not telling us."

"What?" Otter shot him a look of annoyance. "What do you mean?"

"Oh come on, there's only one Forrest in the area who also goes by Frosty, and that's that evil king's stepson. Do you not pay attention to our bordering kingdom's politics?"

"You're the one who goes out and trades," Girth sniffled.

"Yes, and it's my fault this happened. I should've realized he was in danger. That he would be too trusting … that …" Whisker began to bawl anew.

There was nothing Philip could say. Nothing he could do other than look down at Forrest's handsome face and dream of a better time, when they could be together.

Maybe it was wrong, but he just had to kiss him. He couldn't go the rest of his life wondering. And so he bent down, brushing his lips against Frosty's. Their beards tangled and brushed against each other, the wiry whisks scratching his cheeks unlike anything he had ever experienced.

He pulled back, staring down at the only man he could ever love. The smells of sandalwood and bourbon lingered on his beard. Masculine. Intoxicating. How could he go on without him? But as he went to step back, Philip noticed pink coloring returning to Frosty's cheeks. His lips returned to their rosy hue, and his eyes, his eyes fluttered open, revealing the deep blue of the ocean. An endless amount of water Philip would happily forever drown in.

"Forrest?" Carnal whispered beside him.

Otter peered into the casket. "Guys, he's moving! He's alive!"

Frosty sat up, a lopsided grin on his face. "Wait, did I just miss our first kiss?" he asked the prince.

Philip smiled back. Their eyes locked on each other. "Maybe, but if you're nice, I'll let you remember the next one."

Frosty reached out, grabbing Philip by the front of his shirt. He pulled him in and with a heavy growl, whispered above his lips, breath warm and heady, "You better." And he smashed his lips against Philip's, their mouths becoming a tangled mess, both eager never to be separated again.

And if Frosty didn't like ruling Philip's kingdom, well, he'd just have to get used to it, for Philip was next in line to the throne and would do everything in his power to keep them together. Even if that meant going to war with his future stepfather-in-law.

THE KING STOOD IN FRONT of his vanity, his face sunken with time and sleeplessness. "Mirror, Mirror, in which I peer, tell me who has the most luxuriant beard?"

The mirror once again paused. He knew Forrest Snow was alive and well, already whisked off to another kingdom. Would the king wage war over this? Over who has the most luxuriant beard? The mirror did not remember the king being this cruel before. How did he ever love such a man once upon a time?

The king glared at the mirror; impatience was written large on his face. "I said—"

"Yes, yes I heard you. You're just not going to like it." And the mirror showed him the handsome face of his stepson, his beard freshly trimmed.

"How? How can this be?" The king banged his fists against the table. "It's impossible. I've done everything. Everything."

He continued his tantrum. The king walked into his bedroom, ripping his dresser away from the wall. Ripping down curtains. Throwing his pillows and blankets onto the floor. Like a petulant child, he raged. Until finally he returned with a globe of glass.

"That stupid wizard. He told me to make a wish. To make a wish and whatever I wanted could be mine. I could have it all. I wish for a kingdom and I get the attention of the future heir. I wish for the location of the best oils for my beard and I get it. I wish ..."

He turned towards the mirror and yelled, his voice a desperate plea, tears streaming down his face. " ...I wish for my lover to be able to stay with me and I get that too."

The mirror stared at the globe. There was something wrong, he thought, with that piece of magic. "Your Majesty?"

"But it was all for nothing!"

He threw the globe.

Like a cannonball, the globe smashed into the mirror. The mirror felt like he was breaking into a million pieces, shattering on the bathroom floor. A heavy pounding ruptured in his head and exploded through his cranium, returning years of memories. He had a life. He was a person. He had a name.

"Michael?" the king whispered.

The mirror—Michael—lay naked and cold on the tiled floor. But what was cold? A sensation he hadn't felt in years.

And the king, he was frowning and rubbing his head.

"How did I forget you?" the king whispered, his face frozen in shock or horror. "What have I done?"

Michael looked at the shattered globe. Dark smoke leaked up and drifted out the window. "George, I think that was cursed."

"I ..." The king, of course, had a name, and hearing Michael utter it brought back so many memories. "I didn't know what I was doing. It was like, like a chunk of me was stolen. Like I only lived for—"

"I understand." Michael glanced at his hands. "It happened to me too."

"I'm so sorry." George anxiously tugged at his beard. "I'm so sorry. I don't ... I don't deserve ..."

He moved swiftly, lifting the nearby shears to his beard. In one sudden movement, he started hacking away at so many years of great labor and grooming.

"No, I won't let you feel sorry for yourself," Michael said. "Someone cursed you. Someone cursed *us*." Michael approached, grasping George's wrist, stopping his destruction. "But it's over."

"I have to apologize to him," the king said. "I have to make up for this."

George was talking about Forrest, Michael knew. Just like Michael knew how sweet George was before all of this. How he had only indulged the prince's attentions as a means to avoid the life of a pauper. At the time, George's merchant had recently burned down. He had no way to pay his debts. But then, unexpectedly, love developed between them despite George's machinations.

Luckily, the former mirror thought, the huntsman had also fled the kingdom before the king could enact any unforgivable revenge.

"Of course," Michael replied, rubbing George's arms, enjoying the feel of the king once again. Memorizing the warm, muscular shape of his body. "But first ..."

Michael lifted the royal straight razor and helped smooth George's face, removing the only thing that had mattered to the king in years.

George reached up, his fingers brushing against the jeweled crown. "I don't think I can do this anymore."

"I loved you as a merchant," Michael said. "I stayed with you as a king. I think we could try again as men."

With a sad smile, George brushed warm fingers along Michael's head and pushed the errant, shaggy locks of hair behind an ear. "Good. I'd like that."

It was unprecedented, a living king abdicating to his stepson. But the kingdom accepted the announcement with barely an objection. George had ruled with fear, not loyalty, and so the people celebrated the rise of the royal son.

And afterwards, as George stepped away from the crowd, the advisors and royal council departing to spread the news far and wide that Forrest Snow could once again return, return and rule, Michael leaned in, meeting George's lips with his own, stealing what had always belonged with him. Every sunrise and sunset they'd been together, but still apart.

Now, they could finally be whole.

THE MAN WHO DREW CATS
ALYSHA MACDONALD

THEY TRIED TO MAKE A farmer out of Shiro. They raised him in the hot sun with mud caked up to his knees, grinning to themselves as he stooped and planted row after row of rice in the flooded paddies with his cousins. They told them stories at night of how, though it was true that emperors were the direct descendants of the sun goddess, Amaterasu, that it was the peasants who were her actual favorites. After all, the emperors stayed away from the sun by hiding in their large homes and traveling solely by covered wagon. They were tucked away safe like pretty gems, while Shiro's family was raised beneath Amaterasu's glory. They grew tan from her presence. They broke out in sweats and sometimes collapsed in the water, then waved up at Amaterasu to go rest behind the clouds, so that they could have a moment of peace in the shade.

Shiro was to his family what nobility was to Amaterasu. He hid in the long grass and jumped out as his cousins passed. They cursed and hit him with their hats, hissing that he'd scared them half to death by thinking he was a kappa. When his sisters got angry after finding him stitching small birds into their clothes, they pinned him down and shaved the top of his head so that he better resembled the monster. After that, everyone started calling him the little *Kappa*. He leaned into it. He wrestled his cousins and ate cucumbers with sharp, quick snaps. He hardly worked. He saved up red clay in a jar and painted swirling patterns on their ox, himself, their floor, and once his mother's lips when she was laid out for funeral.

He was an amusement to them. While his family took turns hitting him over the back of the head to get him to focus, they never hit too hard and they never hit a second time. They saved his drawings and etchings, but years passed and Shiro grew into an idle teenager, which was not as endearing as an idle child.

His father came to him one day, watching as Shiro played with a spider by keeping it imprisoned in the circle of his hands. He sat down next to him and Shiro scrambled to his knees, the spider running free as Shiro realized that his scythe had been discarded outside. There was no feigning work.

"Sometimes," his father said. "People grow straight and upright like the bamboo. They bask in the sun, keep true and tall, and then are felled when it is their time."

His father placed a hand on his head.

"And sometimes," his father said, "a person grows like a vine. A vine needs to grow in shaded places or up sturdy walls. It can grow nearly anywhere and it can grow well, but it cannot grow up among the bamboo. It'll die in the ground if it tries."

Shiro watched him.

"There's a place for you, somewhere, and you'll be happier there," his father said. "You've an idle body but an overworking mind."

Shiro gave his father a small smile, but he caught the spider again after and sat with it for a long time, watching as it fled from palm to palm but was given no escape. His uncles brought him to town a month later, and Shiro followed a band of monks to a monastery far up some old mountain.

If farming had made him strong, then the monastery padded him out. He ate as much rice as he could after prayers and, sometimes, by sneaking in bites during them. Each taste brought him back home and, if he chewed long enough, he could imagine the ox's plowing, his family laughing and gossiping as they worked, and the slush of bare feet through knee-high water. He traded the rest of his allotted food for others' rice cups and sometimes took out a small clump at night, placed it on his tongue, and let it turn to starch in his spit. With every pound he gained, it felt as though he was adding a new layer of his home to himself. He loved the soft give of his body. He would press his hand to his stomach, feel the hair, and pretend it was the paddy grass. He would press harder and wish that his softness could extend outward and into his life. Where he could have an existence different from the restrained lives that monks were supposed to lead.

He was resentful at his father for sending him away, then resigned and, after a handful of long-winding years, grateful. He learned to read, how to use critical thinking, and about his nation's history. There were endless young men and visiting scholars. Sometimes, a brush with one of them left him with his robes askew and Shiro grinning to himself later during prayers.

Then, one afternoon, he was given a brush and told to write with it. He dipped it in the ink, watched the black blend with the horsehair, breathed in, and pressed it to the *washi* paper. It bled out thickly and smelled of forest. The brush raised, droplets of ink dripped onto the paper.

He'd drawn and stitched throughout his childhood. He made endless little crafts, but he had never made something as beautiful as a single brush stroke.

He sat crying over the paper while watching as his tears dripped down and blurred in with the ink. An older monk went up to him and placed a hand on his shoulder, saying that not everyone could write their name on the first try, so he needn't weep over it. Shiro smiled up at him and, for the first time in his life, focused. He drew *Kanji*, swirling flowers, and sold calligraphy prints for the monastery in town. In a different world perhaps, he would have done so until his body bent into death. Where he would be a master by then, unbound by want or desire, and would use his last moments to scrawl out a *jisei* on golden paper.

Perhaps, had it not been for the cat.

Shiro had learned of the many seducers of monks. The forests were rife with *yokai*, ghosts, *oni*, and spirits. One straying step and one didn't just lose their way, but their life.

Shiro's unraveling was far subtler than any demon's influence. The cat arrived with the pond, which had been his duty to build. He spent a spring digging, then lining it with rocks, and finally ordering the silver carp to fill it with. When they were safely settled, he practiced calligraphy with his feet dipped in the water.

It was then that he saw his first cat.

He knew that cats existed, of course, and had seen them as running blurs or white glowing eyes from hidden spots in town, but never in the open. He sat watching the feline weave out from the woods, tail high and proud, and then pad a lap around the other side of the pond. It sat sunning itself and stretched out limbs that seemed unconstrained by physics. He'd heard of ghosts who could turn their heads around. He'd seen a monk fall from the temple roof and lay crumpled at wrong angles on the ground. But when the tabby stretched out so impossibly, it did not seem to be in any pain.

It captivated him.

He wasted all of his paper drawing it before he realized what he had done. When it tried for a carp, but found it too big, he left out a wad of rice for the cat to eat and retreated. He watched from around a tree, while the cat went up to the rice, sniffed, and turned away in disgust.

The monks who saw him with the creature said it must have been some demon cat, a *bakeneko* perhaps, because it so thoroughly led Shiro astray. He abandoned his art. He ducked out during prayers or the middle of the night, stealing a carp and breaking its spine on a rock, before slicing off small cuts for the cat. Soon, the cat grew to cats, and they bred. The monastery was slowly overrun by the furred creatures, until monks couldn't sit in peace without a cat coming up, rubbing against their back, and then pawing at the adornments on their robes.

Shiro cared for nothing but his cats. They said he drew them into existence. He slept by the fish pond in the summer, wrapped up in a great furred blanket of whites, greys, blacks, and calicos. When he moved, the cats all moved with him. His ink was spent for nothing but drawing each one, his calligraphy only used to scrawl their names in the corners. When they took away his inks, he got an old stick and drew out the cats in the dirt, laughing as they swapped at the end of the stick in fake lunges. He walked with kittens in his pockets, wearing a cat as a scarf around his neck, and even started growing back his hair.

It wasn't out of hand until it was. Locals wouldn't come to the shrine because the cats' territorial squabbles destroyed any sense of peace. The place started to smell and, when a group of new initiates drowned sacks of cats in the pond, Shiro exercised no detached patience after finding out. It surprised them too, because Shiro was not a violent man. The numerous frustrations that they vented to him over the year was met with Shiro's friendly response that, as Buddhists, weren't they supposed to treat all animals as equals? As such, weren't the cats not pests, but actually their guests?

Thus, when Shiro saw the bodies of the cats drowned in the water, he felt an anger he had never known. He'd been annoyed plenty of times before, but had never experienced a flashing, fiery sort of hatred. He tackled the initiates into the pond and cursed at them for not respecting the lives of creatures, big or small. When they yelled back that *he* was the one not respecting the lives of *his* own fellow man, he shook his head and got off them. His cheeks flushed with shame. His clothes dripped and clung to him. He went to one of the head monks and the man, who had been the one to whisper to the initiates to carry out the killings, met Shiro with a bag packed for travel. Shiro paused at the door, letting in cat after cat in between his legs. He went there to report the monks' misconduct, but paused upon seeing the bag.

"It's become clear to me that this might not be the life for you," the monk said.

"You would turn me out? For this? Because I was kind to small creatures and sheltered them?"

The monk walked up to him and gave a small, encouraging smile. "Once you leave, the cats will disperse. We're doing them no good by locking them away here and letting them breed. They've killed all the fish and they'll starve without you here to feed them. You shouldn't stay here either or you'll starve, too. Mentally starve; spiritually starve. There's no shame in leaving. You don't have a monk's soul. You're too attached to life and so ... this is not your path, but we'll care for your cats until they leave."

"No," Shiro said. "After the cruelty I've seen today, they will leave with me."

"Then you'll learn loss, finally," the man said. "And I wish you the better for it."

Shiro tried to keep the cats with him. Before he left, he bought a bucket of eggs and cracked one open every hour of walking. The cats scrambled and fought over the yolk, but he could not keep them all. They dropped off, one by one, and he couldn't follow them into town, up trees, or into the mouths of foxes. He held to what he could, but every day brought fewer cats and pieces of his heart slipped away each time one ran off to a new territory. There was no holding such fluid creatures. They squirmed, hid, and climbed. Some went to farmers or the arms of smiling, happy children. Others were trampled by a horse or taken by a bird. He buried every one that he found dead. The leaves fell. He awoke to snow on his face. He sat up shivering and saw that the last of his flock had left him.

He was alone in the forest.

He bowed and contemplated their tracks in the snow. Already, the snow was blanketing them. Three cat trails in different directions—what was the point in choosing one to follow?

Shiro breathed out. Was this what his father had meant, years ago, when he called him vine-like? As an adult, Shiro knew that vines were weeds that destroyed whatever they clung to. Perhaps that was his father's message and never one of love. That he clung to pointless things and crushed them with his desperate, clawing grasp until everything around him suffocated.

How could he return home as a failure? He'd been away for years. By staying in exile, he could keep his childhood locked neatly away in memory. He didn't have to face any news of deaths or suffering. He couldn't bare the thought of traveling back, only to see the house gone entirely and his family moved on or murdered.

But where was he supposed to go? He'd spent his life listening to what other people wanted him to be, but what did he want?

He took out his art tools, sat with his back to a tree, and drew out his home in long, loving brush strokes. He drew cats in place of his family. They slept atop the roof and jumped up in fright from the water. He placed the paper down, drew a fire and some food with a stick in the snow. Then he slept, feeling strangely warm and nourished, with the echoing of meowing in his ears and the crackling of imagined flames.

WHEN HE AWOKE, SHIRO FIGURED he had made such a poor drawing that he was cursed into a landscape painting. He was atop a snowy mountain peak, pressed into the top branch of a pine tree, and clung to it with a start after seeing how high up he was. The beard he was growing was not yet long enough to shield him from the biting cold.

A coo of laughter came from the next tree over. A tengu peered down at him from the topmost cedar. His black wings flicked about in the wind while he gripped to the bark with sharp, black-nailed talons. The rest of the body was squat, but undoubtedly human. The tengu watched him from behind a long-nosed *gigaku* mask with its hair a mismatch of black and feathers.

"Welcome, monk," the tengu said.

Shiro knew of tengu, but their origins changed depending on who he asked. Some called them the protectors of Buddhism, others the reanimated forms of people killed in jealous blood. They were creatures who loved nothing more than to mock, torture, and sometimes murder, depending on the tale. A monk at the shrine had fallen prey to one such being. He disappeared and returned, vacant-eyed, foaming at the mouth, weeping of nonsense and clawing at his own face. Whatever the tengu did to him drove the monk mad.

Shiro didn't mind the thought of a tengu scrambling his brain into incoherency. To some, that would be a fate worse than death, but thinking had only led to sorrow in his opinion. Perhaps he would find some peace in the insanity.

"You've brought me to a nice view, friend," Shiro said.

"A nice view of the heights?"

"Of course. And a nice view of you."

The tengu snorted.

"Did your fellow monks not teach you how to address us beings? You repent *first* and then you flatter me. If you do it well, then I'll bring you back down the mountain. If you don't, well ... There are no riddles from me; no trickery. Humble yourself in exchange for your life."

Shiro thought for a moment. He took a slow, careful seat on the branch and tried not to think of the drop. "Can you tell me your name?"

"My kind doesn't give out their names freely. What's yours?"

"Humans don't either, at least, not to demons. Monk is fine."

"Hmm. Then you can call me Crow."

Shiro nodded. He still had his belongings and wasn't injured, which was good. The tengu didn't seem particularly bloodthirsty, so Shiro scooted close to the trunk and proceeded to climb down the tree. The tengu paused, flew over to a branch above him, just out of reach.

"What do you think you're doing?" Crow asked.

"I didn't think you would help me down. It's no issue. I'll manage the climb on my own."

The tengu jumped branch after branch, until he squatted and rested his arms on his legs, mask pointing at Shiro with an accusatory glare. "I kidnapped you to repent. You're failing your task and cedars don't have branches at the base. What is your plan?"

"What do you know about me that needs repenting?"

"I know you're a monk, but your hair is long. That you are fat and slow and that the items in your bag are expensive. I saw you with your cats. Did you think you were some little god who ruled over the felines? How quick they abandoned you. And now you're all alone."

"You've been watching me for a while, then?" Shiro stood on a branch and smiled upward. The tengu leaned forward, bowing his branch so that a dusting of white snow covered Shiro's shoulders. "I think *you're* the one trying to flatter *me*."

"Human," Crow cautioned.

"You're no different from a cat. You inconvenienced me for attention, I imagine. Or because you were bored." Shiro laughed. "If you were really going to kill me—"

The tengu jumped down to his branch, bent it enough to send Shiro off balance, and slapped him once with the back of his wing. If it weren't for the snow, the fall would have hurt him more. As it was, it still hurt him some.

Shiro stared up at the tree, dazed.

The tengu leaned forward.

"Run away, monk! Return to your people and tell them to never set foot in my woods again."

The tengu made to leave, but paused after extending his wings, staring down as Shiro made an awkward limp away. "That's not much of a run."

"The fall hurt my ankle," Shiro said.

The tengu hesitated. "Consider yourself lucky that I didn't eat the eyes from your head instead."

Crow left him to his hike.

Shiro was used to cats. Once he was aware one was around, he heightened his senses to their little tells. The shuffle of feet, the creak of wood as they jumped atop it, or the sound of nails in tree bark. Now that Shiro knew he was being followed, he hobbled slowly down the mountain and could sense the tengu nearby. Shiro found himself laughing. He was used to being left alone, not stalked. When he got halfway down the mountain and a break in the woods showed him some of the valley, he studied the miles of wilderness, the small town miles off, and the trade route cutting straight through it all.

If he was to go out and make something of himself, then these demon-haunted woods seemed a good a place as any to settle down.

CROW TERRORIZED HIM.

Shiro would wake in a cave, a cliff, and once, was adrift in a river. He often spent the better part of the day returning to his home, though once it took him almost a week. The villagers got used to their new, self-proclaimed artist stumbling through town for water with dirty, torn clothes and a bemused expression. No danger ever befell him on these mandatory sojourns, however. Whenever he heard the growl of a wolf or some other nightmare, there was a yelp and then silence. Sometimes, he talked aloud to Crow the entire way back, but there was rarely a reply. Only the occasional sigh. And, even rarer, a quick laugh from high above.

Seasons slipped by and Shiro drew them, but never failed to add in a cat. He became well acquainted with his immediate country and soon found it easy to navigate, until his longest wanderings only took three nights to traverse back to his home. Shiro came to love nature in a way he never had as a farmer. He didn't have a knack for trying to bend it to his will or organize it, but he enjoyed building a home amidst the chaos. He cut trees, went fishing, trail-blazed a path to the main trade road, and took to lazing about, shirtless, in his wildly unkempt garden. When Crow kidnapped him and brought him somewhere new, Shiro had the feeling that Crow was trying to show off the prettiest parts of their valley.

Each time that Shiro made it back home, Crow flew ahead to wait for him on the perch of Shiro's roof. As though Crow hadn't been following him the entire time. The tengu laughed while mocking him—his state, his late timing, his skin burned from tan to red by the sun.

He yelled down, "Have you gone mad yet, monk? You're more hair and beast than human! How can you call yourself anything but a failure? Look at this little lean-to in the woods you call home and despair. I've seen nests sturdier."

Shiro stood by his door each time, arms crossed, craning his neck to see the tengu.

"I see you've stopped by," Shiro said. "Are you coming in?" But the tengu never did.

Shiro had never been cunning enough to insult others, but he fought back in small ways. He spent a summer's day threading a large nest atop his roof and, when the tengu arrived to land, Crow became all fluster and feathers. He cursed him and kicked the nest from the roof, claiming that he was no ordinary songbird, no pet. Shiro collected the fallen feathers. He hung them from his door and when villagers came to look at his art, they seized the huge feathers in their arms, whistled, and asked what beast they came from.

"Just a pest," Shiro said with a smile.

Once a season, a traveler would stop by for the night, offering their life story or a trinket for board. Some were flings; most were strangers. Some asked to be painted, but Shiro said he was cursed to draw cats—only cats. Some travelers he drew as cats, and they laughed together at the portraits. Some knew of the tengu that haunted him, and asked if he needed help getting rid of it. Shiro shook his head. He had already spoken to the local monastery a year ago about Crow and they knew of him. They said that Crow was the least of their concerns. Monsters far deadlier lived only steps from the road, the monks told him. Besides, this wasn't Crow's territory at all—couldn't he tell?

Shiro could. He saw it in the bent branches around his home, where Crow undoubtedly slept. He saw it in Crow's ever watchful eyes when he peered out at their surroundings as they talked. Or when Crow was scuffed from some fight. He wasn't too different from a cat in that manner, both being creatures of predator and prey.

When Shiro turned Crow's discarded feathers into a cloak, the tengu refused his gift, hissing, "Would you consider wearing a shirt of your own hair or shoes from welded toenail slivers?" But the present was gone the next day, either way. And, a week later, Shiro received his first and only gift from Crow.

He woke up on the nearest mountain and spent most of the day scaling down it. He stopped in town for food, then met Crow sitting atop Shiro's home. Clenched in the tengu's foot was a cat. He threw it down at Shiro and Shiro dove to catch it. When Shiro put the cat down, he saw that something was wrong with the feline. It moved on front paws, bore a broken, bent back and was a missing tail. It was still young. Not yet one year old. On the street, it wouldn't survive much longer. The wounds were old, though, so Shiro discounted Crow as possibly being the predator to paralyze it.

"Do you like my gift? Long may you look at this whelp and know that it suffers endlessly. Long may you be too weak to kill it and give it peace. And long may you know that, in your weakness, you will let it limp on like this, hurt and broken for all its days."

Shiro bent down and held out his finger.

The cat gave a nervous, though curious sniff.

"Crow, this is the kindest thing anyone has given me. Thank you."

The tengu said nothing, but watched him bring the cat inside. After Shiro made a bed for the cat to sleep in, he turned and saw Crow's long-nosed mask peering around the doorway.

"It will have no companions," Crow whispered. "If you bring another cat home, I will kill it."

Shiro offered him a cup of tea.

"Monk, why would I drink your dirt water?"

"It's Shiro, actually."

And the tengu didn't cackle or curse him. Or fly off. Crow paused, lowered his face, and whispered something to himself.

It was the closest Shiro had gotten to Crow. And he knew enough about beasts to know when approaching would scare one off. Shiro kept his hands at his sides instead of reaching out like he wanted to. He sat at the table and Crow took a tentative step inside. The cat ran its awkward, sliding run under paper scrolls and hid from the tengu. It peered out with bright green eyes.

"Shiro," Crow repeated.

"Shiro of the family of rice planters. And you?"

"I don't remember my name. But ..."

"But?"

Crow hesitated. "My family was from the coast. Fishing folk, I imagine."

"They say tengu are born out of the souls of people who have been killed."

"Some do."

"The souls of vain people."

"Yes, so it seems."

"Won't you sit?"

"I would never stoop so low. I'd rather sit on the floor."

"The floor is open."

Crow remained standing.

"I've been wondering, Crow. Do you have some unfinished business? What is it you want? After all these years, I can't imagine."

"I'm not a common ghost. What makes you think I want a thing from you?"

"Do you remember your previous life?"

"Our lives are seeds, aren't they? You fell the crop that grows and in its place a new one sprouts. That's what you monks seem to think, anyways."

"Who knows? I don't remember a single past life."

"Not the most enlightened, are you?"

"No." Shiro laughed. "I was far from it as a monk. I still am."

Crow sighed. "I shouldn't be wasting my time on somebody that isn't a real monk. Or somebody who is selfish, though, somehow, not vain. That's not what tengu do."

"I'm glad you do, though."

"I figured."

The tengu looked over his room without moving from his spot. He stretched a wing and knocked stacks of drawings over, which further sent the cat hiding. "You're not even good at being an artist. You haven't made a profit from it, after all these years. You never moved away to richer places."

"You do keep a man humble," Shiro said.

"It is my purpose."

"Well, perhaps I'm content here in these backwoods. With crates for chairs and you watching over me."

Crow looked to him. There was something in that stare that made Shiro continue, emboldened.

"Tell me, friend, who is it you've been protecting me from? This isn't your territory. The monastery says these are dangerous woods, but I've never had any trouble."

"Don't flatter yourself. I torment and protect a great deal of other forest homes."

"From whom?"

Crow folded his wings back up, and gave a low huff. "The Goblin Rat. But don't worry your little empty head about her. She won't bother you."

"Why?"

"You're a poor artist. What makes you worth a thing to a rat?"

"It makes sense. In the end, I suppose I'm only worth a thing to a crow."

As Crow turned to take his leave, he paused by the door. "There's nothing vainer than infatuation."

Whether Crow said that to Shiro or to himself, Shiro did not know. Either way, Crow didn't come back.

Shiro regretted his words and spent long nights thinking them over. The truth was, he wanted a demon in his home. He wanted a tap on his door, Crow's black eyes, and the sneak of a monster crossing the room to his bed. He wanted hands on his throat—murderous at first glance, but softening to loving. Until the two of them were nothing but bed and feathers.

Still, Crow did not come back.

Shiro was left alone for the first time in years. He kept to his cat and his art, trying uselessly to draw something not feline. But when his brush pulled away from the paper, he was left with a cat-bird hybrid. He didn't let it dry, but tore it apart in long slivers.

PERHAPS CROW WOULD STAY AWAY forever. Perhaps the best way to banish a demon was to make them uncomfortable with the prospect of love, then never see them again. There were endless tales of monsters seducing humans, but what of humans being the one to reach out? By extending one arm, did monsters run away screeching? He didn't want to think that Crow had fled out of physical repulsion. Shiro knew he was not handsome, but he was proud of the man he'd grown into. His hair was graying and starting to thin, but he was a human and humans were shaped by the world around them. He could trace the farmer, the scholar, and then the secluded artist in his features. He had callused hands but a taste for laying around, savoring others cooking, and going to town on festival nights.

Just as Shiro didn't try and tame nature, he didn't attempt to tame his appearance. He was how the world had shaped him. He was himself—hairy, burly, and with a moustache that refused to grow without a bald patch in it. There was no use trying to alter his body into what others wanted in order to appease them. And those others included Crow.

Sadly, tengu were creatures built on vanity and Crow spent more time preening every feather into its perfect place than he did flying. Shiro hoped that his friend wasn't so shallow as to think lowly of him because of his looks, but Shiro was unsure. Crow was guarded, and now he was gone.

Shiro sat watching the changing, cycling world and petted his sickly cat. He had come to enjoy those silly kidnappings. He didn't travel without them. Instead, he holed up in his house and kept the door open, inviting anyone to come and take him to some new mountain or forest path. He slept, rolled up amongst sheet after sheet of paper, with ink stained to his skin.

His number of visiting travelers dwindled. When people rested in his home for the night, they now only spoke of the Goblin Rat and her cohort. They asked if he knew anything at all about how to beat her or if he could sell them talismans, but he wasn't magically inclined. He gave them sheepish smiles and said he didn't do much but draw cats, really.

The Goblin Rat terrified the valley, but not because she was a warmonger who left scores of people slaughtered. In truth, her cohort didn't kill many people at all. But rats were rats, and they were nearly impossible to keep out. She could fit through the smallest crack in the floor. She worked silently. While never maiming entire homes, her rats burrowed their way into the mouths of sleeping people. They attacked too quickly for the victim to scream. Then, once the rats choked the person to death with their own bodies, they took over and walked in the person's corpse. They pulled at the human's vocal cords and neck muscles, making them talk. The rats worked as a team for the Goblin Rat's plans. What those plans were, nobody knew. But her corpse-walkers traded in town, bought weapons, jewelry, and the finest of foods, before hauling it all back to the woods. Nobody knew how many had been killed by the rats, but a young boy was struck by a cart and, to everyone's horror, when he fell down with a shattered bone poking through his thigh, there was no blood. A rat's sniffing snout emerged from the body, startled. It alerted a pack of rodents that expulsed from the boy and into the streets until all that remained was a husk of skin and bone, everything else eaten clean away.

Perhaps the rats inhabited only one person; perhaps the rats had taken over half the town. People started cutting their hands to show that there was clean blood beneath. A few died from infections this way.

Shiro started to wonder if Crow hadn't simply run off. Or maybe Crow was killed by the Goblin Rat the very night Crow told him about her, as though speaking her name aloud had summoned her.

It was reckless to live in the woods alone, but the Goblin Rat had never bothered him. Sometimes Shiro found the torn corpses of rats around his woods. Still, he knew his cat's disability prevented her from taking down something half her size.

But he didn't understand the tengu. If Crow was going to keep watch over him, Crow might as well pester him. It seemed unfair to have a friend who risked his life for Shiro without bothering to drop by for tea.

It made him feel pathetic.

Shiro took his brush out from the case, laid out his floor with paper, and stood over it. His cat went from scroll to scroll, trying to find the best place to stretch out and nap.

He breathed out. Talismans. He had seen monks and demon hunters use them before. There couldn't be too much to them—could there? The worst-case scenario was that they did nothing but make the townspeople feel safer. He tried to make them ornate, but his characters slowly started looping and he made up the kanji he needed as he went, thinking of lofty and vague words (Justice, Begone, Protection, God's Blessing).

When he stepped back from his first drawing, he saw he had drawn out the face of a cat in characters. He bit his cheek, thinking it looked childish instead of legitimate. Surely the townspeople wouldn't think something so silly would save them.

He made hundreds of such cat faces. He ran out of words and started writing sentences, commencing with: "The Monk Shiro commands that you leave this house alone". He replaced his name with more powerful monks instead. Finally, he broke down into tired scratchings of, "Go away. I eat mice. Die."

The townspeople were mostly illiterate anyways. What did the words of a talisman matter if the intent was the same? He let the various cat faces, poses, and paws dry before giving them away.

He was ready for people to laugh at him, but instead villagers scrambled for a painted talisman. They offered payment, anything at all, but he asked only for more paper and ink. He spent the next weeks writing out words made of cats. Shiro had no idea if they were working or not. The number of corpse-walkers remained unknown. When a new one was discovered, it was impossible to tell if the person was changed pre-or-post talisman. Eventually, it would be clear if the talisman were working, though. Those possessing one of his talisman would either all be alive, or dead.

But maybe they did do something. For when the fall leaves were at their reddest, the monk Mitsue stopped by. Mitsue was a wiry fellow who had visited years ago to welcome him to the valley. Welcoming him meant that Mitsue had really come to chastise Shiro, saying that he shouldn't wear monk robes if he wasn't a monk anymore. Shiro did stop wearing the adornments, but always made sure to wear his robes when visiting the monastery—mostly to annoy the man who scolded him.

Mitsue caught him mid-painting. He stood in Shiro's doorway with clenched hands, all smiles and shyness.

"Good afternoon. I've come on behalf of the monastery. Do you think, great artist Shiro, that you could paint some talismans for us too?"

Shiro looked up from his page.

"You don't need to treat me with reverence, my friend, just because these are trying times."

"Of course. Endless apologies."

"There's no need to apologize. You can take some of these back with you, though I'm sure that your own talismans would work better. I remember something about not being considered a real monk?"

"We have a big monastery," Mitsue replied, ignoring him. "We thought you could paint our *Shoji* screens. You must understand—holy ground is always a target for demons. They would love nothing more than to slaughter us all." Mitsue smiled at him.

Shiro didn't know what was so amusing about it. "I can paint your walls," he replied.

"That's great news. We'll pay you with whatever you'd like."

"I don't need payment."

"Then we can offer you as much ink as you need, so long as you protect our monastery."

This was surprising, but not unpleasing. "But some more kindness from the monastery would please me," Shiro replied.

The monk laughed, but when Shiro invited him in for tea, Mitsue backed up and bowed. "I really have to get back, although if you wouldn't mind stopping by tomorrow, that would be most appreciated."

Shiro didn't think it was a strange meeting at first, even if Mitsue was overly formal with him. Perhaps he had to be, being on official orders from the monastery and all. But when Shiro walked up the monastery path in the morning, he was taken by how queer the woods had gotten.

The forest, by day, should have been anything but peaceful. He listened for rustling creatures or birdsong, but even the wind seemed muted. There was the occasional gust of leaves caught up in wind, but nothing else. His footsteps were muffled by the unkempt steps. Perhaps the monks were too afraid to leave their domain to sweep away the leaves. Perhaps the valley was in worse shape than he thought.

When he arrived, breathing heavy, at the top of the hill, nobody was there to greet him. The monastery should have been full of hundreds of monks, but he only saw a handful scattered about the grounds. They were in prayer or walking, their hands behind their backs. He breathed out, waved to a few, and they waved back. He found Mitsue by the entrance and the man ran to greet him.

"This place is nearly abandoned," Shiro said.

"The Goblin Rat scared most of them off. But that was months ago, now."

"I didn't know."

"You don't pay attention to most things. That is ... if you don't mind such an impetuous statement, honorable artist Shiro."

"The Goblin Rat is that powerful?"

"Of course!" The monk shook, more emoted than Shiro had ever seen him. "She could rule this entire valley, if she wanted to."

"Do you think that's her goal?"

"It's impossible for somebody like me to know the goals of a being so awe-striking. It's beyond comprehension."

"Well, you could still guess," Shiro suggested. "Sometimes it's fun to guess at things."

Mitsue didn't seem to understand.

Shiro dropped the subject and the monk left him alone to paint the cloister screens. He worked straight through the day and made cats large and small. Three hours into his task, Shiro realized he had made a fatal mistake.

For these monks were most likely all corpse-walkers.

Shiro painted anyways. But his grip tightened to keep his hand from shaking. As a former monk, Shiro knew that routine was ingrained deeply into every monk's day, but these monks seemed to have no plans. Even if dwindled down to a few scared monks, he couldn't imagine them abandoning the faith. If anything, people stuck to routine more strictly when faced with so many unknowns. Instead, these monks lingered. They peered into the woods and didn't speak to one another. There was no bell for prayer; no chanting. They didn't seem to notice time at all. It had taken Shiro years to stop planning his day around the ingrained call to prayer and sometimes, even on the road, he would find himself humming at sunrise and sunset.

Maybe this was his fate. That a disgraced monk should be torn apart by imitations of his own order.

Mitsue came to check on him, flanked by the other monks.

Shiro lowered his paintbrush.

"You plan to kill me, I take it," Shiro said by way of greeting. "If you don't mind, I'd sooner kill myself than be murdered by rats. Can you at least give me that option?"

Mitsue's laughter was the sound of hundreds of squeaking rodents held deep in the monk's frame. "You're not our high prize. You're bait, so we keep you alive."

Shiro paused. "Haven't I killed scores of you? This isn't revenge?"

"Killed us with your words and pictures? Of course not! Your little follower is the scourge. And he'll come out of hiding if your life's forfeit. The Goblin Rat comes tonight. We'll slay you both."

"Crow won't come for me," Shiro said. "He gave up on me months ago."

The monks laughed as they assaulted him.

Despite the blood rising from their bites, he held no anger against them. No rage. He did nothing but clutch his brushes closely. They ripped open a screen and dragged him by the hair through to the prayer room and threw him on the cushions as though he might plead to some higher power to step in and help.

He didn't pray. He pressed the blood on his face and pulled his hand away, staring at the redness.

They didn't guard him. They didn't think he was worth the bother. Shiro sat alone in the prayer room. There were no life-threatening wounds, but dozens of bites and scratches. They had fought animal-like. That had probably saved him some agony; humans fought far more cruelly than rats. Humans flayed and tortured and knew what pain was. These rats had only nipped.

He didn't think Crow would come. Crow hadn't come when people went missing or were turned to corpse-walkers, but the rats seemed to hate the tengu. He sat wondering, feeling useless. But wasn't that the fate of humans? In a world of myth and demons, what were people but pathetic creatures? Not even worth posting guards for.

The false monks waited outside for the Goblin Rat or for Crow to arrive. He hoped neither did. He hoped each would sit outside from day to night then day again, feeling foolish.

His talismans had done nothing. How could he think some scribbling on a paper could fend off demons? The monks taught that the world was illusion and, thus, the world was meaningless. He didn't know how they could teach that because he found so much meaning in everything. Even if comprised of pictures and the two-dimensional, didn't that still have meaning?

He pressed the paintbrush to a gash on his arm and drew a hand-sized cat on the floor beside him. He wouldn't mind being a haunt to this place. If they killed him, then he wanted to tie himself to the monastery. He was addicted to the world. To material things. To life. If they murdered him, perhaps in a hundred years' time the Goblin Rat would move on and Crow would perch on a tree nearby. Shiro would peer out, specter-like, from the abandoned monastery, and talk to him again.

He might as well be a ghost. Might as well be an illusion clinging to a material object.

He painted with his blood. On every surface he could reach, he drew a cat. When his blood dried up, he mixed his blood with his ink. The ink turned the lines from red to black. His iron and cells were embedded in that color. It was his ink; his drawings. He marked the world again and again, claiming his stake in it. That he was worth something, if only a scribbling. If only an etching on the wall.

When night came and he heard yelling, then fighting, outside, only then did he pause. It sounded like a bloodbath.

The Goblin Rat had come. She would discover Crow was nowhere to be seen and walk into the monastery to shred him. He sat on a cushion and closed his eyes, waiting.

He wouldn't scream in death. He wouldn't fight. He would drift from his body and they could do what they wanted with the corpse he left behind, though he didn't have much pull in town, so how could he be worth imitating?

When the screaming quieted and the door slid open, Shiro opened his eyes. The Goblin Rat was a murderess. She must have attacked her followers because Crow had not appeared.

He faced his death head-on, expression placid.

But standing there was no goblin twisted with savagery; standing there was Crow. Or Crow in pieces, for his wings were gone, and his arms hung limp with chunks of feathers torn out. His mask was cracked down the middle, barely holding in place. Everywhere, his feathers were tufts, the ends shredded.

Crow also bore older wounds. His wings were months' scabbed over. The tengu walked with a limp. Shiro saw that Crow bore two severed claws on his right foot. These were fresh. The third claw, front and hind, was slick with red.

Shiro gasped. "I didn't think—"

"You should think more, it's a good talent," Crow said. He staggered and fell forward.

Shiro wasn't quick enough to stand and catch him. But he ran to Crow and crouched down until they were close. So close that he smelled iron and salt.

"You came for me," Shiro said.

Black, beaded eyes stared up at him. "I did, didn't I? It makes me a bad tengu."

"But it makes you a good man."

Crow laughed, but with pain. "It seems that I'm the one that's been driven mad by a human."

"You were watching over me all this time? All this time you've been keeping away and just watching? Even when I kept the door open? Even when I walked around at night looking up at the trees? Why? Do you really find me so repulsive, just because I reached out one time? I didn't need your undying love if you were so disgraced at the thought of being with me."

Crow stared at him, surprised.

Shiro wasn't used to raising his voice or edging over to anger. He breathed out and sighed. "It doesn't matter."

"You think I'd find you repulsive? The disgrace is mine, Shiro. You should be the one turning away."

Shiro watched him. He saw how self-conscious Crow was about Shiro looking at him, how much more tense about that than being in pain. It was true that tengus were vain creatures. Crow had spent so much time trying to appear beautiful that he was fearful of not living up to the tales that told of what a tengu should be. That he had a role that he'd been placed into, the same as Shiro had been, but whereas Shiro had made his own way, gaining the kind of confidence that only comes in knowing oneself, Crow had hidden all of his insecurity behind pride. With his wings gone, Crow seemed more disgusted with himself than with anybody else.

"I was trying to keep away," Crow said.

"Why?"

"Because they would have killed you sooner," he said. "But it looks like they'll kill us all the same. They found what would lure me. Even when I tried to hide it."

"If I may?" Shiro asked.

He used one of Crow's uninjured talons to rip off a strip of his shirt and wrapped the material around Crow's foot. The makeshift bandage did little to staunch the blood.

"You could have stayed," Shiro said, "if it didn't matter. You could have stuck around and we could have been killed then. Instead of months of silence. And me, thinking I was fool for following a bird."

"You are a fool for following a bird," Crow whispered. "And I'm a fool for coming."

"Do we run? Do we fight?"

"They own the woods. And now I am worthless. The Goblin Rat is on her way. When she arrives, she'll sniff us out. She'll have everyone in the woods looking. We should seek a more merciful death."

"Let me understand. You stayed away because she took your wings? And you only came because I was going to die either with you at my side or alone, so you chose to stay with me?"

Crow said nothing.

"Did you really think I'd care to see you without your wings? Did you really think I'd drive you off?"

Crow stiffened. "Isn't that all I am to you? Some pretty bird?"

"Of course not."

"I didn't want to be like your cat, either. I was afraid to be a pity case."

"You aren't a pity case to me."

"Then what am I to you? How can I be worth a thing as a tengu, with no wings?"

"'Tengu' is but a title. And I know your name. You are Crow."

Shiro looked around the darkened room. The moonlight illuminated what it could. He could barely make out outlines. His drawings were no more than shadows. Shiro lifted up Crow in his arms.

The defeated tengu did not resist, which Shiro found heartbreaking. He walked with him around the room, looking for anywhere to hide, and eventually came across a linen wardrobe. He opened it and tried to fit around the sheets. He kicked at them until they loosened and he could just squeeze the door shut, but they were both full-sized men. They took up most the space and the clean sheets absorbed their blood.

"She'll find us here," Crow whispered. "Nothing keeps a rat away."

"I don't care." He fumbled in the dark, trying to find Crow's face amongst all the feathers. When it was close, he pressed his forehead against the mask and breathed out. "If she comes, if she kills us ... then it will be like when you kidnapped me. We'll be reborn and show up somewhere else, won't we? And then we can wander and find each other again."

"That's a nice dream, it is. But it's a dream all the same."

"I think I love you, Crow. I think I've loved you more than I've loved anything else. Even cats. And I love cats so much."

"Even though she tore off my beautiful wings—"

"Love is the deepest cut and the darkest stroke. My heart cares for yours.

It beats faster than your wings ever did. Can you not say the same for me?"

"Fully." Crow's word echoed with emotion.

In the doomed and shadowed prayer hall, Shiro kissed the crack on the mask. In the dark, they were both blind.

Crow pressed the side of his face to Shiro's. "When I died, I woke upon a shore. I was in a body bloated by the sea and, slowly, I pecked my way free until I was panting in the sun with sea water dried to salt on me. My old flesh was nothing more than rotten skin, a husk."

"How did you die?"

"I—I don't remember. Drowned, probably. There was rope around my legs and it was frayed at the end. I was killed for a reason, probably deserved."

"But you don't remember?"

"No. I have never wondered why. But now I want you to know my past."

Crow's mask split down the middle with the sound of a nut cracking in one's palm. He pressed his head closer to Shiro's, who felt the sharp turn of a beak against his neck.

"I don't think I mind getting killed," Shiro said. "Even if it's by a rat."

"No, I believe I don't mind much, either."

When the Goblin Rat came, she spoke in a tongue that Shiro did not know. He kept his breath quiet, though Crow was unconscious from his injuries. They smelled too much like blood, the two of them.

He waited for a long snout to push through the crack in the dresser and grin at them. Instead, the Goblin Rat yelled at whoever was with her. The sound of dozens of sniffing, snorting human-rats filled the monastery. He heard her nails clicking on the floor.

She taunted him in her demon tongue.

He felt Crow stir, but pressed a hand to his beak to keep him quiet. Shiro didn't want to be butchered. He figured that nobody ever did, but life was cruel and took and sometimes turned a person into lunch. It would be a brutal but quick death.

The Goblin Rat was close now, close enough for him to hear her claws against the door.

She hissed.

The hiss carried from the mouth of one to another. Well, there was a hiss, but perhaps it wasn't her.

Shiro wondered if she had an army of hissing monsters at her side, but the Goblin Rat suddenly went quiet.

The hissing continued, loudly, then gave way to growling, yowling, then fighting.

Shiro held his breath and listened to terrible screaming, but from whom he could not tell. The violent fight shook the cabinet and woke Crow, who tensed against Shiro. They waited in the dark, together.

For whatever was fighting would come for them next. It felt giant. Monstrous. As tall as trees and strong as fire. It fought and growled until all Shiro could smell was blood.

Then, silence. Then, the two of them close together, hearts racing.

They didn't dare come out. Not for hours. Not until the sun pressed against the crack in the wardrobe and Shiro could finally see Crow with the sliver of light. His face was that of a bird's, the beak pointed straight, trying to look outside. For hours, they sat there.

His entire body hurt to move, but Shiro opened the door, carefully.

The prayer room was a ruin.

Claw marks covered nearly every surface. Half the walls were torn down. Blood painted the floor.

Shiro would never know what the Goblin Rat looked like, truly, because she was a mess of shredded red skin and white bones. There was nothing left but remnants and the corpses of the torn monks, their bellies emptied of slaughtered rats.

Shiro stood with the tengu leaning against him, surveying the wreckage.

"But what creature could—?"

"Your cats," Crow said, gesturing at the walls.

And there, Shiro's cats of ink and blood looked down upon them lazily. They were still paintings but not in their original poses. They grinned, rat fur matted in their mouths, blood staining their incisors.

He felt a faint purring vibrating out from the walls, but the cats did not move. They remained perpetually happy from their feast.

Shiro's cats had saved them.

He and Crow waited for somebody to come, but of course nobody would. The monks had fled months ago. Nobody stopped by a haunted monastery. When the birds and animals returned to the woods, they were alone. Not a single rat was left scurrying alive.

"It seems you've finally won your territory," Shiro said.

Crow sat on the *engawa* with his back to him. There was no re-growing the stumps where his wings once were. No more silent movement or flight. He couldn't walk without stumbling, but that would heal. They both knew that, with so many scars, he was no longer a tengu. That he would never roam the skies again.

Crow did not weep. He seemed both destroyed and relieved.

Shiro sat beside him.

They looked out at the forest.

"I can't hold a territory, not anymore," Crow said. "I could barely protect myself once the Goblin Rat took my wings. I didn't want you to see me like that. I still don't. Those wings were my pride."

"Maybe you could protect a smaller range. Here with me."

Crow blinked a moment. "This monastery?"

Shiro lifted his arms. "*This* monastery abandoned to the woods. I'll be its keeper, but you are its protector. We'll root out any remaining rats together, if there are any. Help out the town."

"The monks won't come back?"

"Not if we lie and say it's cursed."

"And when something bigger and stronger comes to claim this area as their own? What will we do then?"

"Then we'll kill them or we'll die. But we will die on land that we've made sacred. Do you think that's so bad?"

Crow laughed, his neck feathers ruffling outward. He shook his head. "No, it's not the worst thing."

"There's one stipulation though."

"And what is that, Shiro?"

"Once you heal, I plan to kidnap you."

Crow cocked his head. "Do you, now?"

"Yes. I'll tie you up and throw you over the back of a horse, then leave you by the seaside. Then you'll have to spend days wandering around to try and find me."

"And what will happen when I do find you?"

Shiro leaned close and took Crow's hands in his own. "Of course, I'll attack."

HEFT
MARK WARD

Those thin men, skeletons
in tight flesh. They say you've
    put on weight since
the whole 'new clothes' affair—
but at least there's no more pretence.
    They were sure of your
shame, but instead you revelled
in how your body moved, let those
    knights aspire to tautness—
you installed mirrors, had seconds,
took to walking around the palace
    naked and gloriously feckless.

I had left home, being the youngest
and having eaten them out of it, I found
    a job as a footman; yours.
You liked to inspect us yourself
(which caused a whisper) when
    company was coming—
some queen and her stable of princesses
to dangle under your nose. That day,
    you wore a robe, just about.

My uniform didn't fit and I bulged
out of it, embarrassed. We didn't speak
     but a week later, one arrived,
tailor-made. The others noticed and
the first footman told me to go and
     say thank you.
At your room, the maid said you were
in the library. Asleep naked in a chair,
     your book had slid down, covering

nothing—you awoke and stared at me,
still half-asleep, before realizing your body
     had woken too. You were embarrassed,
something no one had seen you be since
that day the whole town laughed at you,
     not for your body but your gullibility.
You had swooned over the tailor, you later told me,
his barrel-chest, his measuring tape covering every
     inch of you. You wanted it to be true.

Now, you reached for a robe and covered yourself,
abashed. *I'm sorry for interrupting, Sire.* And you
    laughed, smiled. *You didn't. Jones, isn't it?*
I instinctively straightened up. *Yes, Sire.* And you
didn't speak for a long minute. *I'm glad to see that*
    your new attire suits you well. I wanted you
to be comfortable in it, a handsome man like yourself.*
The next day, dressed, you sat and spoke with me,
    about small things, palace life, everything.

Within a few weeks, our visits were twice daily.
You asked if I would be happy to spend my time with you
    as your personal footman. You stared at the ground,
nervous I would say no. *I'd really like that but there's*
just one thing. You sighed, regretting saying anything.
    The clothes you've been wearing have got to go.
You smiled but said, *I can't, not around you.* I undid your buttons,
your breeches and kissed you, embracing your heft. I stripped too
    and brought us to the mirror to see us in our finery.

EL MUERTO'S GODSON
EVEY BRETT

I DO NOT REMEMBER THE night my father took me out onto the road, though I heard the tale many times as I grew. The tall *saguaro* cacti watched like sentinels and the desert air was damp with the threat of rain. Owls and coyotes made an uneasy chorus while my father held me against his chest, full of despair.

"Thirteen," he muttered. "Twelve children I can handle, but thirteen is too many! I already work day and night just to put bread on the table. No, no, this one must go; I will give him to the first godfather I can find."

We were out on the road for some time when there came a man on a white horse, his jacket embroidered with fine silver thread and inlaid with pearls. In the moonlight, he sparkled so brilliantly he might have been one of the stars come to earth.

"Please, sir," my father said, "I love my child, but I have twelve others to feed. Can you find it in your heart to be a *padrino* to this one?"

The man gazed down at me with nothing but love in his expression. "I would be honored to do as you ask, *señor*. I will hold this child at his christening and see that he is happy upon the earth."

Something in the words made my father wary. "Who are you?"

"I am the master of the heavens," he said. "The creator of all."

"Then I change my mind," my father said stubbornly, and gripped me hard enough that I squirmed. "You reward the rich while leaving the poor to starve."

And so saying, my father turned his back and continued down the road.

A second horse came thundering up, this one sleek and wild with a hide as red as blood. The *caballero* astride him was handsome and dashing in a short coat of black studded with crimson jewels. My father repeated his plea, and this man said, "Of course I will take your child. I will shower him with gifts and riches, the likes of which you cannot imagine."

This, too, raised my father's suspicions. "Who are you?"

"*El Diablo,*" he said with a grin that lit a fire in his eyes.

My father hugged me close. "Then I do not choose you, for you are a liar and a deceiver."

El Diablo just laughed, and rode away as madly as he'd come. My father stood stiffly on the road, anger mixing with misery. He could not keep me, yet he was losing hope of finding me a suitable guardian.

And then, so stealthily we did not hear him approach until he was upon us, came a third man. He wore gray, such a dusty, light color that he was nearly lost in the night. His steed was a sturdy, dappled gelding that reminded me of my father's plow horse.

"I will take your child," he said in a voice that rasped like dead leaves. "I am *El Muerto*. In my eyes, all are equal, and he who has me as a friend lacks for nothing."

At this, my father's hope rekindled once more. "Then I choose you, for you make no distinction between rich and poor. The christening will be Sunday at noon; will you come?"

"I will," said *El Muerto*, and he kept his promise.

The adobe church was tiny, barely large enough to fit my family along with the priest. If any wondered who my strange *padrino* was, they did not ask.

Afterwards, my *padrino* cradled me in his arm and carried me outside. As he did, the storms broke, bringing the life-giving rain to the desert and giving me a baptism of a different sort.

And thus I began my apprenticeship.

"FOR EVERY LIFE, THERE IS a death," was the first lesson I was taught. "And for every death, a life."

My *padrino* would take me out into the desert and show me everything, from hawks and coyotes preying on hares to buzzards and maggots feasting on the corpses. I saw snakes eating lizards, and once, a kingsnake battled with a rattlesnake, twisting and writhing until it managed to swallow the rattler whole.

I witnessed births as well, from the summer rains bringing forth seedlings and drawing toads from their year-long slumber to mate and find puddles in which to lay eggs that would become toads in a matter of days. Doves and woodpeckers tended their young in their nests. Sometimes the babies lived to fly. Sometimes a falcon or snake got them first.

Never a harsh word did my *padrino* speak, and never did I fear him. Life and death were one, an endless cycle that he worked to keep in balance with some algorithm that I did not yet understand, but assumed that one day I would.

Later on, he took me with him to sickbeds where doctors worked to heal their patients. Sometimes they managed; often, they didn't. As I grew, I had a keen sense of awareness. I had but to glance at a person to *know* what ailed them, and if they might live or die. The strange thing was, none of those near death did anything about it.

"*Padrino*," I asked one day, "don't they know they're going to die? Can't they feel it?"

He shook his head. "Few are so aware. When you're of age I will teach you, more about it. For now, just watch and listen and learn."

So I did.

Over the years my childish fascination grew to keen understanding. And while my mind changed and adapted, so did my body. I began to have lurid dreams, and while the resulting reactions did not frighten me, I found them disconcerting. I was a man, after all. I'd seen animals rut and create a new life.

But I was also different, and not just because *El Muerto* was my godfather.

He was old beyond measure, and if he ever felt a young man's stirrings, he had forgotten them long ago. When I overcame my embarrassment enough to ask him, he said nothing but took me with him on one of his nightly journeys, making sure no one saw us.

I witnessed girls laughing and flirting with boys who tumbled them in the hay. There were the working women of the *pueblo*, the ones who gave themselves to the soldiers in exchange for money. Other men beat their wives into submission, caring little for their protests in the bedroom. And, thankfully, there were the married couples who were truly in love, and treated each other tenderly when they offered up their bodies.

And last, we came upon a pair of *vaqueros* alone guarding a herd of cattle. They were both naked, entwined on a saddle blanket and rutting the way I'd seen a stallion do with a mare; thrusting and grunting and making odd moaning noises.

My heart skipped, and I felt a strange tingling within me that had not happened with the other couples. Longing stirred, and with it, my cock.

Cheeks flaming, I turned away so my *padrino* could not see the result of my excitement. Even so, he must have noticed, because he said, "There are many kinds of love."

Feeling mollified that he thought me neither strange nor unnatural, I asked, "Have you ever loved anyone so?"

He was silent for a long, long time before he said, "Once."

But no matter my pleading, he would not say more. I wondered who he might have loved, and who could have loved *El Muerto*.

A FEW NIGHTS LATER, HE took me on another journey, this time to a secluded grotto at the base of the black mountains. There was a pool there, fed by water bubbling up through the earth. Around its edge grew an herb I'd never before seen; it had small, pointed leaves and sported tiny white flowers.

"What I show you is our secret, and to be used in our work and only as I bid you. Do you understand?"

I nodded, wondering what this was. My *padrino* was rarely so grave. "I do."

He plucked a few sprigs of the herb. "With this, the *hierba vida*, I give you the gift that is your destiny. You will be a *curandero*, a healer. And when you are called to a patient's bedside, I will be there. If I am at the head of the bed, you may give the patient this herb and they will be well. If I am at the foot, you will say that all remedies are in vain, and the patient cannot be saved. And beware of using the *hierba vida* against my wishes lest ill befall you."

"*Sí, Padrino.*" Never before had I gone against my guardian; I could not dream of anything that would make me do so.

He taught me how to prepare the *hierba vida*, by drying it then crushing it into a fine powder that could be mixed with either water or wine. A sip or two would be sufficient. Under his supervision, I prepared a batch and kept it in a small gourd that served as a flask. I ached to try it, to see what would happen, but I knew better than to disobey my *padrino*.

He found me a hut at the edge of the *pueblo*, one with just enough room for myself, my medicines, and a patient, who was not long in coming. The *pueblo* had a physician trained in Madrid, but many either could not afford him or were too shy to ask such a well-dressed man for help.

My first was a shy little girl who simply held out her reddened hand, which I guessed had been burned in a fire. This I did not need my *padrino* for; I knew well enough which medicaments would heal without resorting to the *hierba vida*. So I tended her wound and bade her be more careful around the cookfire. She mumbled something in thanks and handed me a pretty green stone she must have found while out playing. I smiled and set it on a shelf so I could be reminded of my first patient.

Soon after, a man about my age arrived at my door, breathless. "It's my wife. She just gave birth, but she's ill. And so hot ...."

I grabbed the gourd of *hierba vida* and followed him through the *pueblo* until we reached a small adobe house. Inside, a basket with a swaddled infant sat beside a bed on which a young woman twisted and thrashed, face covered in sweat. To my relief, my *padrino* stood at the head of the bed.

My hand shook as I held the gourd to the woman's lips. She batted at me and refused to drink; I bade the husband to hold her arms while I steadied her head and trickled the medicine down her throat.

I waited for one long breath. Two. And I began to fear that I had done something wrong in preparing the herb, or worse, that my *padrino* had lied to me about its efficacy.

Then, with a gasp so sudden and loud that I jumped, she went limp and relaxed into a normal sleep. I put a hand on her forehead. The fever had broken.

"It's a miracle," the husband said, and kissed me on the cheek. I was pleased; more than pleased. I checked the infant over as a precaution, and was soon certain that both mother and child would be well and healthy.

My next patient, however, was not so fortunate.

"Please come, *señor*," said the young farmer twisting his straw hat in his hands. "It's my brother. There's been a terrible accident."

There was no time to saddle my own horse, so I clung to him as we rode, ending up at a farmstead. I saw the blood trailing from the field and into the house, and thought if my patient were still alive it would be a miracle.

The family had gathered around his bed, weeping. My patient was young, not even sixteen.

I peeled away the cloths pressed against the grievous scythe wound in his leg and knew, even before I saw my *padrino* standing at the foot of the bed, he would die.

"Send for a priest," I told the brother. "There is nothing I or anyone can do for him."

The brother ran, and the priest arrived mere moments before my patient succumbed to his injury. I snuck out, pained and aggrieved.

Even though I had acted rightly, the loss stung. The *hierba vida* could have staunched the blood and saved him.

"It was his time," my *padrino* said, and I did not argue, however much my pride stung. "For every life that goes, another takes its place."

"But how do you decide whose time is up?"

"I don't decide. I simply know."

The answer frustrated rather than helped. Try as I might, I could not make sense of who lived and who died. There were the elderly who had lived a good life, although some were ready to leave their ailing bodies but could not. Others were children stricken with fevers or consumption, fighting valiantly to live while their bodies grew too broken to continue.

One night, after I'd been forced to let a man die of a snakebite, I railed at my *padrino*. "Don't you care who lives and who dies? The wife has lost a husband. She loved him deeply, and now will pine for him. Have you no pity, no compassion?"

He didn't answer, but simply faded into the darkness as was his habit. Usually, I let him go, needing time to myself, but this time I followed him, desperate for some answers to the questions plaguing me.

One of my many lessons had been stealth; I employed it now, staying just far enough behind him so that he would not detect me. We traveled through the desert, the air scented with creosote and hot stone. The unyielding heat of the day remained, even after dark.

We went up a rocky hill until it leveled out into a mesa overlooking the *pueblo*. I figured this must be some vantage point of his, where he could watch the people pass below and count the days they had left. I'd never been here before and hadn't even realized there was a usable path to the top.

I crouched behind a boulder while my *padrino* stood, quiet and contemplative. Anger flashed within me; how dare he lecture me on life and death yet be so callous to the anguish of others?

I was ready to confront him, to call him on his deception when he made a choked, strangled noise.

El Muerto was weeping.

The sight twisted through my gut, filling me with shame. I turned away, having intruded on something too personal, too intimate. I was so used to his passivity in all things that this display of emotion utterly unnerved me.

I dared not move until long after he left, then, gathering my courage, went to inspect the area that had undone him. There was naught to mark the place but a few stones, but even so, I knew it was a grave.

A pang struck my chest. How strange to think that *El Muerto* had once loved someone and still mourned, yet, the revelation filled me with resolve. I didn't want to be like him, to wander through the years alone and pining. I wanted a living lover of my own.

ONE DAY I WAS PASSING through the market on my way to the tavern with a delivery when I couldn't help but sense the excitement rippling through those gathered in the plaza. "Don Lorenzo has returned!" I heard, although I wasn't sure who he was.

I went inside the tavern, already bustling with soldiers and *caballeros* drinking and eating heartily. Juan, the owner welcomed me with a smile as I handed him the bottle of medicine to give to his wife, who was still recovering from a fever.

"*Gracias, señor,*" he said, sliding a cup of wine to me. "Please. On the house. Just arrived from California."

I thanked him. I turned to face the crowd, leaning idly against the bar when I saw him: a finely dressed man with a sword strapped to his belt and a stomach so large that I would not have been able to wrap my arms around it. He sat at a table with two companions, helping himself to a full plate of venison, rice, beans, and fresh tortillas.

My amazement must have been obvious, because Juan said, "That is Don Lorenzo, Don Esteban's son."

The name clicked into place. Don Esteban was a wealthy *caballero*, having made his money from cattle and could afford to send his son away for schooling. To me, the son had returned much the better for it. That Don Lorenzo was fond of food was obvious; he was far larger than the other men in the *pueblo*, yet I could also sense his health and vitality.

My loins quickened, and I turned away, suddenly shy. I was no stranger to bodies and their workings, yet none of my patients had elicited such a reaction before.

Juan put on a mischievous smile, took my arm, and led me over to the table. "Don Lorenzo, may I be so bold as to introduce our *curandero?* Many of the people say he works miracles. I will vouch for him; he saved my Magdalena from a fever."

"Perhaps he can cure what ails you," one of the companions said with a jab to Don Lorenzo's ribs.

I gave a slight bow, hoping it would hide the flush in my skin. "At your service, Don Lorenzo, though please, do not bestow upon me the gifts that belong to the gods."

"Ah, he's humble, too," said Don Lorenzo with a grin. "A pleasure to meet you, my friend. I have just returned from my schooling in Madrid, and while I have not been home long, I have heard much about you."

I bowed again, wondering what strange spell this stranger had cast on me to leave me trembling and unsure.

"Come to the *hacienda* this evening. I have a complaint that no physician has been able to remedy; perhaps you will be more successful."

"Of course," I said. "I am at your service."

He clapped a hand on my arm, which sent a jolt through my body. When he let go, I felt weak and dizzy and had to grab a nearby chair to steady myself.

I don't think Don Lorenzo noticed; he'd already returned his attention to his meal and friends. I felt an unwelcome pang of jealously and was taken by a sudden image of being dressed in a fine suit and proud to sit next to such a handsome man.

Then I tossed it away. I was a *curandero*, and such thoughts were not professional. I had my job to do, and I could not let my own desires get in the way of my patient.

At least, that's what I kept telling myself.

A SERVANT MET ME AT the door of the *hacienda* and led me to the drawing room where Don Lorenzo waited.

"Come," he said, and gestured at me to follow. "I would prefer privacy."

He led me into his room, which was as elegantly furnished as the rest of the house, and at least twice the size of my home. A carafe of wine sat on a small table alongside a plate of peaches and pears.

My *padrino* was not present, which gave me a measure of relief. This visit was not about a life or death ailment. What, then?

Once inside, he unbuttoned his jacket and pulled it off, breathing a sigh of relief as he did so. Sweat stained his linen shirt. "Forgive me. It's this damnable heat. I've never gotten used to it."

I kept my eyes averted, too aware of the excitement coursing through me. I could not lose control of myself. Not here, not now.

We made courteous small talk, and I spent some time examining him, checking his pulse, looking into his eyes and throat. I did not get a sense of anything overtly wrong, but whatever ailed him, Don Lorenzo was too embarrassed or too ashamed to admit.

That is, until he said, "I have seen many beautiful women, some whom expressed a desire to be my wife, and yet I feel nothing for them. I have accompanied my friends to brothels, but I find I am ... unable to act as a man should."

He paused, having to take a deep breath before continuing.

"The physicians have given me countless remedies. Some say I ought to lose weight, and I have tried, to no avail. So now I beg of you, a humble *curandero*. What ails me? Why can I not be a man?"

Dios was cruel, taunting me this way. I strove to be professional, to keep my longings at bay, but I found it difficult. The answer to his complaint was as clear to me as a cloudless summer day, yet I had to approach it carefully. "Have you ever shared a bed with another man?"

"I did while I was at boarding school, but it was only in jest. Play. The kinds of things boys will do. When the headmaster found out, he whipped us."

"And, these times of play...did your manhood function then?"

There was a long, empty moment before his voice dropped almost to a whisper. "Yes."

I said nothing, waiting for him to come to his own conclusion.

He did, suddenly startling. "*Dios*. Is that why—with women—nothing happens? Because I like *boys?*"

I didn't miss the note of panic. "Boys ... or men?"

He became quite still as he pondered this information. At last, he said, "I had wondered for some time. This is not a new revelation, only an unwelcome one."

"There is no shame in it, and you are far from unique in this matter."

"No. I suppose not." After a while, he gave me an odd, piercing look. "You're like me, aren't you?"

"It makes no difference. I am here as your *curandero*, and I mean to ..." My voice caught.

"Mean to what?"

My heart pounded, making me dizzy. I could not think. I, who knew so well how bodies worked and what they needed, suddenly became a slave to mine.

Outside, thunder rumbled. A few raindrops fell, then more until they became a steady beating on the roof.

"There," Don Lorenzo said, "now your departure must be delayed, unless you want a thorough soaking."

I should have gone anyway. A voice inside my head told me to flee, to leave before this vague sense of dread took hold.

"The servants won't come, if that's what you're afraid of. I've bidden them to go to bed, and they won't disturb us until morning." He came to me and fiddled with the laces on my shirt.

I pulled back, suddenly shy.

"Haven't you ...?" he asked.

There was no way to explain the sort of isolated, cautious childhood I'd had. "No."

He laughed. "But you want to."

I could not answer. I dared not.

"Come," he said, taking my hand. "Cure me of what ails me."

He peeled off his shirt, exposing the rolls of flesh I'd been longing to see. A fine black mat of hair went from navel to chest, and at the sight of it, I lost the last of my inhibitions.

I ran my fingers through his chest hair, breathing in the scent of his sweat. He wasted no time in yanking my shirt over my head and running his hands over my skin.

"Yes," he said, and it was almost a growl in my ear. "I think you're right, *curandero*. It's the men that call to my manhood, not the women. Shall we continue, just to make sure?"

He kissed me, long and hard and deep, and I tasted the remnants of wine on his tongue.

Gently, he lifted me onto the bed where he busied himself unbuttoning my pants and yanking them off, spying for the first time since I was a child what no one other than my *padrino* had seen. I lay there, vulnerable, while he shed his pants and let me see the cock jutting forth between his ample thighs.

I sat up and grasped it, fascinated by the way it stiffened in my hand and how the lightest touch made Don Lorenzo moan with ecstasy.

Too soon he tugged at my legs until they were spread wide around his waist. He spat liberally on his fingers then reached down to my asshole. One finger slid in, then two, teasing some inner point that shot fire through my loins as he readied me for the inevitable.

And when it came, I let out a cry of utter pleasure. I'd spent so long worrying about bodies that were ill and broken that I'd never guessed what a healthy one, let alone my own, was capable of.

After the initial climax and a bit of rest, we tried again, going more slowly. I took my time exploring his body, marveling at the structure of his muscles and the folds of skin. I'd healed any number of hurts to men, and thought I knew their bodies well, but here, with neither shame nor my profession to hide behind, I discovered new, unimagined points of both pain and pleasure.

When it was my turn, he spread me wide on the bed and went over every inch of me with lips and hands. He was a large man, bud he did not lack for strength. When he tucked me beneath him, he was careful not to let his full weight rest on me.

The closeness was sheer, utter bliss. I'd never known feelings like this were possible; certainly not from my *padrino*, who always guarded what few emotions he had. Even after witnessing others in the midst of passion, I had not guessed what they were truly feeling.

Now I knew, and I did not want this newfound happiness to stop.

WHEN I RETURNED HOME, MY *padrino* waited for me. I was still full of energy and exuberance, eager to tell him of the new pleasure I'd found.

But I had no need to tell him, after all.

"Be careful," he said. "Some lives are shorter than others."

Would that I had heeded his words, but I, being young and in the first throes of love, paid them no mind at all.

TWO DAYS LATER I WAS summoned back to the *hacienda*, not for Don Lorenzo, but for his father, Don Esteban.

The *pueblo* doctor gave me a look of impatience as I strode into the sickroom, though he left without complaint when Don Lorenzo dismissed him.

I knew the diagnosis, of course; it was easy to tell from the old man's blue-tinted lips and harsh breathing. I pulled Don Lorenzo aside. "It's his heart."

"So the physician said. Is there nothing you can do?"

I glance back at the bed. There my *padrino* stood at the foot, gazing down at *Don* Esteban. "No. Nothing. He will not last the night."

I had rarely seen a man weep, but Don Lorenzo did. "I've only just returned. I don't know enough about the *hacienda*. I love him; I'm not ready to let him go."

And because he was pained, so was I. I sensed his grief, felt it wash over me like a summer storm. Guilt followed soon after. The cure rested in my pocket. I had but to give Don Esteban a dose of the *hierba vida*, and he would heal.

But there my *padrino* stood, and I had promised to obey him. As long as he stood at the foot of the bed, my patient must be allowed to die.

And there, like a spark to tinder, I had an idea. "Help me turn the bed."

Don Lorenzo gazed at me, uncomprehending.

"Just do it."

It took both of us, as well as two servants, to shift the heavy wooden bed and its occupant, but we managed. Now, my *padrino* stood at the head of the bed.

Quickly, I dosed Don Esteban with the *hierba vida* and fussed over him enough to disguise what I'd done. It didn't take long for color to return to his face and his breathing to return to normal.

"You've done it!" Don Lorenzo threw his arms around me, and his relief sunk into my bones. "You *are* a miracle worker." Then, into my ear so no one else could hear, he whispered, "I love you."

"YOU DECEIVED ME," MY *PADRINO* said when I returned home. His raspy voice held an uncharacteristic edge of steel, and I froze. "It was *Don* Esteban's time to die, yet you took it upon yourself to trick me so he did not. Why?"

I had the feeling he knew, and I felt ashamed. *Don* Lorenzo loved his father deeply, and I could not bear to cause him pain.

"You tamper with the natural order of things. Old men die. Sometimes the young do too. It is the way of life. Have you learned nothing?"

"*Si, Padrino,*" I said, chastened. "But Don Esteban is a good man, loved by his people. He takes care of his workers and treats them well. His son—," here I choked, thinking of the night we'd shared, "—his son needs his father to guide him into manhood. There is much love between them."

My reasoning did not sway my *padrino*. "One mistake I will grant you, for you are my *ahijado*, my godson. But break your promise again, and I will take your life myself."

"*Si, Padrino.*"

I had no doubt he meant what he said. For the first time, I feared my guardian, who had never once gone back on his word.

THE POUNDING AT MY DOOR woke me from a sound sleep. I rose quickly, wondering what sort of emergency had arrived, and pulled open the door.

Don Lorenzo stood there, a saddlebag over one shoulder, fine clothes askew, breathing hard. "My father lives, and I have you to thank for it."

He shut the door and bolted it. I was not afraid, although I sensed the wildness within him. He quickly shed his sword belt and stripped off his shirt. I had only a moment to think before he thrust me against the wall and rucked up my nightshirt, exposing the cock that rose eagerly to meet his hand.

Then he was on his knees, hands tangled in fabric, nuzzling between my legs, taking my length into the wet heat of his mouth. I groaned at the sensation.

Just when I thought I could hold back no longer, he released me and flung me onto the bed sideways, so my legs dangled off the side. Hands grabbed my buttocks and pried them apart, making way for his tongue and, moments later, his cock.

His belly slapped my ass as he drove into me harder, faster, until I thought I might expire from desperation. His thick fingers gripped my waist so hard as to bruise, but I welcomed the pain.

He came with a howl that rivaled any coyote I'd ever heard. While still pulsing inside me, he pulled me close and reached down to grasp my cock, rough hand sliding up and down the shaft until my body convulsed in release.

"Don't leave," he told me when it was over and I splayed over his belly, taking in the warmth. "I need you, more than you know."

I twirled a finger in his chest hair. "I have my duties to the people and ... elsewhere."

He grabbed my hair and jerked my head back, leaving me no choice but to accept his kiss. His tongue slid between my teeth and I shuddered at the invasion. "I love you."

The words stunned me, yet I felt answering warmth deep in my chest. "I love you, too."

He grinned. I should have known he would not arrive empty-handed. From his saddlebag he withdrew a veritable feast; tortillas, dried beef, pears, apples, cherries, and fried bread along with a jar of honey. We shared a meal, with him taking great pleasure in dangling a bite above my mouth before feeding me and watching for my enjoyment. I was used to simpler meals, and these treats were a welcome addition.

He left just after sunrise. I watched him go, aching, wanting him back. With him, my loneliness had eased, and I began to consider happiness rather than mere contentment.

But such things were not meant to last.

Not for the godson of *El Muerto*.

A MONTH LATER, I GOT word that Don Lorenzo had fallen from his horse.

It was Don Esteban himself who rode out to fetch me. "You are known throughout the *pueblo* for working miracles," he said. "You must come and provide one for my son."

I grabbed my bag and headed out, riding hard beside Don Esteban.

But when I arrived, my *padrino* stood at the foot of Don Lorenzo's bed, expression neutral as he gazed down at him.

I ignored him and examined my patient anyway, desperately seeking a means to cure him that meant I need not use the *hierba vida*, but my hope quickly died. Don Lorenzo must have hit his head on a rock when he'd fallen, because there was a deep gash in the back of his skull. I tugged open his eyelids, only to see the pupils fixed and dilated.

"Please," Don Esteban wailed. "Save my son as you did me!"

"*Por favor, Padrino,*" I said so only my guardian could hear. "Please change your mind. Do not take him."

But my *padrino* gave no answer. I knew it was foolish to ask; not once in all the years I'd known him had he been swayed by tears, pleas, or love. I thought now of his warning: *Some lives are shorter than others.*

He'd known my lover was going to die, and had done nothing.

"Please!" Don Esteban said again. "Just save him, and I will give you anything you desire. Money, a fine estate, a place here, at my son's side."

His offer cut with a pang. I wanted nothing more than to be Don Lorenzo's companion. He would have to father a son, at some point, to carry on the family name and hand down lands, but otherwise he could be mine. We would ride together, care for the estate during the day and make love at night. I wanted his body against mine; heavy flesh snug and warm.

I looked once more at my *padrino*, who cared for his duty and for the life and death of every living creature, but who understood nothing about love. If he did, how could he allow so many terrible deaths to happen? His face remained passive as he waited patiently for Don Lorenzo to die.

Then, in a sudden fury, I pulled the sheets from the corners of the mattress and tugged and tugged until I got Don Lorenzo turned fully around. The servants and Don Esteban must have thought me mad, but I didn't care. Now that his head was at the foot of the bed, my *padrino* was at the end meant for healing.

I dared wait no longer; I thrust the gourd of *hierba vida* between Don Lorenzo's lips.

A heartbeat passed. Another. And another.

Don Lorenzo gave a great, deep sigh and opened his eyes.

The moment he did, *El Muerto* grabbed my wrist in his icy fingers and yanked me into the night.

THERE WAS A SICKENING SENSE of disorientation, a swirl of blackness, then flickering brightness that caused me to blink. When I could see once more, I found that I was in a huge cave filled with hundreds of thousands of candles lined up in neat rows. Some were tall and burning well, others so low as to be nearly sputtering. Here and there lights went out, only to spring up elsewhere on fresh tapers. I dared not move, lest I commit some infraction.

Yet my *padrino* moved among them effortlessly, causing no breeze to threaten the flames. "Do you know what these are, *ahijado*?"

I shook my head, still stunned by the abrupt transition from sickroom to cave.

"These are lives. Here," he pointed to a lengthy candle, "is a child, just born yesterday. And here," he gestured to one nearly burned out, "is an old woman with a mere handful of days left."

It made sense, now that he knew where and when to appear in a sickroom. "Which is mine?" I asked, expecting to have one of the taller candles, or at the very least, one half-burned.

Instead, my *padrino* gestured at a candle sputtering in melted wax.

"*Ai, Padrino,*" I said. "I have only just discovered love. I risked your anger for the well-being of another. Would you see my life cut so short?"

"I warned you. From the first day I showed you the *hierba vida*, you knew not to disobey me."

Even so, I was hurt beyond measure that my guardian would take my life himself rather than make an exception. "After all this time, I have served you well, cared for you, done as you bid. I have asked for nothing. Will you not grant me this one favor?"

"You are but one brief life among so many."

I could not believe he was so truly lacking in compassion. "I know you have been at your duty for years beyond count. You've treated me with kindness and patience, and although you seem to be passive and indifferent in all your actions, I know you are not incapable of feeling something deeper."

Frightened, desperate, I played the one card I had left. "I saw you one night, up on the *mesa*. You wept as I have seen few men do. It could only have been for love, for someone lost to you forever."

His pale eyes flashed, and I could see him struggling to maintain his equilibrium.

"I am your *ahijado*. Do you not love me as well? I, who have been your only family? Light another for me. Let me be with my beloved. Let us live a happy life together." I was pleading, and hating myself for it. "You know the pain of loss. Don't wish that upon me as well."

At last, he slumped, and I could see defeat written in his gaunt form. "I cannot light another for you."

My heart sank. "Is there nothing you can do?"

He went down a row of candles and lifted one that was half burned. "This is your Don Lorenzo."

I watched, perplexed, as he took a wick and threaded it carefully into the melted wax of the candle.

"Once I join yours to it, the candle will burn twice as fast. And when at last it is extinguished, you will die together. This much, I can give you."

Relief and gratitude made me giddy. "Thank you, *Padrino*."

I kissed him on his papery cheek, filled with affection and relief. "I swear, on my life, that I will never deceive you again."

"No. You will not." He spoke with such finality that there was no chance of argument.

Heart pounding, I watched as he lifted the remnants of my sputtering candle to the new wick in Don Lorenzo's. The flame caught, flared, and I had one moment of intense brightness and warmth before the cave fell away ...

... and I came to on the road leading to Don Esteban's *hacienda*.

I NEVER BREATHED A WORD to Don Lorenzo of what had passed in the cave. It would benefit no one, and it was no kindness to a man to know that his life had been cut short.

Don Esteban, true to his word, made me welcome in his *hacienda* and provided me with a workshop to create and mix whatever medicines I needed, although I kept my little adobe home near the *pueblo* so patients could visit me there. And if the servants or Don Esteban had any issue with Don Lorenzo and I sharing rooms, none spoke of it. That is, other than an occasional lament from Don Esteban about wanting grandchildren.

This, too, was solved when I was sent to the bedside of a family newly arrived from Spain but stricken with smallpox. The parents passed on, but their son, a healthy two year old, survived, and Don Lorenzo was given leave to adopt him. Don Esteban happily acted as grandparent, and took the child with him on rides around the estate.

"I need not fret about a son now," Don Lorenzo told me one night in bed. I was tucked up against him, comforted by his bulk. "All will be well, as long as we are together."

I had no doubt of that, although I always kept an eye on the foot of the bed, watching for my *padrino*.

EVERY SO OFTEN I WENT back to the base of the black mountains to that small, beautiful grotto. I'd kept that secret as I had so many others, and was just gathering the *herbaria vida* when I felt my *padrino* nearby.

"Is it time?"

"Not yet. But soon."

Soon, to him, might mean ten days or ten years. Either way, I was content.

I stood to face him. "Thank you. For everything."

We'd had little chance to speak over the past few years, despite the number of times I saw him at a bedside. He hadn't changed; still faded and thin, yet his finely embroidered coat showed not the slightest hole or loose thread.

"*Ahijado.*"

From his tone, I knew he had something serious to speak of. So I waited, puzzled and curious.

"I did love, once. Her name was Lucia. She knew me for who I was and did not fear me, but her candle was short, her flame so brief. I did nothing to help her and I've regretted it every day since. You, I do not regret."

It was the closest he would come to expressing his love and affection for me, and I accepted it as it was. "*Gracias, Padrino.*"

His fingers brushed my cheek, and then he was gone.

Perhaps a month later, I returned home after tending to a patient to see Don Lorenzo seated by the fire. A plate of food rested on a table beside him, but it worried me to see it only half finished.

Taking his hand in mine, I asked, "Are you well?"

"Never better." He rested his other hand on his ample stomach. His belly hadn't shrunk with age; if anything, it had grown, and I loved him all the better for it.

"Come to bed. It's late."

He came with me, straining more than usual to climb the stairs. His breaths were harsh and he lacked the strength to undress himself, so I did it for him, then bade him lie down.

As the godson of *El Muerto*, I knew, of course, but I did not fear.

I made love to him that night, slowly, tenderly, taking in every part of him, whispering sweet words into his ears. He smiled, contented, and drifted into sleep.

In the hour before dawn, my *padrino* came to the foot of the bed. There were no more tricks, no deceptions. He held out his hand and I went to him, grateful for a life well-lived and well-loved.

LESSON LEARNED
ROB ROSEN

A LONG TIME AGO IN a land far, far away lived a prince, namely me, Prince Theodore, who was imprisoned by his father, namely my father, King Henry, for doing unspeakable acts. Repeatedly. And with various men employed by the castle. And with various men not employed by the king. And by myself around the castle grounds when various men were not to be had. By me, that is.

In any case, imprisoned I most sadly was, forced to live high above that aforementioned far away land in a long-unused tower until such a day that my father deemed that I had learned my lesson, though what that lesson was remained a mystery. Again, to me.

Did he mean sleeping with men? With various men? With too many men?

Or was it the quality of the men and not so much the quantity? Because, fine, he might have had a point there.

These questions were moot, however, because how could I answer them while locked away in the tower, fed through a hole in the door, no one to talk to, no one to do unspeakable acts with, mainly because there was no one to speak with, let alone to do acts with?

Though I tried. Because there was still a hole in the door. And any port in the storm, I always say.

Alas, the hole was promptly plugged and placed far too high to do unspeakable acts through. I know this because still I tried before promptly falling off of various bits of furniture piled on high. And landing from up on high while attempting unspeakable acts was, ironically, a lesson learned, though, alas again, not the correct lesson.

So alone I did live, if you could call it that, staring out at the trees and birds, missing my life. And the men. Various and lowly though they that might have been.

My father would visit me from time to time, to see if my lesson had been learned, but, seeing as I did not know what lesson he spoke of, his visits proved less than fruitful.

Still, years into my ever so lonely banishment, I did have yet another visitor. A woodsman. I could not see him, my perch too lofty, but I could nonetheless hear him as he felled a nearby tree.

"Hello?" I shouted down, belly fluttering with butterflies at a chance for company, however distant said company might be.

"Hello?" came the response from below. "Where are you?"

I tossed an apple core from my window. "Up here! I am imprisoned!" I shouted his way. "Afforded meager rations!" Well, meagery. I mean, I was still a prince, after all.

"Too bad!" yelled the woodsman. "Why are you imprisoned? Murder? Thievery? Treachery?"

I paused. "Um," I ummed, before adding, "Buggery!" To which I also added, "Repeated buggery!" At least I thought that's why I was imprisoned. Sadly, I was quite good at buggering, and so it truly was a shame to be imprisoned for it.

"Were you any good at it?"

Again, I laughed. Again, I cried, "Very!" I wiped tears from my eyes. "Or so I was told." Repeatedly.

"Shame, then!"

I eagerly nodded my agreement. "That's what I say!"

His name was William, a woodsman employed by my father to thin out the trees around the royal grounds. Made it easier for hunting, he said. Or, rather, hollered. I pictured him as a big man, a burly man, which is to say, William the woodsman's deep voice caused my own wood to grow to tree-limb proportions.

It would not be the last time this would happen.

He visited me the next day, in fact.

I craned my neck and chest out, but the building was slightly wider atop, narrower below. I could just barely see a hand, a shoulder. He moved away from the tower, but at my perilous height, he looked small and squat, the boulder looking more like a pebble.

We ate lunch together. I tossed him a whole apple this time, and all the times thereafter. Over the course of several weeks, he told me about his life in the woods—or shouted about it, his voice bouncing off the ages-old trees as if to surround me like a cocoon.

He lived alone, worked from sunrise to sunset, tending to the woods as need be. It was a solitary life. In his retelling of it, he sounded sad. Or he echoed sad, but still.

I told him while we ate, day after day, of my life. Of what it was like to be a prince, eventually relating my exploits in and out of numerous beds. In my retelling, I too sounded sad, which was surprising, given how much fun I seemingly had.

"Sounds lonely!" he shouted. A moment later, he added, "I mean you!"

Me? I thought. *But that does not sound right.* And yet, up until I'd met— well, sort of met—William, I had been alone. At least come morning. Or at least come come. I had everything I wanted. I had nothing I needed. Was that my lesson? Had I at last learned it?

When my father came to visit a fortnight later, he said, "Theodore, you are indeed looking older, but it is wiser I was hoping for."

I nodded. William told me that the tower was abandoned because locals thought it cursed by its former occupant, a wizard with severe social anxiety. Magic explained why I now possessed a beard of golden hue that reached my knees. "I have become wiser, your highness," I explained. "I have learned that to want for nothing is not a goal in life, that to need for more than the fineries is more important, and that one can be lonely even when surrounded by servants." Randy servants, but still…."

He nodded, smiled, the skin around his eyes bunching into wrinkles. He had also grown older. "Yes, my son," he said. "I see that you have grown wiser, but this is not yet what I need from you in order to set you free."

I sighed, my head hung low. I thought of William pressed against me.

Of me beneath the bulk of him. Of meeting him face to face. Or other body parts to other body parts. Of simply of a kiss.

THE DAYS ROLLED INTO MONTHS, the seasons changed, but my one true constant remained William. I did not know what he looked like, but my heart swelled each time I heard his voice from the woods below.

I leaned out each day, perchance for a better view, but as always, I was simply too high up.

"Your beard, Your Highness, has grown long," he noted one day. In truth, it filled up so much of the tower room that I often draped some of it out over the window ledge. Brushing it took *forever*.

"The hairs on my chinny chin-chin ache as I ache to be nearer to thee, William," I told him, trying for a rather poetic tone.

He laughed, a flock of pigeons taking wing at the sound. "You should write that one down," he yelled. "Maidens would swoon at your prose!"

"And what of a certain woodsman?"

There was no answer.

Worried, I moved to the window.

"I ...," he started. "I ...," he started again. "I would rather tell you my thoughts in person!"

I sighed. Yes, good luck with that. Unless he grew wings, meeting in-person was not to be.

Or was it?

For an idea came to me.

"William, with your axe why don't you break down the door to this tower and climb the stairs and tell me how you feel?"

"Of course," he said and laughed. Minutes later I could hear the sound of him hacking away at the locked door at the base of the tower. Only, soon I heard William curse.

"It must be enchanted wood for it shattered the blade of my axe," he called out. "I shall search high and low, Your Highness, for a better axe."

And William left me, and I sulked the rest of that day, all of that night, feeling despair. And when he returned with three brand-new axes and still could not break down the door, I shouted down for him to stop.

"Could you not fell one of the nearby trees. It will fall against the tower, and then you can use it as a ramp to reach my window!"

"Possibly!"

It took him two days, misery swelling within me during those two days. Though, at the edges, there was hope.

The sound of the tree crashing against the tower's stonework echoed throughout the forest.

I looked at the tree, it wasn't one of the verdant pillars I saw throughout the forest. The word *scrawny* came to mind. And I voiced my doubts that its trunk would bear his glorious heft aloft.

"It will be enough," he replied. "Trust me, my prince, it will be!"

I trusted him. I trusted him with every ounce of my being.

"In person at last," I cried out, my heart nearly bursting forth from my chest. And as I cried, I stared down below, all while he climbed. "Hurry, William! Hurry and be careful!"

He laughed. "If you're a religious man, Theodore," he shouted, "now would be a good time to pray!"

I wasn't a religious man, though I did sometimes shout, "Oh God!" during certain unspeakable acts. But I tended to doubt that counted. And still I prayed. I prayed for William. I prayed for us.

He reached the top branches, which were so thin that they shook with every step he took. I glimpsed the top of his head. The top of his head met the end of my beard. He looked up, his round face smiling broadly, the blue in his eyes twinkling like the stars in the heavens.

"You have blue eyes!"

"Thank you for noticing." To which he added, "I'm too low." He needed the tree to be at least another twenty, maybe thirty feet.

I leaned out farther as he stretched his arms up to me. But still we were far apart.

"Wait," I yelled. My third idea I hoped would be my best. I grabbed as much of my long beard as I could and pushed it over the window sill until it become a shimmering, soft stream flowing down and down and down.

My heart momentarily stopped pounding. "Can you reach it?"

With a grunt, he said, "I … I think so!"

As I felt several firm tugs, I braced my feet against the wall of the tower, my hands against the rim of the window, and pulled back as he began his climb.

"Your beard is so soft and luxurious, Your Highness."

I blinked. "Thank you for noticing!" was my pained reply. "And?"

"And it makes it difficult to move fast!"

I nodded. I clenched everything I could clench. And then I waited. And then I waited some more. And at long, long last, the feather of his red hat came into view, and then, finally, those eyes of blue.

I reached down and grabbed his arm. I reached down as he reached up, and with all my strength, I heaved him up and over, both of us falling into my room, him on top of me, me below him, the feeling utterly indescribable.

He smiled as he huffed, and I smiled as I huffed, and we simply lay there staring as we fought to catch our breath.

"I believe," said I, finally with no need to shout, "you had something to tell me in person, good woodsman."

He nodded into my chin, the red of his beard blending with my blond one. He gulped and said, "I love you, my prince. I love you with all my soul even having never seen you before. My eyes, after all, do not need to see what my heart surely feels."

I grinned. I grinned, then kissed him. Then kissed him again. "Seems we are both rather poetic these days."

It was then I learned my lesson. I knew it as sure as I knew I loved the bear of a man that pressed into me, the pebble finally a boulder, the fur of his arms tickling the fingers that held onto him for dear life.

DAYS LATER, MY FATHER PAID me his standard visit. He flung the door open and strode in before coming to an abrupt halt. He was shocked to see two men greeting him instead of the usual one.

He sucked in his breath but then smiled as he noticed the hand in mine.

"Ah," he said. "And what lesson have you thus learned, my son?"

I smiled as I gripped William's mitt of a hand in mine. "Love, sire," I replied. "I have learned love for someone other than myself."

"Took you long enough," said my father as he moved away from the door to allow us to pass.

"Tell me about it," I replied as I tripped over my beard and into the world outside.

BEARS MOVE IN
ANN ZEDDIES

AUREN CAPELLI, SCROLLING THROUGH SUMMER apartment rentals ads, snapped to attention when his roommate, Drew, called out "Yo, there's a moving truck in front of that house next door."

He dropped his phone into the cushions of the couch, and Ashley, his other roommate, rushed to the window sill before he could; he was forced to peer around their heads and shoulders to see the latest development about the local mystery.

He glimpsed a squad of movers, unloading a full-sized semi. They emerged with an endless series of boxes from the truck's depths, then an eclectic collection of furniture in at least three distinct styles. Then the movers banded together to drag out exercise equipment. Contrary to all logic, they hauled the gear precariously up the rear exterior stairs and up to the third floor.

"Look at the different types of machines," Drew said, craning his neck to watch, though once the equipment was safely transferred without anyone falling off the steps, he lost interest.

"Lucky you're moving out," he told Auren, "I bet all that stuff will make a terrible din when they turn it on."

"I suppose…"

Auren wandered back to the couch, and Drew plopped down next to

179

Auren to lace up his cross-trainer shoes. Moments like these both enticed and repelled Auren. He enjoyed the smell of Drew's sweat and Axe, the proximity to his bare shoulder. All that coiled muscle right next to him. Drew was everything Auren felt he was supposed to want, with the additional spice of presumptive straightness.

"Well, you have two weeks to figure out where you want to live this summer," Ashley said. "Just let me know if you find another place. My cousin and his friends could use your room."

Drew smacked Auren on the shoulder and jumped to his feet. "Sure you don't want to come with us to the gym? I have the membership till the end of the month. I can still get you in free as my guest."

"No thanks."

"All the guys on Grindr are ripped." Drew lifted up his shirt to show his abs.

"How do you know about Grindr?" Auren asked.

"I'm very aware—"

"Thanks, but the gym is just not my thing." Auren found working out only made him feel lonelier than ever, even when the place was crowded with sweaty, grunting men. His roommates might not believe it, but Auren liked exercise, being flushed, out of breath—when he was a kid, Auren snuck out at night sometimes to run across the nearby golf course, deserted at that hour, and surrounding thickets. He jumped walls, climbed trees, and felt strong, powerful, invulnerable, in the magical cloak of night. But the gym seemed like a performance he had never rehearsed for. Truth was, ever since he was a kid, he felt his chunky frame embarrassed him, and the golden hairs that sprang up all over his chest and arms and legs only made him feel even more like an outsider. His high school gym teacher once referred to him as a cryptid.

Drew picked up his gym bag and smart phone and headed out the door.

Ashley called out to him to "Always swipe right!"

Auren laughed. "Should we be placing bets when Drew comes out as bi?"

She shrugged. "Let's not change the subject away from you. What about that guy you used to go out with?" she asked. "Jack? Or Zack? He seemed like he was connected. Maybe he could hook you up with someone who needs a roommate for the summer."

"We don't talk much." Auren would rather even go back to his parents than rely on Zack for help. But he wasn't about to explain that to Ashley.

A horn honked outside.

"My ride's here—gotta go." She left in a swirl of blonde ponytail and cute athletic skirt.

Drew relaxed into the musty old couch, grateful for the silence. An interrogative mew announced that his cat, Bear, was emerging from his hiding place behind the couch. Bear glared suspiciously at the door to make sure the other humans were gone, then trotted over and plumped his considerable weight into Auren's lap.

"Meh," the cat commented.

Auren stroked Bear's fluffy fur.

"Me too, Bear," he sighed.

He'd lived in this shabby condo just off the bus line with Drew and Ashley for the last two years. This summer, they both had other plans, and because Auren couldn't afford the rent on his own, his friends were subletting their rooms to Ashley's cousin and his friends. Summertime had become the beginning of the end.

From his bedroom window, Auren had often gazed at the topmost gables of the old house next door. It was a Victorian edifice, three stories high, cluttered with spires and gingerbread. An architectural monstrosity, it still seemed attractive to Auren after his years spent in dingy, cheaply-built student housing. He wished he could magically transport himself and his belongings down the block, to reappear in a hidden nook in the old house. The place had stood empty for some time. No one seemed to know who was the property manager.

Now he felt punched in the gut that someone else had found a way to rent the mystery house.

His parents would have been happy to have him move back home. He could have lived with them all through college, and let them pay for everything. But he couldn't tolerate the numbing vapor of faint hope and perpetual disappointment that wafted toward him every time he made a choice that wasn't their favorite.

Being gay wasn't the problem; it was never any secret. His parents had never paid attention to his dating life, or lack of one, until after he graduated from high school and briefly joined a student group on campus, met people, and brought a date home. There was a brief flurry of interest and support from his parents over his newly activated gay identity. His father the surgeon and his mother the bank manager got along famously with Zack, an aspiring entrepreneur. Clearly, they hoped he would be a good influence—that Auren would finally choose a lane, get some direction, lose weight, join a gym, maybe make some cool friends who owned art galleries or did CrossFit. But when he showed no signs of turning into anyone different from his usual self, his parents once again gazed at Auren sadly, as if he was a home improvement project that never quite worked out.

Zack had never really broken up with him. They had just parted company after an awkward evening—a drinks party with faculty and graduate students at the business school. Zack had dressed to impress, and Auren felt happy to be with someone so sharp and confident. Then Zack gate-crashed a group gathered around a celebrity professor. He never even introduced Auren, and the circle eventually closed up, including Zack, leaving Auren to contemplate his tonic and lime while trying to make small talk with a girlfriend who was similarly excluded.

After the party, Auren made a rare attempt to reach Zack's heart. "I felt like you ditched me to impress someone more important. It made me feel disrespected," Auren told him.

Zack groaned—for a moment, Aurel feared his boyfriend was going to stop the car in the middle of the road and ask him to get out. "Listen, it's a tough world. If you want respect, you have to go out and get it. I saw an opportunity and grabbed it. If you can't keep up, that's on you."

Auren texted him the next day. No reply. After a couple of weeks, he saw Zack sitting with someone new in the front row of the lecture section they both attended. Auren caught up with him in the hall afterward.

"Does this mean we broke up?" Auren asked Zack.

Zack shook his head without meeting Auren's eyes. "Dude, we were *never* a thing."

"Apparently being gay is one of the many things I don't do right," he told Bear.

The cat purred and sank prickly claws into Auren's thigh muscle.

"Ouch! Stop that. And the worst part of it is...my parents, my roommates, even my stupid ex- (we *were* a couple, Zack, no matter what you think)…I don't have a clue what I'm doing."

He held the cat up so Bear seemed to stand on his hind legs. Auren made him march to and fro.

"Look, it's Puss in Boots, he's Puss in Boots! Oh, Bear, why can't you don your magic boots and grant me my wish? Just find me somewhere I can fit in."

The cat gave an angry huff, wriggled out of his grasp and jumped to the floor, where he washed himself thoroughly, as if disdainful for Auren's nonsense.

"And my best friend is a cat," Auren said gloomily. "How sick is that?"

THE NEXT WEEK WAS CHAOTIC. Drew and Ashley sorted through their possessions, leaving stacks and heaps all over the living space, waiting to be bagged and trashed, or boxed for moving. Auren found it hard to settle down to the task of finding somewhere else to live. Whenever he shut himself in his room with the laptop to search, someone would pound on the door to ask for his help in moving furniture or question him about a missing bill.

The roommates cleaned the refrigerator—*Finally!* Auren thought—and piled the trash bags on top of the dumpster already full of discards. The next morning, trash was strewn around the woodsy strip behind the condos. Ashley declined to wear rubber gloves and assist, and Auren refused outright, so Drew had to clean it up himself.

"Auren, you'd better make sure the dumpster lid is shut tight," Drew declared when he returned inside, as if the problem wasn't of his own making. "And tell the kids they'd better watch out too, when they get here. I saw the apartment manager out back, and he says a bunch of buildings in the area have had problems. He thinks it's a bear invasion."

Auren scoffed. "Probably just a dog off the leash. Anyway, I won't be here to tell Ashley's cousin what to do with his trash. I'm leaving."

"Really? Where are you going?"

But Auren hadn't worked that out yet.

When he brought out another bag of trash, Auren looked around the concrete pad behind the parking lot, where the dumpsters stood, surrounded by a chain-link fence. The fence had a gate, but it was almost always left ajar. It was a nuisance to unlock while carrying anything bulky. The dumpster served both the condos and the house next door. Auren noticed that apparently there were people in there, because they had dumped some detritus—packing materials and such. He also noticed footprints in a damp patch at the pad's edge. They were blurry and hard to read, but he discerned a five-toed pad far too big for a raccoon. The tracks would have been big for a dog, too, unless someone had a Hound of the Baskervilles running around loose. Auren still didn't believe it was a bear, but he was extra careful not to let his Bear out at night.

Drew and Ashley didn't make that easy. They and their friends were constantly in and out the doors, banging them open, slamming them shut, propping them ajar for greater ease in moving boxes. Auren took refuge from the chaos in his room, where he tried to do a little packing of his own. He tried to keep Bear with him, but the cat was adept at escape maneuvers.

One evening, when welcome silence hinted that Drew and Ashley had gone out, Auren ventured out to find that they had left the back door ajar. Bear was nowhere to be found. Auren searched the apartment, but there was no sign of him. He stuck his head out the back door and called, but Bear didn't come running. With a knot of anxiety in his stomach, Auren walked out the back door, looking from side to side into the shadows and calling.

Bear sometimes escaped briefly to stalk birds or mice in the yard, but he always came back. Auren worried that the commotion in the house drove him away for real this time. Auren still didn't believe in bears, but there were all kinds of creatures in the strip behind the condos: stray dogs, raccoons, maybe even coyotes.

Auren heard a mew near the dumpsters.

Relief flooded him, only to be displaced by terror. The mew became a high-pitched yowling and wailing, a cat in distress. Worse still, the cat noises were answered by low-toned snarling and growling, and the clanking of something big rattling the fence. Auren pictured the worst—Bear attacked by a big stray dog, possibly rabid.

"Come, Bear," he cried. "Come, kitty!"

He didn't want to go near this situation, but he forged on into the semi-darkness. The reality was worse than he'd imagined. Bear huddled on the far side of the fence, his tail and fur fluffed out to twice his normal size. He was wailing and stabbing with an extended paw at a massive dark shape that seemed to have him trapped.

"Come, Bear! Come, kitty, kitty, kitty!"

Auren knew the cat could climb the fence and come to him. Perhaps he was too terrified to turn his back on the creature menacing him. It bore furry bulk, round ears, massive paws and big white teeth like on no dog he had ever seen.

"Oh my god, oh my god, it *is* a bear," Auren muttered.

Yet it didn't attack the cat, or Auren. As he approached, the bear jerked backward, releasing a cry of what sounded like pain. Auren realized why it wasn't moving. One paw was stuck in the chain-link. The bear yanked again at its tethered paw and whined. It no longer sounded threatening, but Auren was no less terrified. The cat shrank farther into the corner and yowled. Clearly, Bear was not going to save himself, but was insistent that Auren should save him instead. But Auren didn't know how. Call Animal Control? Who knew what could happen by the time they showed up—if they ever did.

If he cut the fence and freed the bear, maybe it would run away.

Bolt cutters, Auren thought.

But where would he get them?

Drew probably had some.

Auren was dashing back toward the house even while telling himself this was a crazy idea. The bear, set free, would probably eat both him and his cat.

He discovered that Drew had already emptied his closet. Auren tore open box after box in search of tools. Rifling through a mess of cables, rope, plastic containers of nails and screws, pliers, and a hammer, finally he found wire cutters. Thank you, Drew, for once, he thought.

"I'm coming, Bear," he called, returning outside.

Then, he slowed down.

What kind of insanity was he contemplating? What if the bear went after him as soon as it was free?

He took a deep breath. With any luck, the bear would run. Or maybe he and his cat could make it to the back door before the bear came around the fence.

Auren reached toward that killer paw, his hand nearly brushing it as he cut the first wire. That wasn't quite enough. He had to wrestle the cutters through link after link before the opening was big enough for the creature to jerk its paw free.

The bear bellowed, Bear wailed, and Auren yelled simultaneously.

There was a thunderous crashing in the underbrush. The bear fled into the night.

"Bear, come!" he cried again.

The cat crouched in place and mewed.

Auren realized he was going to have to go and get Bear. The last thing he wanted to do was take even one more step toward the direction the bear went, but he forced himself to. He reached out for the cat, but Bear moved backwards, away, tail lashing.

"Rowrrr," Bear said in an almost conversational manner this time, poking with his paw at something on the ground.

"Oh, for fuck's sake, what is it now?" Auren said. "Get in the house before you get us both killed."

He bent down cautiously, hoping to seize Bear before he could flee. Something glinted under the cat's paw. A big key, old-fashioned in shape, its brass dark with patina.

"Huh. Someone probably didn't mean to throw this away." Auren picked it up and stuck it in his pocket. "Now will you come here?"

The cat scrambled into Auren's arms as if he had always had that in mind.

Auren's legs shook as he hurried inside, and slammed and locked the door, good and tight this time.

In the morning, when the frightening encounter seemed far away and even kind of funny, he examined the key.

It was substantial and old, and looked like a real key, not some decorative imitation. He wondered if it might belong to the new neighbors, perhaps thrown out accidentally with the trash, or dropped in the confusion of the moving. Maybe someone in the house would recognize it, and be grateful to get it back. And giving the key back might gain Auren a look inside the place he found so intriguing.

He checked the view at his window frequently, hoping for a glimpse of the new tenants. Around suppertime, two cars appeared in the driveway—

an intimidating black Navigator and a sporty crossover. He waited a decent time after the supper hour, and then, in the early evening, knocked on the front door.

The man who answered was not much taller than Auren, but he was an impressive presence, his chest broad and his belly substantial. His shining dark hair was combed in luxuriant waves, and his black beard curled magnificently. He wore a fine cotton sweater, a procession of bears knitted into the pattern, and elegant leather slippers. He bore the air of someone ready for well-deserved relaxation after a productive day.

"Hello, I hope I'm not intruding," Auren said. "I'm your next-door neighbor, and—"

"How delightful," the man said. "Please, come in. So kind of you to make a visit so early in our stay here. Very courteous! And welcome!"

Auren looked around with interest. The kitchen was cozy, but rather small. The house must have been renovated. He imagined this might once have been a front sitting room. It didn't seem large enough to be the original dining area for such an expansive residence.

Auren perched on the chair the man offered. It didn't seem quite wide enough, or tall enough. He had to sit up straight to keep his balance.

"I was just making a cup of tea for myself," the man said. "Will you have tea? Do you like chai?"

"Sure, thank you."

"But I am remiss! I haven't introduced myself! I am Chandrakant Asvala. Very pleased to make your acquaintance."

"Auren Capelli."

They shook hands. Mr. Asvala's hand was warm and plump, but firm.

The man turned to put the kettle on, and Auren resumed staring around the room. Even in the dining area, one whole wall was filled with bookshelves. Mr. Asvala had literary tastes. Tastefully bound classics. Auren noticed a well-worn copy of *Goedel, Escher, Bach*, and a shelf full of newer volumes about artificial intelligence.

"I see you have a lot of books about AI," Auren said. "If you don't mind my asking, is that a professional interest?"

"Yes, indeed. I work in design for a robotics firm. And you, Auren—if I may call you that?"

"Oh, sure."

"And you must say Chandra. It means "the moon." My full name is Chandrakant—beloved of the moon is the meaning, but it is just a name in these modern times."

Interesting, Auren thought. But he had trouble thinking of this impressive person as anything other than *Mr. Asvala*.

"Are you a student? What are your interests?"

"I'm just a business major at State right now. I'm doing a minor in history, though."

"Really?" Mr. Asvala brought a tea-tray to the table and sat, regarding Auren with an expression that seemed interested and sympathetic. "What period is your specialty?"

"It's really just a hobby." Auren focused on his mug of spiced, milky tea. "More of a fantasy, really. I just like to read about other places, other times. Times when people weren't so—so confined, I guess. So wrapped up in little cubicles, and tied down to some little group of friends who all think alike. Just when there was more room in the world." He laughed and shook his head. "I suppose it's just a form of escapism. A friend once told me history was dead."

"No, I can't agree at all," Mr. Asvala said. "I think you are very wise to know yourself this early in life. You understand that you were meant for a larger world. This is wisdom."

They went on talking about Auren's plans, and he found himself saying things he had never acknowledged even to himself. Chandra seemed to find everything he said interesting and worthwhile. At times, Auren wondered if Chandra was flirting with him, but dismissed the idea. The man was just naturally charming, he thought.

Suddenly he realized that it was dark, and had been for a while. Fearful of overstaying his welcome, he was about to make his excuses and leave, but Chandra leaned toward him with one more question.

"Forgive my curiosity, but you have spoken of friends, but not of one special friend. Is there no one with whom you share such intriguing conversations as we have had tonight?"

Auren stared at the tabletop for several moments. "Not at the moment. Someone I thought was just that decided we had little in common." It hurt to get the words out, but it also felt surprisingly good to articulate what happened. "He was probably right. He was the kind of guy who always had a goal in mind. I guess I'm not like that. I like doing things just because, you know, I like doing them."

"Doing things for their own sake," Chandra said.

"Something like that. Or maybe I'm just lazy. I don't know why he wanted to be with me anyway." Auren laughed, trying to shrug the topic off and retreat to safer ground.

"Perhaps he was drawn to you for that very reason," Chandra said.

He looked kindly at Auren, and Auren felt his cheeks redden. "Because you enjoyed his company without judging him. But people who judge themselves harshly can never stop for long. So he became uncomfortable and had to leave. Perhaps it was his failure, and not yours."

Auren didn't know what to say. His silence felt uncomfortable, although Chandra seemed perfectly at ease with the pause. "I've imposed on you too long. I should go. I'm sorry—I just go off on tangents. That's what my roommates say, at least. Story of my life." He sighed.

Mr. Asvala stood up, and Auren thought he was standing to usher his guest out. Mr. Asvala was beside his chair, so close it became awkward for Auren to get up.

"I cannot agree with your friends," he said. "You seem to me a young man of great potential, who perhaps needs just a bit of guidance to find his way. Perhaps I might be of assistance in that regard. Allow me?"

Auren took his hand, stood, and found himself chest-to-chest with the other man, the dark curls of the magnificent beard tickling his cheek.

Mr. Asvala bent toward him. Auren felt his warm, spicy breath, and the full, parted lips inches away. There was no doubt of what was happening. Auren almost panicked.

A chubby but surprisingly powerful arm slipped around his waist. He leaned into Mr. Asvala's robust warmth with a surge of desire that took him by surprise. It was like hot cocoa with a shot, comforting and intoxicating at once. He managed to stammer some word of assent as Mr. Asvala guided him not toward the front door, but to an open, welcoming inner door.

When Auren opened his eyes, the room was filled with light. He was alone in a strange bed. Disoriented, he tried to sit up, and found himself tangled in quilts, sheets, embroidered pillows and coverlets. He tried to thrash his legs free and hit his head on an elaborately carved headboard. The bed seemed too cramped for him to stretch out his arms and throw off the covers. He tried to roll over, and fell over the side. He landed hard, still swathed in blankets.

The room felt like a cave, with a coved ceiling and narrow windows. The bed stood high off the floor on claw-footed legs of highly polished old wood. The room was crowded full of curios—antique chests, porcelain objects displayed on shelves—all things he might like to explore, if he wasn't so abuzz with anxiety. He was naked. He looked around wildly for his clothes. They lay folded neatly on a footstool at the foot of the bed. Auren dragged them on hastily and escaped the claustrophobic bedroom to find himself in the kitchen.

Chandrakant Asvala sat at the table, drinking tea and reading a newspaper. The table held scones, a teapot, a jug of milk, and a pot of honey. An extra place was set for Auren.

"My dear boy, how delightful to see you this morning," Chandra said.

Auren didn't feel delightful. His teeth were not brushed, and neither was his hair.

Chandra smiled broadly, waving Auren toward the table. "Sit down, make yourself comfortable. I've prepared some breakfast for you—spiced porridge, my favorite dish. My mother used to make it for me on Saturdays."

"I can't—really, I don't want to take any more of your time," Auren said. He felt he was babbling.

"Nonsense! Sit down."

Auren sat, but he could not make himself comfortable. The narrow, rush-bottomed chair creaked under his precariously balanced weight.

Chandra poured tea for them and served porridge with a flourish.

Reluctantly, Auren picked up the heavy silver spoon. His mind had gone blank. He did not know what people said in these situations. He popped a full spoon of porridge into his mouth to cover his confusion. Thermal heat burned his tongue. Chilies and curry fumed up his nose. Tears sprang from his eyes. He sneezed uncontrollably and recoiled, grasping for a drink, a napkin, anything to smother the explosion he felt rising in his throat. The chair tipped backwards and splintered apart, throwing him to the floor for the second time that morning.

Chandra reached out to help him up, but Auren scrambled to his feet and bolted for the door.

Too embarrassed and confused to form complete sentences, he couldn't even offer an apology.

"Stay—have some tea!" Chandra called after him. "Let me get you water. I did not realize I had prepared this too spicy for you."

"I'm sorry—I can't—I just remembered—my cat—"

Auren jumped over the threshold and didn't stop until he reached his own door. Panting, he flung himself into the safety of the apartment, slamming and locking the door behind him. After the opulence of Mr. Asvala's rooms, the place looked extra shabby, a wasteland of half-filled cartons and dust bunnies, but Auren didn't care. He poured a glass of cold water to soothe his stinging throat. Bear darted toward him, yowling displeasure at this extended absence.

"Oh, Bear, I'm sorry. I didn't mean to be away so long. I won't do it again, I promise. Are you all right?"

He sat down. Bear jumped into his lap. He diligently sniffed Auren, as if trying to determine what he'd been up to, then settled down, purring. Auren was surprised to be forgiven so quickly. Usually Bear snubbed him for an hour after such a dereliction. Auren calmed himself, stroking Bear's plushy fur and telling him about his adventures. Bear blinked wisely, as if he knew all about them.

"Now, I really have to do something about finding a new apartment," Auren said. Standing up to get his laptop, he felt something hard in his back pocket. The key.

"I'm such an idiot. I never even asked him about it."

Later that afternoon, after more packing, he made a few calls. The most promising places were already filled, and his second choices didn't pick up, or said they would call back, but didn't. Worry burned in his chest.

As twilight dimmed the windows, he felt more and more restless. He couldn't sit still and focus on ads and listings. He paced around the room. In the absence of roommates, with no one to ask for an explanation, old habits called to him. Out in the dark, he didn't need an identity. No one would expect an apology. Bear followed him to the door, but he pushed the cat back.

"No, Bear, you stay here. You know what happened last time you were out."

"Mmmph," Bear said disapprovingly.

Stepping out into the night, Auren felt the familiar excitement. He slipped like a wild thing through the overgrown bushes that separated the condo from the house next door, the branches brushing his face, the breeze toying with his hair. He meant to veer toward the alley on the far side of the block, but the dark bulk of the house looming against evening clouds brought him to a standstill.

The key still weighted his pocket. There was a faint glow of light behind the curtains on the first floor. The upper stories were dark and still.

With only a few steps, Auren could find himself climbing those tempting back stairs to the mysterious third floor.

Knowing just how stupid this might turn out to be, he felt for the key in his pocket and set foot softly on the first tread.

He moved stealthily. At the landing he paused. The moon stared at him, seeming almost level with his eyes. He saw over roofs and empty streets. The sense of height was exhilarating. It would be fun to live up here, he thought, and enjoy this commanding view.

The darkened windows showed no sign of life. He continued to the top. He didn't see any signs warning of security measures, and when he looked in the windows, he saw nothing, no little lights blinking. He tried the doorknob, cautiously, wondering how fast he could get back down the stairs if a warning sounded. To his amazement, the latch clicked, and the door swung open. He needn't even try the key.

His heart pounding, Auren knocked softly on the edge of the door. "Hello? Anybody home?"

There was no answer. He stepped inside and closed the door behind him. Using his phone for light, he looked around like an explorer examining a newly-discovered cave. The large room was set up as a bedroom. The occupant had not yet finished moving in. An enormous super-king size bed took up most of the space to the right of the door, under a set of windows. On the other side, the matching window was partially blocked by stacks of boxes and an immense and complicated exercise machine whose iron arms loomed like some kind of torture device. French doors stood open into an adjoining space.

Drawn by his curiosity, Auren tiptoed into the deeper shade within. His little light showed a desk on the left, with a large adjustable desk chair. Auren sat down, and felt dwarfed. His feet barely touched the floor. The high ergonomic back stretched up above his head. He shone his light on the wall above, illuminating a gallery of framed photos, award certificates, and shadow boxes containing medals and jerseys.

The photos showed a ferocious-looking man, with a thick dark beard, grinning beside even larger men, or clasping hands with them, with a paw the size of a ham.

Auren's mouth felt dry. If this was who lived here, maybe he should leave right now.

He peered closer at the certificates. Apparently this giant's name was Grysz Medved. Auren didn't even know how to pronounce that.

Even though Auren knew he should get out, he couldn't leave without sating his curiosity. He slid down and moved to the next room, careful to tread softly and not bump into anything, finding his way around more boxes, into the kitchen. The appliances were super-sized, the counters high. He felt like a child in a giant's kitchen. The stainless-steel refrigerator gleamed like a monument, daring him to peek inside.

Besides several six-packs of Duchy beer and a bowl, the cavernous interior was disappointingly bare. Curious, he reached for the bowl, stoneware and the size of a soup tureen, covered with plastic wrap. Auren hefted it in his arms and carried it to the counter, hoping it might be a delicious dessert. He peeled back the plastic and sniffed. Not a promising scent. The fridge's light revealed a pale, smooth mass that could be pudding or cream. With two fingers, he scooped out a portion and popped it into his mouth, prepared to dash to the sink and spit if necessary. Not horrible, but not the treat he had hoped for. It tasted faintly of berries and nuts, but the main flavor was some kind of bland protein powder. The temperature was cold, the texture clammy. Auren resealed the plastic and pushed the bowl back onto the shelf.

"Okay, that's enough—now we'll go," he assured himself.

Then he felt the vibration of heavy footsteps coming upstairs. He froze for a moment in panic. He couldn't tell if the footsteps were approaching by the back stairs he had climbed, or the interior stairway. He decided to flee the way he had come in rather than blunder through the interior darkness and possibly get trapped in a narrow hallway. But no sooner had he hurried into the bedroom than he realized the footsteps were indeed climbing the exterior stairs. He looked around wildly for a hiding place. There were no closets that he could see. The boxes were jammed too tightly against the wall, leaving no space for cover. With effort, he lifted the immense bed cover to see if he could hide under there, but it was a platform frame.

The steps were at the door.

Auren dove beneath the covers just as the door opened. He found himself engulfed in a vast duvet and a heap of pillows. He flattened himself into the mattress and prayed no one would ping his phone.

The door slammed shut. A light snapped on.

He dared glance from beneath the edge of the duvet, and saw a massive pair of brawny legs passing by. Footsteps thumped out into the kitchen. The refrigerator opened and closed. A beer can popped open. After a brief pause, another can cracked. Water ran. A toilet flushed.

Auren was thinking about making a dash for the door, but the footsteps returned.

Clothing hit the floor. Boots landed into a corner. There was a massive sigh and yawn, and the light went out. The mattress rocked with the weight of its owner throwing himself onto the bed.

Auren's heart was pounding so hard he was afraid it would shake the bed. He sensed those giant limbs settling themselves just inches away. Body heat radiated through the covers, and a scent came with it, a musky, powerful aroma that was not unpleasant, but tickled his nose and made him tingle with apprehension. Such wildness was unpredictable, dangerous. Terrified that he would sneeze, Auren hugged the edge of the bed and prayed the other occupant would not roll over.

He caught himself almost wanting to be discovered, to be captured in those massive paws. And then what? He breathed silently through his mouth, willing the disturbing images away.

Mr. Medved of the unpronounceable name thrashed about briefly, perilously close to flinging an arm over Auren.

Auren's heart leapt into his own mouth.

The oblivious bedmate settled into a comfortable position and relaxed. His breathing slowed, and he began to snore lightly.

Auren moved a fraction closer to the mattress edge, froze again, waited. There was no reaction from the other side of the bed. He repeated the process a couple of times, until he had one foot extended toward the floor. With breath held and fists clenched, he slid out of the bed, crossed the shadows that lay between him and the door, turned the handle as quietly as he could and burst out into the moonlight. He didn't look behind or slow down until his feet touched the ground, and he ran faster than he would have believed he could, to the safety of his back door.

"Oh my god, oh my god," he gasped. "I thought I was going to die."

He checked the view cautiously from the corner of his window, as if someone might be looking back at him. But no lights went on next door. There were no shouts of discovery. Everything was quiet.

Auren scooped Bear up and held him under his chin. "I was so scared," he said. "That must have been the craziest thing I ever did. Even crazier than last night. I am losing my mind. Bad enough that I'll probably end up living with my parents. What if they had to come and bail me out after I got cuffed and hauled away for trespassing?"

But once his heart stopped thumping, a smile stole across his face.

"I got away with it, though. It was really kind of an adventure. It was wild. And if the police come around—well, I've been here all night with my cat. Wasn't I, Bear? You'd testify for me, wouldn't you?"

Bear struggled free and jumped down. "Nawrr," he said grumpily.

Auren thought that if a cat could have shrugged, he would have.

Auren slept uneasily, buffeted by dreams of escaping from dark spaces into wild forests full of unseen life, dreams in which his body burst its bonds and ran through the night unhampered, dreams of massive paws and thick furred limbs, of wrestling, tumbling, pressing close, of snuffling and tasting, of heady scents of musk and honey. He woke up tangled in his blankets, sweaty and disheveled.

Taking a quick shower to clear his head, he knew what he had to do: finish packing, then make a last-ditch effort to find another apartment. If nothing turned up in the next day, Auren would have to bite the bullet and call his parents. Even that seemed better than waiting for Ashley's junior cousin and friends to arrive.

One final loose end remained.

"This key," he said, waving it at Bear. "This is what got me into all this trouble. It got me thinking about that house next door. It's all your fault, you know."

Bear stared at him meaningfully, his pupils wide and dark.

"I'm going to return it for sure this time, and then I can forget this whole thing forever. I won't be gone long this time—I promise."

He watched from the front window until the burly, confident form of Chandrakant Asvala strode down the driveway, got in his car, and departed. Only then Auren dared walk past the front entrance of the house and around to the far side. As he hoped, Auren found the entrance to the only apartment he had not yet visited. A short flight of steps led to a second-floor porch and a door with a mailbox beside it, neatly labeled ART BRUNO.

Auren pressed the antique brass doorbell, half-hoping no one would respond. Then he could put the key in the mailbox and return to his own mundane problems. He tried to repress the thought that he might, instead, try the key in the lock, and if it fit, walk in. But that possibility was deferred as he heard steps, the rattle of the knob, and the door opened.

The powerful, well-proportioned man before him filled the door frame perfectly.

"Mr. Bruno," Auren blurted. "I've just come to—"

"To ask about the carriage house?" the man said. "Listen, I'm just about to have breakfast, so—"

"I'm very sorry." Auren hastily reached for the key. "I won't take up your time, then."

Before he could take it from his pocket, the man stood aside and gestured for him to enter. "Not at all," he said. "I was about to say, 'Come on in and sit down'. We can talk about it over coffee."

Brushing past him through the doorway, Auren felt the other man looking him over. Mr. Bruno's smile widened appreciatively, as if he liked what he saw.

Auren felt himself blushing. He wasn't used to such looks.

With a hand on his back, Mr. Bruno guided him to a seat at a cheerful kitchen table. The chair he offered was a generously built captain's chair, the polish gleaming but mellow, the wide seat cushioned. Substantial and comfortable, it suited Auren perfectly.

"Have you eaten?"

"No, but—"

Mr. Bruno held up a hand to stop Auren's protests. "Can't make good decisions on an empty stomach."

He handed Auren a bowl of oatmeal to match his own. He poured coffee and gave his own cup a warm-up. "There you go. Help yourself to brown sugar, cream, raisins—however you like it."

The bowl steamed appetizingly. Auren poured cream and watched it swirl through the coffee's perfect shade of darkness. He knew this was all a mistake, but after all, why not find something good out of a misunderstanding? He stirred melting brown sugar into the steel-cut oats and tasted them. With a chaser of hot coffee, they warmed him to his core.

Mr. Bruno nodded approvingly. "That's better. Now we can talk."

"Thank you, Mr. Bruno. This is really good. But—"

The other man laughed. "Please, call me Art. Just how old do you think I am?"

Auren blushed again.

"You're the next-door neighbor, aren't you?" Mr. Bruno ... Art extended his hand across the table.

For a moment, Auren paused before shaking it. A neat white bandage wrapped the knuckles.

Mr. Bruno saw him hesitate. "Oh, this is nothing. I had a run-in with some wire fence the other day. It's just about healed up now. I forgot all about it."

The man's handshake enveloped Auren's hand in a strong grip that tested his own.

"I'm Auren. Auren Capelli."

"Nice to meet you. So, does this mean you're looking for a change of residence?"

"I am, actually. But—?"

"That's why you're here, isn't it? We put out the word that we need a tenant for the carriage house in the back."

"Carriage house?" Auren hoped he didn't look too stupid. He had never noticed there was a carriage house. He'd assumed it was just a garage.

"Yes, and it's important to us to find someone who fits in."

"Us?" Auren heard himself repeat, but couldn't stop.

"Yes, Chandra, Grish, and I have shared space for years now. We find we get along very agreeably, so we'd like whoever moves in to be the same."

"And you think—you think I might—"

"I think you could be just the right person."

Something about Art's big, easygoing grin made Auren feel so comfortable. He still didn't understand how this could possibly be happening, but he didn't want to do anything to mess up the impression.

Still, he thought of his confused exit from Chandra's apartment, and worried about what Art would think if that came up.

"What about the others?" he said awkwardly. "Is that going to be all right with them?"

Bruno smiled. "I'm sure they'll be glad to have you. I think you already met Chandra. He spoke of having tea with 'that nice young man from next door.' He said you were a young man of great potential, but he was disappointed that you had to leave so suddenly. He'll be delighted to see you again."

"But what about the other one, on the third floor? Mr. Medved?"

"Oh, you met him too?"

"No, not really. Just saw him in passing. But he's, um, intimidating."

Bruno laughed heartily, white teeth gleaming in his neatly-trimmed, brown beard. "Grish is a teddy bear when you get to know him. He'll be glad to have the place occupied. He says he's heard some prowlers recently."

Auren's cheeks flushed, but Art's eyes were twinkling. He put a hand on Auren's shoulder.

"If you've had enough coffee, why don't we walk over to look at the carriage house and see if it suits you?"

"I'd love to."

"Now, where did I put that key?" Art mused. His gaze landed on the key rack by the door. He put his hand in his pocket. He frowned, uttering a little growl of puzzlement.

Oh my god, I never told him, Auren thought. *Why do I keep forgetting?*

"Actually, I came to see you about this." Auren held out the key. "I found it by the dumpster. I wondered if someone had thrown it out by accident."

"That's it," Art said. "It must have fallen out of my pocket. You certainly have a talent for being in the right place at the right time." He made no effort to take the key. "Keep it—that's yours now. If you like the place." He cuffed Auren's shoulder in a friendly way, and let his hand rest there again.

But Auren had one last question. He hated to ask, for fear the answer would be 'No', but he had to know. "Is the rental pet-friendly? I have this cat named Bear. He's been with me forever, and he's the best cat. I promise he never does any damage."

Art laughed again. "No problem. Us Bears have to stick together!"

His hand still on Auren's shoulder, Art guided him out the door and across the back yard toward the small dwelling behind the big house. The sun shone, and the grass smelled fresh and green.

Auren felt the warmth of Art's touch like the sun on his shoulder, shooting down his spine like fire. He never wanted Art to let go. For the first time since he could remember, Auren felt that everything was just right.

AFTERWORD
JEFF MANN

MOST WRITERS I KNOW ARE voracious readers and have been since childhood. My guess is that this is true for most, if not all, of the authors in this anthology, and I am no exception.

I spent my earliest years in the mountains of western Virginia, in the grimy, odoriferous paper-mill town of Covington, where my mother worked in payroll at the Westvaco plant and my father taught at the local high school. Some of my earliest memories are of regular visits to the downtown library with Daddy. It must have been there that I first encountered fairy tales, for I have a vague recollection of checking out collections of such stories, volumes named after colors. A quick online search this morning, reveals that they must have been the twelve collections of *Andrew Lang's 'Coloured' Fairy Books*, published between 1889 and 1910, with titles like *The Blue Fairy Book* and *The Red Fairy Book*. At some point during those Covington years, my parents must have introduced me to Hans Christian Andersen's tales as well, for I remember reading "The Little Mermaid" and "The Snow Queen" out on our sunporch.

My enjoyment of such imaginative fare—what today some might label fantasy or speculative fiction—continued when we moved to Hinton, West Virginia, in 1968, during the summer this Leo turned nine. I recall sitting out on the back porch of my maternal grandmother's little house in rural Forest

Hill, West Virginia, and admiring the illustrations while Daddy read to me from the Dover edition of Howard Pyle's *The Story of King Arthur and His Knights*. I was especially fond of Merlin and his magics. Another favorite during that time was Edith Hamilton's *Mythology*, where I developed a lifelong interest in gods, goddesses, monsters, and heroes. My first years at Hinton High School were devoted to yet more fanciful and fantastic fare—Tolkien's *The Hobbit* and *The Lord of the Rings*, as well as comic books.

Then came an important insight and a profound change. My sophomore year in high school, I spent my weekends ranging around the local woods and state parks with members of the Ecology Club, led by my biology teacher, Jo Davison. Eventually, Jo came out to me as a lesbian, as did two friends, "Bill" and Brenda, a couple. Spending time with them helped me realize I was gay. Nothing in my rural/small-town Southern Appalachian upbringing had prepared me for such an epiphany, but my sense of self-preservation surmised that any expression of my newly discovered sexuality would get me into big trouble, put me in danger, and alienate me from almost everyone I knew. How could I make sense of my intense, albeit unwelcome, same-sex attractions? In those days, there were next to no positive depictions of gays and lesbians in the media, in movies or television, certainly not in fantasy novels or comics.

Books once more were the answer, albeit more realistic fare than fairy tales, fantasy, Arthurian legend, or European mythology. At that point in my emotional development, I needed to read about real gay men in the real world so as to learn how to navigate that world. Jo Davison lent me Patricia Nell Warren's novel, *The Front Runner*, about the love affair between an Olympic track star and his coach. It gave me much-needed perspective on my sexuality, and Warren's next two novels, *The Fancy Dancer* and *The Beauty Queen*, lent me role models after which I might forge a gay identity and a personal style, with the former book's butch love interest, Vidal Stump, and the latter book's BDSM leather man, Danny Blackburn. I also took to Mary Renault's historical novels set in ancient Greece, which often included male characters attracted to members of their own sex. After graduating from Hinton High School in 1977, I fled my small mountain hometown to begin my undergraduate studies at West Virginia University, in the more simpatico and cosmopolitan city of Morgantown. In the same years that I was dancing and drinking in my first gay bars and having my first erotic experiences, I was devouring the works of the Violet Quill authors. Realistic fiction helped me make sense of myself and the gay community.

It must have been during my graduate-school days at WVU that I encountered the poetry and prose of a lesbian writer, Adrienne Rich. In her essay, "Invisibility in Academe," she says, "when those who have power to name and to socially construct reality choose not to see you or hear you, whether you are dark-skinned, old, disabled, female, or speak with a different accent or dialect than theirs, when someone with the authority of a teacher, say, describes the world and you are not in it, there is a moment of psychic disequilibrium, as if you looked into a mirror and saw nothing" (from *Blood, Bread, and Poetry*). This statement made me understand more clearly than ever—as both a gay man and an Appalachian—the importance of what so many folks today refer to as representation, where members of minorities might see their experiences reflected in books, films, and other media.

For years, Lethe Press has also published material catering to various subcultures within the LGBT spectrum. When I first discovered and identified with the Bear community in the early 90s, there was very little in the way of literature catering to us, but Steve Berman has certainly changed that. Lethe Press has published many volumes of fiction and nonfiction centered on gay Bears, including, thankfully, many of my own books. In fact, the first time I met Steve—on Royal Street in New Orleans during a Saints and Sinners Literary Festival, in the spring of 2008—I remember that our conversation involved a fiction project he had in mind involving the gay Bear community.

Flip the numerals in sixteen, the age I came out, and what you get is my present age, sixty-one. Here we all are, having made it to 2021, and here's the very first volume of fairy tales featuring Bears. How could I ever have imagined, back in the 1960s, reading Lang's fairy books and the tales of Hans Christian Andersen, that in my middle age I'd be a bushy-bearded, graying "Daddy Bear," delighting in these "burly tales" and writing an afterword to accompany them? What a pleasure to read stories in which I can see my own hairy, bearded and brawny self, ingenious retellings to which I can directly relate, narratives I don't have to "translate" into gay experience, as I would have had they been heteronormative like the vast majority of folk tales and myths.

I've enjoyed every one of these fairy fictions, in all their variety and global range, and a few have even gotten me wet-eyed. The presence of shapeshifting stories certainly makes sense, as we Bears are often reminded that our fur, brawn, and maturity are far from the smooth, slender beauty-ideal of much mainstream gay culture, and, like some of these fairy-tale heroes, we must cast off the curse—in this case self-doubt—in order to come to terms with our bodies. Simply the title of "Bear" also suggests that we are more in touch than many with our animal nature, with its emphasis on physicality, passion, and immediacy. I loved the frequent and very familiar illustrations of erotic longing, courage, determination, and camaraderie, the way the stories so often celebrate both the gift of simpatico companionship and the excitement of erotic potential. Bears are renowned for being some of the most social and gregarious men in all the realm, and there is room in the heart for friends as much as lovers.

When I teach creative writing classes, I often tell my students that there are two major reasons why I read as much as I can: first, to explore and learn about lives very different from mine, and second, to see lives like mine reflected in literature, allowing me to achieve what I call "the recognition click," i.e., "I know how that feels! I've experienced that!" The former frisson gives us a sense of humanity's amazing range and diversity; the latter frisson makes us feel less alone. In these fairy tales, gay bears might garner a bit of both.

In 1938, J.R.R. Tolkien spoke about fairy tales at St. Andrews University in Scotland, a talk written partly in response to Andrew Lang's fairy books. He later expanded this speech into a long essay, "On Fairy-Stories," which appeared in his collection, *Tree and Leaf*. In it, he says that fairy stories can give the reader "a fleeting glimpse of Joy, Joy beyond the walls of the world, poignant as grief." He continues, claiming that a "good fairy story… however wild its events, however fantastic and terrible its adventures…can give to child or man that hears it…a catch of the breath, a beat and lifting of the heart, near to (or indeed accompanied by) tears, as keen as that given by any form of literary art."

I have found that joy while reading Tolkien's own work and in much of the fantasy and speculative fiction I've relished, both in books and on television and movie screens. I've found it here, gleaming like red-gold rings in these stories, after a long, dark year of global pandemic. I hope you've glimpsed some flicker of that joy in this volume as well. My guess is that you have.

—JEFF MANN
Pulaski, VA
March 2021

Artist: Jazz Miranda

ABOUT THE STORYTELLERS

EVEY BRETT is a queer writer who lives in Southern Arizona with a three-legged Carolina dog and some cats that like to interfere with her writing by jumping or sleeping on the keyboard. She's had numerous short stories published with Lethe Press, Flame Tree Press, three Darkover anthologies, and elsewhere. She's attended Clarion, Taos Toolbox, and the Lambda Literary Retreat for Emerging LGBT Writers, and is a first reader for *The Magazine of Fantasy and Science Fiction*. Visit her online at eveybrett.wordpress.com.

B.J. FRY grew up on the hill of a repurposed rock quarry, near a local nuclear power plant. After she moved, graduated from college, and stopped glowing at night, she started an exciting career reading insurance policies. She's married to her own Prince Charming and together they have two sons, a streetwise dog, and a totally not obscene number of cats. Inspired by her spare-time hobbies of reading romance novels and playing video games, she began pursuing her interest in writing by focusing on short stories that titillate and entertain.

JOHN. T .FULLER hails from the north of England. He works with computers by day, writes by night and enjoys walking, real ale and hair metal. You can pick up a copy of his novella *When the Music Stops* or his short story collection *The Trojan Project* (jointly authored with Richard Rider) online. He hangs around on Twitter as JohnTFuller and cannot promise not to put sausages on all of his book covers.

JOHN LINWOOD GRANT is a professional writer/editor from Yorkshire, UK, and has had some sixty short stories and novelettes published during the last few years in venues such as *Lackington's Magazine*, *Vastarien*, *Weirdbook*, and *Space & Time*, and in several award-winning anthologies. He writes dark contemporary fiction and period supernatural tales, both queer and straight. He is also the editor of *Occult Detective Magazine* and various anthologies. His first collection, *A Persistence of Geraniums*, was set in the Edwardian era, and a further collection of his weird fiction, *Where All is Night, and Starless*, will be out from Trepidatio in 2021. He is ageing, sarcastic, and has his own beard.

JONATHAN HARPER is the author of the short story collection *Daydreamers* (Lethe Press), a *Kirkus Review*'s Indie Book of the Year for 2015. His writing has been featured in such places as *The Rumpus*, *The Rappahannock Review*, *The East Jasmine Review*, *Chelsea Station*, as well as numerous anthologies. He is currently at work on a novel. Visit him online at thejonathan-harper.com.

ALYSHA MACDONALD is a writer, birder, and New Englander living in Germany with a semi-feral cat. She received her bachelor's in English from Suffolk University and, like many of her fellow graduates, works in a field unrelated to her degree. You can find her on twitter @AlyshaMac_ or at alyshamacdonald.com.

JAMES K. MORAN's speculative fiction and poetry have appeared in *Icarus*, *On Spec* and *Glitterwolf*, among other publications. Moran's articles have appeared via *CBC Radio*, *Daily Xtra*, where he wrote for over 16 years, and *Rue Morgue: Horror in Culture & Entertainment*. Lethe Press published his horror novel, *Town & Train*. Moran's first short-story collection, *Fear Itself*, will appear from Lethe Press in 2021. He blogs about peccadilloes at jameskmoran.blogspot.ca and is findable on Twitter @jkmoran.

CHARLES PAYSEUR is an avid reader, writer, and reviewer of all things speculative. His fiction and poetry have appeared in *The Best American Science Fiction and Fantasy, Strange Horizons, Lightspeed Magazine*, and many more. He runs Quick Sip Reviews, has been a Hugo finalist fan writer, and can be found drunkenly reviewing Goosebumps on his Patreon. His collection *The Death of Paul Bunyan and Other Strange Stories* is due from Lethe Press. When not hunting Hodags across the wilds of Wisconsin, you can find him gushing about short fiction (and his cats) on Twitter as @ ClowderofTwo.

Multi-award-winning and best-selling author/editor/anthologist ROB ROSEN (therobrosen.com) is the author of *Sparkle: The Queerest Book You'll Ever Love, Divas Las Vegas, Hot Lava, Southern Fried, Queerwolf, Vamp, Queens of the Apocalypse, Creature Comfort, Fate, Midlife Crisis, Fierce, And God Belched, Mary, Queen of Scotch, Ted of the d'Urbervilles*, and *Sort of Dead*. His short stories have appeared in more than 200 anthologies. He is also the editor of *Lust in Time: Erotic Romance Through the Ages, Men of the Manor*, multiple editions of *Best Gay Erotica of the Year*.

MARK WARD is the author of the chapbooks, *Circumference* and *Carcass* and a full-length collection, *Nightlight*. He was the Poet Laureate for *Glitterwolf* and his poems have been featured in *The Irish Times, Poetry Ireland Review, Banshee, Skylight47, The Honest Ulsterman, Assaracus, Tincture, Cordite*, and many more, as well as anthologies, including Lethe Press' own *The Myriad Carnival*, whilst the most recent of which is *Hit Points: An Anthology of Video Game Poetry*, forthcoming in 2021. He was highly commended in the 2019 Patrick Kavanagh Poetry Award and in 2020 he was shortlisted for the Cúirt New Writing Prize and selected for Poetry Ireland's Introductions series. He is the founding editor of *Impossible Archetype*, an international journal of LGBTQ+ poetry, now in its fourth year.

M. YUAN-INNES loves fairy tales in all shapes, shades, and sizes, and has rewritten Cinderella ("Golden Fish, Golden Slippers") and Little Red Riding Hood ("Sharp Teeth") in China, as well as Snow White with an anatomical variation ("Death and the Mother"). She writes the critically-acclaimed Hope Sze medical mysteries under the pseudonym Melissa Yi. When she's not creating new worlds, she hangs out with her currently-bearded husband, their two children, and Roxy the Rottweiler. Find her on Facebook (Melissa Yi Yuan-Innes), Twitter @dr_sassy, and her website, melissayuaninnes.com.

ANN ZEDDIES is the author of the acclaimed Typhon series of novels. Her short fiction has been featured in *Boys of Summer, Magic in the Mirrorstone,* and *Speaking Out: LGBT Youth Stand Up.* The editor of this volume believes she is one of the kindest souls in all of existence, and may have written this bio for her.

MATTHEW BRIGHT is a writer, editor and designer. His short fiction has appeared on Tor.com, *Nightmare's Queers Destroy Fiction, Lightspeed, Glittership, Harlot Magazine, Clockwork Iris, Queen Mob's Teahouse* and others, collected in Lambda Literary Award Finalist and Kirkus Best Indie Books of the Year selection *Stories To Sing In The Dark.* He is the editor of several anthologies, including *The Myriad Carnival, Threesome, Clockwork Cairo* and the Lambda Literary Award Finalist *Gents.* By day, he pays the bills as a book cover designer in Manchester, England.

JEFF MANN, who kindly provided the afterword, is the award-winning author of poetry and gay romance and erotica. He adores men and food, and both in generous proportions. His *Salvation: A Novel of the Civil War* won both a Lambda Literary Award and the Pauline Réage Novel Award. He has also been inducted into the Saints and Sinners Literary Festival Hall of Fame. Mann teaches creative writing at Virginia Tech in Blacksburg, Virginia.

STEVE BERMAN has edited numerous anthologies of queer and speculative fiction. He has been a finalist for the Andre Norton, Golden Crown Literary, and the Shirley Jackson Awards. He won the Lambda Literary Award for the unique erotica anthology, *His Seed.* He resides in Western Massachusetts.